R L McKinney is a native of Boulder, Colorado but has lived in or around Edinburgh since 2004. She studied social anthropology at Edinburgh University and has worked in academia, the voluntary sector and local government. In previous lives, she has tended bar, trained horses, worked in bookshops and taught creative writing. Her short stories have appeared in several anthologies and journals. She lives in Midlothian with her husband and two children.

BLAST RADIUS

R L McKinney

SANDSTONEPRESS

HIGHLAND | SCOTLAND

First published in Great Britain
and the United States of America
Sandstone Press Ltd
Dochcarty Road
Dingwall
Ross-shire
IV15 9UG
Scotland.

www.sandstonepress.com

Editor: Moira Forsyth

The publisher acknowledges subsidy from Creative Scotland
towards publication of this volume.

ISBN: 978-1-910124-06-2
ISBNe: 978-1-910124-07-9

Cover design by Brill
Typesetting by Iolaire Typesetting, Newtonmore
Printed and bound by Totem, Poland

For my family in Scotland and America

Acknowledgements

This is the story of one fictional veteran after this country's most recent war, but he could be any veteran after any one of too many wars. This book has been informed and inspired by more sources than I can credit, from Remarque's *All Quiet on the Western Front* to Michael Herr's *Dispatches*, Pat Barker's *Regeneration* trilogy to Gregory Burke's stunning play *Black Watch*: factual and fictional accounts of war and the psychological scars it inflicts on the men and women who experience it.

I might never have written anything at all without the encouragement of some special people: my parents Alan and Peggy Frank, who raised me with eyes and ears for the world; my university roommate Erika, whom I subjected to my late-night scribblings on a regular basis; my aunts Pat and Nina who surrounded me with love and amazing talents; and my uncle Red Davis, who let me steal just a little bit of his story and run with it. Thank you also to the members of Dalkeith Writers Group for making me better at this craft, and to Moira Forsyth at Sandstone Press for gentle but wise editorial insight. Claire Lamond – friend, filmmaker, artist – thank you for reading, commenting and continually inspiring.

Finally, to my husband Craig McKinney, for his eternal patience and love, and to Jamie and Susanna: thank you for being here and for understanding why I do this.

A blast radius is the distance from the source that will be affected when an explosion occurs. A blast radius is often associated with, but not limited to, bombs, mines, explosive projectiles (propelled grenades), and other weapons with an explosive charge.

Wikipedia

War does not determine who is right – only who is left.

Bertrand Russell

I

Sad bastards. This town is full of them. You know the ones I mean: the men who wear a rut in the pavement between the bookies, the dole queue and the pub, shuffling along with no clear purpose in life except to survive until the next day. When I was at school I used to watch them and think, *you sad, sad bastards*.

Now I'm one of them; fate's a funny thing. A half-deaf, twitching, psyched-out prick, wandering down Civvy Street with no job and less prospect of getting one than a one-eyed, hump-backed whore. That's me. Sean McNicol: sad bastard. I still have all my teeth and I don't smell of piss, but the rate things are going that could change. I even have a beard. A beard is prerequisite for Saddo status. I've given up shaving because I don't like to look in the mirror. When I look in the mirror I have to go through the tedious routine of asking how the fuck I got here.

How the fuck did I get here? I followed the directions that I was given, and somehow I ended up here. Right back in Saddoville where I started out. This isn't bloody right!

Ok, Mitch told me one time, *so there's only two fixed points on this map. You can't go back to the first and you sure as hell can't avoid the last, but everything in between is up for grabs.* If you look at it that way, I suppose every decision of your life is a crossroads, from

1

which there can be infinite possible roads toward that second and final fixed point. The only thing I can't work out is how you know which is the right one, because it seems to me that up to now this life has been a series of wrong turns, leading to other wrong turns, and then to those places you can't get back from, carrying me faster and faster toward that inevitable final stop.

Anyway, that's why I don't bother shaving.

Helen, the librarian, smiles at me as I make my now predictable appearance on a Monday morning. I've more or less read my way through the entire Mystery section (it's a small town and we have a small library) and am now working on True Crime. True Crime's pretty good reading as a matter of fact, and it reassures me that there are still some folk out there whose lives are more fucked up than mine.

Helen's a canny wee woman. She was a friend of my granny so knows me from the bad old days. She is mostly deaf and has to read lips, but she sees more than most folk. She knows what it's like when you can't hear very well: how your world closes in around you and your own thoughts echo like thunder.

I hand her my book about John Gotti. American crooks are so much more interesting than Scottish ones.

'How are ye the day, Sean?' she asks in the way you'd ask a cancer patient.

'Still here, Helen.'

'Afore ye go, here's something ye may be interested in.' She bends and retrieves a piece of paper from beneath the counter, slides it toward me.

VAN DRIVER/REMOVAL PERSON NEEDED, IMMEDIATE START, it reads.

'Harry over the road asked me to put it on the notice board, but I saved it for you.'

'The job's probably gone already,' I say.

'He was just here ten minutes ago, son.'

Ya beauty! Get over there, Nic, your name's on this one. This is Mitch. He shouts in my bad ear when he thinks I need a kick up the arse. I don't know why I hear him in my bad ear and not my good one, but anyway that's how it is.

I read the notice again, looking for the inevitable fine print. *Clean driving licence required. Heavy lifting involved.*

'Aye, ta Helen,' I say, and fold the notice into the pocket of my coat. I leave the library and head down the street, chin tucked into my collar and eyes averted in case any of the other local Saddos clock where I'm going and beat me to it.

The Once Loved Furniture Company occupies what used to be the carpet factory, the town's largest employer after the pits. It kind of sums the place up: we don't make anything anymore, we just sell cast-off shite. I push open the door and enter a cavernous room crammed full of the kind of furniture that filled more or less every living room in Britain twenty years ago: overstuffed suites in an explosion of floral prints, lots of grey and pink, MDF, yellow pine. Smells of mothballs and furniture polish, dusty carpet and upholstery imbued with stale fags and cat piss. Against the back wall are at least two dozen old boxy televisions, perfectly functional but discarded for the latest flat screen models.

I see a man on his knees at the back of the shop, slowly rubbing a bit of sand paper along the leg of an upturned chair.

'I'm looking for Harry,' I say and he turns, gets to his feet with some effort, and gives me a lopsided smile.

'Office.'

3

'Where's that?'

He sighs, makes a show of dusting his hands on his trousers. 'Show ye.' Then he moves off toward the back of the building, dragging his left leg. As I follow him, a couple of the other staff watch me. None of them look exactly the full shilling, if you know what I mean, and I realise that this must be one of those places that exists to give unemployable losers a token job to keep them off the streets. Saddo Central. I want to run a mile, but seeing as I'm one of them, there's no point.

The old boy leads me to a blue door at the back of the shop, knocks twice and then opens it to reveal a small office, cluttered with stacks of paper and pieces of furniture – table legs and broken lamps – strangely like disembodied limbs.

'Felly to see ye,' my guide says to the man at the desk: a chunky wee guy with a grey beard and a Fair Isle jumper.

'Thanks Al,' he says, rising from the chair and crossing the room to shake my hand. Gas-flame blue eyes lock onto my face and I immediately look down at my boots. 'Harry Boyle. I'm the manager here.' Throaty voice, accent that is vaguely Scottish but impossible to place, possibly public school.

'I'm here about the removals job.'

'Ah, outstanding.' He pulls over a chair. 'Sit down just now and we'll have a little chat.'

I sit, and immediately my legs begin to jiggle. Once upon a time I knew how to be still as a chameleon on a branch. I could do it for hours. But now I jitter all the time. *Don't blow this,* Mitch mutters at me. *Don't tell him any more than you have to.* I force my legs to be still.

Harry Boyle opens the bottom drawer of his desk, shuffles through some files and pulls out what looks like a job application form. Then he sits opposite me.

4

'The thing is I need someone who can start right away. Our driver left without notice on Saturday and the jobs are already backlogging. There's not much to explain about the job, really. We're a charity, we provide affordable second hand furniture. Luton van, load the furniture in, take it to customers. Or pick up from customers, bring it back here. Most of the time, you'll have another person in the van with you to help with the lifting. Be polite and courteous to the customers. Don't turn down any furniture; what we can't sell, we recycle or ship out to Africa. That's about all you need to know up front; you'll learn the details on the job.'

'I'm strong enough. I have an HGV licence. I can start anytime, I'm . . .' The word *unemployed* smacks of desperation. 'Available.'

'Excellent.' He nods and turns the gas flames on me again. I wouldn't like to be interrogated by this guy. He picks up a pen. 'What's your name, son?'

'McNicol. Sean.'

'Sean . . .' he repeats, jotting this down, then scanning toward the meatier sections of the form. 'Can I ask about your past work experience?'

This should be the easiest question in the world to answer. I've only ever had one job in my life. But it panics me. Most of my skills are non-transferable, no matter how you package them.

'Royal Marines. Since I left school.'

He gives away nothing. 'Did you have a specialism, Sean?'

'Ehm . . . reconnaissance, latterly. I passed the Mountain Leader course in 2008.'

He writes this down and if it impresses him, worries him or means nothing to him, it doesn't show on his face. 'How long have you been out?'

5

'Pardon?'

He looks up at me. 'When did you come out?'

'About a year ago.'

He smiles and cocks his head slightly to the left, and somehow I think he already knows the answer to the question he is about to ask me. 'Can I ask why you left?'

'Medical discharge.'

Mitch starts muttering, and I clear my throat to shut him up. 'I . . . ehm . . . was injured in Helmand, but . . . I'm fit enough. Physically. I can lift. I can still run forever. I'm just a bit deaf in my left ear. It's not a problem most of the time.'

Go on, Nic, tell him about me, I dare you. Tell him about the voices.

I press my lips together.

'It's a little awkward to ask about this, but is there anything else that might affect your ability to work? Mental health, wise? Please don't worry that this would stop us considering you, but we do need to know so we can make sure we support you.'

Oh no, not at all, he's perfect apart from the fact that he'll hit the deck if someone drops a pencil. That, and the dead guy he talks to.

My jaw is so tight I can feel the muscles pulsing in my cheek. Then I sigh. The only reason he's asked is that he can see it on my face, so there's no point lying.

'I was diagnosed with Post Traumatic Stress, whatever that's supposed to mean. Sometimes I . . . get a bit . . . nervous, but I can work. I don't need *support*, I need a job.'

Whoa . . . whoa . . . whoa! Crash fucking bang boom, you're losing it mate. You're blowing cover boy, and you call yourself a bootneck.

'My old C.O. will give me a reference. The thing is I haven't even been asked for an interview before now.'

Shut the fuck up now, Nic. My jaw snaps shut. The general purpose machine gun in my chest rattles away at my own private Taliban.

'Work's pretty thin on the ground these days,' Harry says quietly.

I nod, biting my lower lip so hard I can taste blood.

'How would you feel about a two week trial? See how we get on? I can't lie and say this job will make you rich, but we believe in paying a living wage so . . . at least it's better than the dole.'

He hands over a note of the terms and conditions, and I scan this quickly. Pay: tolerable for an antisocial bugger who lives with his sister and never goes out, but barely. Pension: you'd need a microscope to see it. Benefits: you're having a laugh.

'You're serious? You'll have me?' I resist the urge to fall crying around his ankles.

The creases at the corners of his eyes deepen. 'That's not an easy thing you just told me. A lot of people under-value honesty, but to me it's all important, especially in a charity. You find yourself having a hard time, just let me know and we'll deal with it.'

'Aye . . . ehm . . . okay. When do you want me to start?'

He leans back in his chair and laces his fingers behind his head. 'What are you doing this afternoon?'

II

When the dreams come I don't even bother trying to sleep. Sometimes in the wee hours I go for a run up the Rosewell Road and onto the old railway line that leads through Roslin Glen. Places are different at night. You see things you'll never see during the day. Every once in a while, you see people who make beds among the trees and stare at you with wild animal eyes as you go past. They're not like the Saddos in town during the day. These are more like feral people, who have forgotten how to live in the world of rules and manners and expectations, survivors of an apocalypse that slid by unnoticed by the rest of us. The only traces you'll see of them during the day are the remains of their bivouacs: bits of tarpaulin, a few charred fire rings, discarded bottles and torn, rusted cans.

I don't twitch when I run and I'm light on my feet. Running is the only way I can get away from Mitch; I guess it's pretty hard to keep up when you've had your legs blown off.

It starts to rain and the icy needles prick my face, but I don't turn back. The track begins its long descent into the glen, down through the ancient woods toward the river. Because of the strange muffling effect of my deaf ear, I feel like I'm in a long tunnel which is funnelling me down and down into some dark place. Off to my right, across the river, is the site of the Battle of Rosslyn, where the mud turned red with the blood of 25,000 men. This same mud now sucks at my feet like the hands of the dead, but I keep running, leaving the railway line and heading down the brae, over the river, past the ruined gunpowder mills and back up onto the road that climbs out of the glen.

Janet is having breakfast by the time I get home, soaking wet and mud-splattered. She looks up from her tea, sweeps a lock of limp, greying hair away from her face and gives me a look: pity mixed with irritation. She's never had any kids, but she's ten years older than me and in her time she's been more of a parent to me than our mother ever was. When the Corps finally accepted that the growing catalogue of electrical faults in my brain amounted to a critical overload, Janet appeared and said, 'There's a bed made for you, Sean.'

My sister lives in the same house in the huddled ex-mining town where I spent my first eighteen years. It's the gable end of a grey, rough-cast terrace, literally the last street in town, overlooking a windswept field which slopes up toward a stand of elderly and wind-bent Scots pines. Their silhouettes above a blanket of ripening wheat used to remind me of the trees on the African high veldt. Sometimes I used to run along the narrow footpath toward them on summer evenings and pretend I was on the trail of a lion or an elephant.

Many of the fields I used to run through have since been buried under pavement and houses, trimmed and lifeless patches of lawn and monoblocking: dull-as-muck suburbs for dull-as-muck people. But my little patch of Africa hasn't been built on yet, and it's one of the few things that pleases me around here. I look over it to the woods beyond and maintain the possibility of escape, just like I used to.

Turn about, look back toward the centre of town, and

all you see is a grey, purposeless collection of houses. Old men who ache with nostalgia for days spent down a black hole, young men who ache for a life that only exists on TV, and women who ache for whatever joy is to be had at the bottom of a bottle of vodka. Fucking No Man's Land. Not exactly what I'd imagined for myself after more than a decade in some of the world's most notorious glory holes, but where the hell else was I going to go?

I kick off my mud-caked trainers and leave them on the mat next to the kitchen door, then fill a pint glass with water and down it in a oner.

'What time did you go out?'

'I don't know. About five, I guess.'

'Sean, your light was still on when I got up for the toilet at three. How can you go to work when you haven't slept all night?'

'Same way you can fight a war when you haven't slept in months.'

Janet presses for more. 'How's that?'

You just do it, that's how. Somewhere in the back of your mind, you know you are desperately knackered: so tired that the idea of dying becomes almost acceptable. And maybe this is the point. You'll walk into a village where a hundred enemy eyes might be watching you from behind the mud walls because you're too wasted to be afraid.

I could tell Janet this, but somehow I think she doesn't really want to know. I stick my glass into the dishwasher and wipe my face on a tea towel.

'You'll run yourself into the ground.'

I shrug. 'It's more restful than sleeping.'

'That's not right, Sean.'

'Probably not.' I laugh softly and catch a whiff of myself. 'I smell like a cowshed. I'm away for a shower.'

'Strip before you go up,' Janet orders, her voice drooping with resignation.

Under the hawkish eye of my sister, I strip down to my pants and leave my squalid clothes in a heap by the door.

****

'Aye, Ah'm tellin' ye, she's suckin' his face off oot there.'

'Oh, you are jokin', Emma, that is minging. Ye seen his fuckin' teeth, man? They're green.'

'Ah ken. It's disgusting. Eh Sean? Rank, innit?'

I've been at Once Loved for a month now, having survived my trial fortnight without wrecking the van or giving away the worst of my psychoses. The work is brainless and physical, and the girls who work the shop floor giggle when I lift a wardrobe or double bed onto my back.

For the avoidance of doubt, their attention does nothing for me. Saddos of the female variety are still Saddos, and even after more than two years of celibacy, I'm not that desperate. Emma and Dawn, the two who are now gossiping as they stir their coffees, are both in their early twenties, pale and doughy, with bad skin and over-styled hair. Emma is slack jawed, mean and thick as over-cooked porridge. Dawn is brighter, meaner, and might have been bonny if she'd ever eaten well, exercised or had her teeth fixed. She has two kids by different men, neither of whom have anything to do with her or the bairns.

Linda, the shop administrator and subject of their relentless gossip, is in her forties and skinny, with a sixty-a-day cough and a drink problem which she doesn't even bother to keep secret. Linda is, if the gossip can be believed, sleeping with Billy, my van assistant. Billy's

11

a scuzzy wee guy who's never been further afield than Princes Street and never had two pennies to rub together. He's nervous and a little paranoid, a fact which isn't helped by Emma and Dawn and their furtive looks.

The best thing I've learned since I got the job is that being half-deaf isn't always a disability. Sometimes it's a downright blessing, especially when I'm in the staff room tucking into a brew and a tub of Janet's stovies, and the Pilsbury Doughballs get into one of their nasty little exchanges.

Emma waves her hand in front of my eyes and I look up from my paper. 'Earth to Sean.'

'What? You saying something?'

They glance at each other and laugh. 'Never mind,' Dawn says with an exaggerated sigh. 'I'll say it in sign language next time.'

'You do that,' I reply, and look down again. 'That way I won't have to listen to your nippy bloody voice.'

Ooooh, NOT very friendly, Nic. That's no way to speak to a lady.

Fuck off, Mitch, she's no lady.

Emma looks at Dawn, and Dawn giggles in a way that makes me wonder if she thinks I'm flirting with her. Imagine shagging that one. For just a moment, I do: acne on her back and a fanny that smells like chip fat.

I check my watch, then push back from my seat and wash my dishes, wiping up the coffee they've spilled while I'm at it.

'Duffers, the pair of you,' I mutter, rinsing the cloth and slinging it over the tap.

Dawn puts her hand behind her ear and shakes her head. Then she sticks out her lower jaw and puts on the slurred voice of a deaf person. 'Sorry, I cannae hear you, Sean.'

Nasty pieces of work. I shake my head and leave the staff room, head out to shop floor to check the delivery schedule for the afternoon. The first thing I notice is that the girls have left the shop unattended. The second is that there is a dark-haired woman examining the leather settee we put out this morning. The settee is ugly – reddish-brown with walnut-effect legs – but the woman is quite stunning. A strong nose, possibly on the big side, full lips framed by high cheekbones and a square jaw. Her hair is sleek and full, waving a little on its way past her shoulders, and she is well dressed in tight jeans, tall brown boots and a dark purple down parka. I only have time to admire the elegant curve of her backside before she turns toward me and smiles.

More like it. Imagination suddenly becomes a much more worthwhile enterprise.

'Hello. I wonder if you can help me.'

Oh, watch yourself here, boyo. This one's officer class. Way the hell out of your league. Bloody essence.

'I'm sure I can.' I smile back, then leap in with both feet. 'Please don't tell me you like that settee.'

She laughs and approaches the desk. 'It's hideous. No offence.'

'None taken.'

'I popped in to see whether I could arrange for some-one to come out and take away a load of old furniture. My father's recently passed away and I've got to clear the house.'

'I'm sorry to hear that.'

She bows her head slightly. 'Thank you. It's lovely furniture . . . antique, a lot of it. Could do with a bit of loving care and repair, but I'm sure it'll sell.'

'You wouldn't rather try to sell it yourself?'

'No, I . . .' she pauses, presses dark red lips together, 'I

13

really just want to be rid of it. Actually . . . if you do full house clearances, that would be even better. Just take everything. But maybe you don't do that.'

Harry is away at a meeting somewhere. I open my mouth to say I don't really know if we do that or not, then catch myself. Dithering isn't an attractive habit.

'Why don't I come out and have a look and get an idea of the size of the job.' I flip through the order book. 'My last delivery today is at four. I can come after that if you like.'

Billy gets dropped off at home after our last delivery, so I won't have to drag that overripe little weasel along with me. Briefly I wonder if I'll have time for a shower.

'Oh, would you?' Her shoulders subside with what looks like incredible relief, and for a second I think she's about to cry. 'Thank you. It's just me, you see. It's too much.'

'Just tell me where to come,' I say softly.

'Cauldhill Farm. You take the road past the old bing at Rosewell, and keep going about four miles.'

'I know exactly. I run up there sometimes.'

Her tidy dark eyebrows arch. 'Do you? From where?'

'Town here.'

'You must be fit.'

I smile. 'I've been fitter.'

'Well, I'm impressed. Two miles is about my limit. Anyway, it's the main house. I'll be there.'

Main fucking house. Told you this bird's worth something. This one doesn't screw men who wear overalls, I can tell you that right now. Bet the old man was a fucking Colonel.

She raises her hand to wave and her wedding ring catches the dusty sunlight. 'See you then.'

Crap.

III

'Dad let the place go a bit, these last few years.'

Cauldhill Farm sits at the base of the Moorfoot Hills, at the end of a road so pitted I have to wonder whether the van will manage it. A couple of green fields bounded by stone dykes and beyond them boggy moorland and heather. And although it still bears the name of farm, it doesn't look as though it's been worked for years. Decades maybe. There are a few rusty bits of farm machinery lying about. Bits of roof have fallen in on the old sandstone barns and outbuildings, and weeds have taken root in the walls. The gate to the walled garden beside the house is hanging on its hinges, and I look in to see a jumble of bare branches and weeds. The house itself, a double-fronted Victorian, looks sorry for itself: flaking stonework, telephone wires hanging loose, filthy windows.

And inside, no joke, it's just possible the lost Roman Ninth might be squirreled away for safekeeping. As she leads me into the kitchen, all of my anal military sensibilities start bellowing so loudly I think I'm going to explode. It's just . . . stuff. The random stuff you collect in life – apparently a very long life, or more likely several long lifetimes – unfiltered and in a state of utter disorder. Every bloody where.

'I see what you mean.'

'Every room's the same. He was a bit of a packrat.'

15

'How can you live in this?'

She laughs, a single sharp 'Ha! I don't. I live in Cambridge, I'm just here to sort things out and get the place on the market.'

'Oh. And . . . how long have you got?'

A shrug. 'As long as it takes, I suppose. We . . . haven't actually introduced ourselves properly. I'm Molly Wells.'

'Sean McNicol.'

Her eyes widen and she fixes them on my face as we shake hands. I wonder if the name means something to her, but she doesn't say anything further so I clear my throat and turn away, make a show of surveying the disaster zone. 'I'm sure we can help, but I'm quite new in the job so I'll have to get a bit of advice on how to price this.'

She replies, but very quietly behind me.

I turn back toward her again. 'Pardon?'

'I said I'm not worried about the price. I just want to be rid of it.'

'Aren't there things you'd like to keep? Sentimental value or . . .'

'No.'

I have seen many women bombed out of their homes, sifting through the dust for whatever they could find: a photograph or a toy or a piece of jewellery to remind them of happier times. And here is a whole house full of memories that nobody wants. I wonder what the Afghan women would make of it.

Molly's face softens. 'I'm sorry, I'm sure that sounded bad. My dad and I . . . well . . . you know. Didn't always get on. I'll help you, obviously, and if there are any little things I want, I can pack them up. Why don't you have a look round the rest of the house, and I'll make you a cup of tea.'

16

'Don't worry about it.'

'I won't. But you look like a man who needs a cup of tea. There's no point denying it. Milk and sugar?'

If it wasn't for that bloody ring, I'd have almost considered myself in there.

'Alright then. Just milk.' I laugh. 'If you can find it.'

'I bought it specially. Just mind you don't get lost.'

'Aye, I will.' I move out of the kitchen, following a corridor past a large dining room with peeling wallpaper. Past the dining room is a smaller office or library. I step inside and breathe in the smells of dusty paper and old pipe smoke. The floor is cluttered with objects: fireplace tools, dustbins, fan heaters, piles of yellowed newspaper, ashtrays. I step carefully past it all and examine some of the books on the shelves: histories and memoirs, mainly, as well as some medical and veterinary textbooks.

My eyes land on a chunky volume about the Falklands war: amazing such a little war could have produced such a fat book. I withdraw it and flick through the pages, automatically searching out the green berets. I've seen these pictures many times; they were so much a part of our collective psyche that sometimes you almost believed you were there, fighting for the Two Sisters. For a couple of minutes, the chaos around me fades into the tunnel.

And then there is an almighty crash and I jerk around so violently that the book flies out of my hands. 'Jesus Christ.'

'Oh bollocks,' Molly splutters as tea splashes onto the tray. She's tripped over the iron caddy of fireplace tools.

I dive forward and move them out of her way. 'Are you alright?'

She puts the tray down on a little table. 'Yeah. Are you? You about jumped out of your skin there.'

My legs are going off the Richter scale and I have to sit

down. Then I make the mistake of grabbing one of the mugs, and slosh tea down my hand. I put the mug down again and tuck my hands under my arms, but Molly has obviously noticed.

She places her long, manicured fingers on my arm. 'God, I'm so sorry. I've given you a proper fright.'

I pull in a long breath and release it slowly. 'I'm fine. I was just . . . in my own wee world for a moment, there,' and I laugh to cover myself. 'I had visions of the whole place caving in.'

Her eyes are still full of concern, but she smiles. 'Have your tea.'

This time I manage to hold the mug without too much seismic activity, and the tea helps to settle my drumming pulse.

'Did your old man live alone here?' I ask to divert her attention.

'Mmm, after we left. My mum was much younger than him, and she left him when I was twelve.'

'Oh, right.'

'So . . . anyway. He was here until he died a couple of months ago. I suggested sheltered housing once and he threatened to shoot me in my sleep. He meant it, I think.'

'Nice guy, eh?'

'Not if he could help it.' She sighs and her eyes turn toward the pink-gold dusky light filtering through the window. Then she looks back at me. 'You don't remember me, do you?'

'Ehm . . .'

'We were at primary school together. You were the year below me.'

Now I have an excuse to stare at her, so I take it. A wisp of memory coalesces into an image: a girl hovering outside a circle of more popular ones, gawky limbs

18

burdened by too much flesh, eyes magnified behind thick glasses, hand dipping into a pocket for sweets.

Disbelief must be visible on my face because she laughs. 'Molly Finlayson. I thought I'd better own up before you recognised me.'

'You've changed for the better.'

'It's taken a bit of work.' She seems amused, but not offended.

'Sorry . . . was that rude?'

She laughs again. 'No, it's fine. I'm glad you think so.'

I clear my throat and ignore the sniggering in my ear. 'You sort of disappeared.'

'My life was such a misery at primary; Mum persuaded Dad to dip into his very tight pocket and send me to Heriots. Not that it was any better there; posh brats still know how to call you a fat cow. I stopped eating when I was fifteen and ended up in hospital with anorexia.' She shakes her head. 'It's mad, you know, the things you do to make people accept you.'

'I never bothered.' I bite my lip. I tried so hard not to bother that most sensible people thought I was a budding sociopath and kept well away.

She narrows her eyes, maybe remembering more than I would like her to. 'You were a proper dark horse.'

'Not really. Just shy and misunderstood.'

'Aye, right. So what have you been doing all this time?'

'This and that.'

She puts her mug down and sits back in the creaky seat. 'Your accent isn't local anymore, which means you've been away and come back.'

'Uh huh. Not to prison, in case you were wondering.'

'Oh God, it never crossed my mind. I'm guessing . . . army?'

Once upon a time, the bootneck in me would have

19

taken this as the world's greatest insult. But now I just hold my hands wide and give her a resigned grin.

'Hair like Jesus and I still look like a soldier. I'm doomed.'

She laughs. 'I'm good at this game. Am I right?'

'Not quite. Royal Marines. I came out last year.'

'Ah.' She nods slowly. 'You've been busy, then, these last few years.'

'A bit, aye.' I drain my cup and put it down, stand up. 'There's only so much of it you can take, eh? If I'm a bit jumpy when things start crashing around, you know why.'

'Mmm. I am sorry about that.'

'Not your fault. Look, I better make tracks. Give me your number, Molly, and I'll phone you tomorrow about making a start.'

She follows me back through the kitchen to the door, then says something apologetic.

I turn. 'Sorry?'

'I . . .' she shakes her head. 'Doesn't matter. Wait.' She tears a scrap of paper off a stack of documents on the kitchen table, and scribbles her number on it. 'I'll hear from you tomorrow, then.'

'Yep.'

'You will phone, Sean, won't you?'

I glance back at her. She's standing on the step, hands clutched in front of her, and I catch the briefest glimpse of the graceless schoolgirl.

'I said I would, so I will, alright?'

She nods. 'Sorry . . . right. Cheerio for now, then.'

'Bye.'

She's gagging for it, Nic, wedding ring or no. You want to know why? Because she wanted your arse in primary school when no lad in his right mind would

20

look at her. It's a memory she wants, not the sad, twisted reality. Don't you forget that.

'No chance, with you here to remind me,' I mutter as I get into the van.

I drive away and Mitch blethers on and fucking on, until I can't stand it anymore and pull over into a passing place. I get out of the van, vault over the stone dyke into a field and run, sprinting as fast as I can through the heavy soil. I stop at the far edge of the field and stand, gasping for breath. Some crows rise in a circle above me, cawing and rattling, and when my breathing has settled enough that I can hear anything else, I hear the wind whistling through the row of beeches at the edge of the field. Lonesome, Scottish sounds. But at least Mitch has shut his gob.

****

Harry is just locking up shop when I get back. He opens the door to let me in. 'Thought you'd gone home. How's your day been?'

'Okay. Actually, I came back hoping to catch you. A woman came in this afternoon to ask if we'd do a full house clearance for her. Her old man's place, Cauldhill Farm out by the Moorfoots. We ever do that kind of thing?'

'We haven't up to now.' He rubs his beard and considers for a moment. 'I don't see any particular reason why not. She's giving us . . . how much furniture?'

'All of it, Harry, and there's a lot of it. Massive house full. I've just been out to recce the place. Valuable stuff. Antiques, everything. The place is like a dumping ground; the old man obviously never threw anything away in his life. It's not going to be done in a couple of hours.'

21

'Right. I'll tell you what. If you can shuffle deliveries about and make time, go ahead. God knows, we need the money. You'll need Billy, I assume?'

'Eventually, but not yet. We've got to unearth the furniture before we can shift it. What do I tell her about the price?'

'I assume she's able to pay a bit.'

'Ehm . . . yeah. I don't get the feeling it's an issue.'

'Charge her the usual rate for removals per van load, plus double your usual hourly rate for the packing up. Give her an estimate for the whole job, and if she wants to haggle, give a wee bit. Not too much.'

'Right.'

'Good lad. Listen, did Dawn give you a bit of agro today?'

'Just a bit of banter. Why?'

'Emma told me she made some inappropriate remarks.'

'Like I say, it was just a bit of banter. What's Emma doing telling tales, anyway? I thought they were mates.'

Harry sighs and buries his fingers in his beard again. 'They are when it suits them. I'm sure you wouldn't but . . . don't encourage Dawn, okay? She can be . . .' he pauses, purses his lips, '. . . temperamental might be the word.'

'Right.' I linger there, wondering if Emma also told him what I said to Dawn, and whether he's telling me off in a veiled sort of way. I'm used to superiors who bellow in your face or tell you point blank how stupid you've been; subtlety is one of the first things they hammer out of you.

Harry pulls his keys out of his pocket and holds the door open for me. I step outside onto the street and he closes the door behind us, locks up and pulls down the shutter.

22

Then he turns to me. 'You want a lift home?'

'Nah, thanks. See you tomorrow.'

He looks incredibly weary all of a sudden, but nods. 'Yep. See you tomorrow, Sean.'

IV

Three days later I'm back at Cauldhill Farm with the van and a load of packing boxes. Molly has agreed to meet me but her car isn't here and she doesn't come to the door. I check my watch and swallow a wave of irritation, then walk back down the front steps and wander toward one of the old stone byres. I swing the door open and step inside, pause on the threshold to take in smells of birds and damp stone, the rhythm of water droplets on the cobbles. The stone floor is wet and uneven, weeds growing up through cracks, thick in some places with feathers and bird droppings.

Light filters through holes in the ceiling in dusty rays. At one end of the barn I find a few fresh owl pellets, so I look up toward the roof beams above to find the pale form of a barn owl. Disturbed from its sleep, it ruffles its feathers and peers down at me, golden eyes deep in a heart-shaped face, but it doesn't apparently find me enough of a threat to abandon its roost. The owl's expression of stoic watchfulness is familiar, almost human. It assesses, waits, closes its eyes again, and I continue my exploration.

There is a rotting wooden trunk against one wall. I squat beside it and carefully lift the lid to avoid a creak, and from inside come the smells of rust and alcohol and old, damp leather. Inside are medical instruments and glass vials, with dried up crusty contents, labelled with Latin names.

Next to these is a smaller, padlocked wooden box, which I lift out and shake gently. Something makes a papery shuffle inside. A moment's rummaging in the trunk yields a long hypodermic needle, which slides neatly into the lock mechanism, and I've got it open within a few seconds. The lid creaks and reveals a small bundle wrapped in old yellow kitchen roll, which I unfold carefully to find two photographs.

The first, black and white and very fragile, is of the crew of an RAF Lancaster bomber. Six men with elbows on each other's shoulders and the seventh turning away, climbing a ladder to enter the plane. It is obviously an original, slightly frayed around the edges, and I hold it gently on my fingertips for a minute before wrapping it up again.

The second photo is in colour and more recent, but still faded with age. It is of a young soldier in dress uniform: tartan trews, Glengarry, the badge of the Royal Scots. He's leaning against the wall on the north side of the Edinburgh Castle esplanade, arms crossed, eyes looking out over the rooftops of the city toward something outside the frame of the photo. Flashes of familiarity in his face fade when I look closely and his features lose their uniqueness; all soldiers look the same at the end of the day. They look like what they are: androids hardwired to send and receive bullets. Handsome young faces like masks, serving only to tug on civilian heartstrings.

I lock the photos back into their box, then sit back on my heels and wonder why they would be hidden in a trunk in the barn. A strange feeling comes over me, an impression of a family boxing up its past and throwing it away.

Over the wind a more substantial sound materialises into tyres on gravel. I stand up and brush off my knees,

25

wander outside and watch the silver Volvo sweep into the drive. Molly parks next to the van and climbs out. Before she sees me, she stoops to examine herself in the wing mirror and rubs fiercely at her lower eyelids.

I approach casually, pretending not to notice the smudged mascara. It's obvious she's been crying. 'Alright?'

'Yep. Fine.'

'Did you know you have a barn owl?'

She turns sharply. 'What? Sorry, no, I . . . where?'

I point my thumb over my shoulder toward the byre.

'I haven't been in there in years. I'm sorry I'm late. Someone phoned and I . . . got delayed.'

'No problem. You want to see it? The owl, I mean.'

She looks past me, her mouth half open, and after a moment shakes her head. 'No, it's alright. We better make a start, I'm sure you don't have all day.'

'I do.'

'Okay . . . fine.' The tone of her voice has cooled from the other day, and I wonder if she's had second thoughts about this whole arrangement. She turns away and marches purposefully toward the front door. 'I've made a start upstairs already. There were some things that were mine.'

'I'll just get some boxes.' I jog to the van and pull out a stack of flattened boxes, then follow her into the house. 'So . . . where do you . . .'

'I don't know. I don't care to be quite honest. It all has to go, Sean, so just pick a room and start packing.'

Her abrupt, frustrated tone is very intimate. She might be issuing orders to a departing husband. A nervous laugh bubbles up into my throat and I bite my lip.

Molly sees me. 'Something funny?'

'Not really.' I about face and take my boxes along to

26

the library. I figure I'll save the bedrooms for when we feel a bit more at ease with each other. Mitch whispers something about my unfailing strategic genius. *Shut it,* I think, and turn my attention to the business of unfolding the boxes and locking their various flaps into position.

It would be easy to waste time perusing the books, but I force myself to stack them into the boxes without examining the titles. Little puffs of dust billow into the air each time I remove a handful from the shelf, and after a while my nose is tingling and my throat feels dry. I fill a couple of cartons and label them *Cauldhill Farm: books,* then straighten up and feel a sneeze building. It comes, followed quickly by three more. When they subside, I pause, survey my progress and wonder where Molly has gone. I think I hear can hear her voice raised in anger from somewhere in the house, but there's no point trying to tune into the words. There is a short exclamation, and then silence. I return to my packing but a moment later there are footsteps behind me.

'Sorry about the shouting.'

I sit back on my heels and dust my hands on my jeans. 'What shouting?'

She thumps a roll of black bin bags onto the coffee table and gives me that sharp laugh again. 'Don't kid on you didn't hear that just now.'

I smile at her, and give her what I hope is an innocent shrug. 'I'm a bit deaf, so shout all you like.'

She tilts her head in scepticism. 'Is that true?'

'Uh huh. My left ear's totally buggered.'

'What's wrong with it?'

'Blast damage to my inner ear. My exit ticket from the Marines, courtesy of the kind young gentlemen of the Taliban.'

27

'Oh God, Sean, I'm sorry. I didn't know. It can't be fixed?'

'They tried. At least it's only the one, eh?'

She takes a deep breath and then squats beside me, peers into the box of books. 'I suppose it could have been worse.'

I glance at her. 'You think?'

'What do you mean?'

My throat constricts suddenly and I shake my head, mouth half open. This happens a lot: the irrational squall of anger at a person for being ignorant of something they would have no way of knowing.

'Nothing. Forget it.'

'I'm sorry.'

'You keep saying that. What are you sorry for?'

I know it's an impossible question for her to answer, and part of me enjoys watching her flounder. Sorry for bringing it up, most likely. Civvies always assume I don't want to talk about it. Or maybe, they're afraid that I *will* talk about it. Afraid of what I have to tell them. Of what happens in the places their government sends us while they're sat at home watching third-rate celebrities eat worms on camera for money.

She doesn't find an answer so I shrug to let her off the hook. 'Don't feel sorry for me, I volunteered for it. I knew what I was doing.'

'I guess you did. *Why*?'

I laugh. 'It seemed a better option than staying here.'

'That's hard to believe.'

'Not really.' I place a stack of books into the box. 'Who were you shouting at, anyway?'

'Peter. My husband.' She makes little inverted commas in the air with her fingers, describing marital failure in a single gesture.

'Oh.'

'He's just . . . frustrated that I'm still here. It's not important.'

'He misses you.'

'He misses my cooking and cleaning and running around after Joshua, but he doesn't miss me.'

'Is Joshua your son?'

A curt shake of the head. 'Joshua is his son from his first marriage. He's fifteen, he hardly needs running after anyway.'

'No kids of your own?'

'No.' A flat, punctuated syllable, which seems like all I'm going to get. Then she elaborates. 'Anorexia fucked up my ovaries, so it seems I'll never have children.'

Too much fucking information for the removals guy.

'That's too bad.' A lame offering but the best I can manage. I look up at the high, damp-stained ceiling for a moment, then reach for another armload of books.

'Are you sure you don't want to have a look at these before I take them away?'

'Positive. I'll get some of this rubbish out of your way.'

We both retreat from our exposed positions and work without speaking for a while. The hands of the clock on the far wall stopped at twenty past seven one day long past, and I mark time by the changing light. It fades from yellow to silver to watery white as the sun moves into the west. Molly crumples years of old newspapers and shoves them unceremoniously into bin bags, compacting them in with her foot to create tight bales. Gradually the space opens up around us, revealing a fine but filthy Persian rug, solid oak bookcases, a grand, tiled fireplace. She keeps her back to me most of the time, and sometimes I think she's having a quiet cry to herself. I pretend not to notice.

29

By the time the sun is settling behind the hills, we have emptied the room of everything apart from the heavy furniture. I have loaded more than two-dozen cartons into the van and am standing on the step, pressing my fingers into the grumbling muscles of my lower back and filling my lungs with fresh, cold air. It smells of coal smoke and wet grass and of winter not quite ready to give up its grip.

A stooped figure is walking along the road with a skinny black and white collie on a piece of rope. An old man in a shabby oilskin coat and boots, with thin grey hair and an uneven gait. He pauses at the bottom of the drive and stares at me. I feel like I've seen him somewhere before, but then pretty much every scuzzy little bar in the county is propped up by half a dozen old pissheads who look just like him.

'That's ma hoose,' he shouts, slurring and spitting. His arm comes up and he waves a knobbled finger in the air. 'That's ma hoose. Ah'm gonnae get that hoose. It's mines.'

'Aye, okay, mate,' I call back, and turn away from him.

Molly is making tea inside. Her face is streaked with dust and there are cobwebs caught in her hair. Before I can stop myself, I raise my hand to brush them away. Her thick hair slides between my fingers, releasing a lavender smell. She freezes, the spoon quivering in her hand.

'Cobwebs,' I say, wiping the sticky silk onto my jeans. 'Sorry.'

'Oh.' A smile flickers on her lips, then fades. She pushes a mug toward me.

'Ta.'

She sits down at the table. 'You can sit, if you like.'

I drop onto a chair across from her. 'So there was this old boy passing just now, said this was his house.'

'Drunk?'

'Steaming.'

A nod. 'Duncan. He's a shepherd. Lives up on the hill with the sheep. Complete alcoholic. He's been there as long as I can remember. God knows how he manages.'

'Why does he think this is his house?'

'Whisky dreams, I suppose.'

'Did he work for your old man?'

'In a manner of speaking. He did odd jobs and helped Dad out with bits and pieces. The sheep belong to the neighbouring farm, but it's still Dad's land. Was, I mean. Dad never worked the farm; he was a veterinarian.'

'That explains the medical equipment in the barn. Old medicine vials and that.'

'You were snooping.' She cups her hands around her mug and regards me through a veil of steam, more curious than angry.

'Just a bit of a recce. I found some photos. Maybe you want to have a look before I get rid of them.'

'Photos? Of who?'

I laugh. 'How would I know? The crew of a Lancaster bomber from the war. Then another one of a soldier in dress uniform, at Edinburgh Castle.'

Molly blinks. 'The first would be Dad and his mates. They flattened cities. The second . . . I have no idea.'

'Your *dad*?'

'Yeah. I told you he was much older than my mum. He was over sixty when I was born. Ninety-five when he died.'

'Wow. Okay . . .'

She sighs. 'Mmm. Well.'

'You want me to bring the pictures in?'

31

'No,' she says, too quickly. 'Dump them. Dad kept too much shit.'

I feel my eyebrows lift. 'Are you sure?'

'I'm sure. If you want to know the truth, Sean, I'm glad he's gone, and not just for his sake. That sounds wrong, I'm sure, but . . .' she trails off into nothing.

Five years ago I walked away from Mum's funeral light as a man newly liberated from jail, and I still can't bring myself to miss her. 'No. I know what you mean.'

Molly acknowledges this with a bob of the head. 'Dad was a surly old bastard who liked animals more than people. At the end there when he was really ill, he asked the doctors to finish him off. He said if he was a horse, nobody would think twice about having him shot. Then he asked me to do it. Can you imagine that? Asking your own daughter to kill you? When I said no, he called me a soft bitch. His final opinion of me: a soft bitch.'

'Charming.'

'Could you have done it? Put an old man in pain out of his misery?'

'I doubt it.'

I can tell by the way her eyes narrow that she doesn't believe me. 'Do you ever get over it?'

'What's that?'

'Killing someone? You *have,* I assume. Killed someone. More than one.'

I laugh stupidly. 'Nobody related to me, as far as I'm aware.'

She tilts her head a little to one side. 'Does it bother you?'

'It was my job.'

'Are you okay with that?'

'It doesn't make any fucking difference whether I'm

okay with it or not. Why would you think that's your business?'

She presses her lips together and looks out the window. 'I'm sorry. I shouldn't have asked, it was rude of me.'

I take a deep breath. 'Not rude, just ... a wee bit personal at this stage in our relationship. I'm sorry I swore.'

Then she puts her mug down and reaches across the table, clasps my hands and pulls them toward her. 'Let me make it up to you?'

Again, crap.

I linger there, my heart hammering and my hands sweating in hers. I want to, obviously. There are any number of ways she could make it up to me, with those full lips and ripe peach breasts. One kiss and all will be forgiven. Maybe two.

I twist my hands and slide them out of her fingers, then flick her wedding ring with the nail of my middle finger. 'This still means something. Call me old fashioned, but I wouldn't do that to the guy.'

Molly stares at the floor and mutters something. Possibly, she has said, 'You wouldn't be the first,' but I'm not quite sure, so I ignore it, get up and dump the rest of my tea into the sink. It's getting late, my back is aching and I still have to take the van to the shop and unload.

'I'd better go before you get me into trouble, Mrs Wells.'

'Maybe you'd better.'

I push back from the table. Her eyes follow me to the door, but she remains rooted to the spot.

'I'll be back on Sunday, alright?'

She nods meekly. 'I'm sorry.'

'It's alright.'

I leave her at the table and drive back to the shop,

33

unload the van, then get changed and head out for a run. It takes ten miles and Green Day on the iPod, turned up loud enough I risk blowing out my good ear, to unwind myself enough to go home.

V

Billy is particularly bedraggled the next morning, colourless hair limp over his forehead and thin grey trackies
tucked into a pair of greasy brown rigger boots. He's
got a sleekit way about him, sharp eyes that never stop
darting from one side to another, hunched shoulders like
a ferret on the prowl. A jerky walk and nervous hands.
He talks a continuous stream of bullshit, showing pointy
teeth the colour of whisky and releasing the kind of bad
breath that makes you think he must be rotting from
the inside out. You can smell the disease in him. Cancer,
liver disease, whatever; I can smell it and he doesn't
even know he has it yet. I'm willing to bet he has never
voluntarily allowed anything green to pass his lips.

Today, just to add to his charm, he's got an almighty
shiner around his left eye. He climbs in beside me and I
roll down the window. Our first job is in Portobello and
as we go rumbling and lurching through the morning
traffic, my cornflakes are churning around in my gut
with the stench of him. He's glancing at me, turning his
cheek toward me deliberately, obviously hoping I'll ask
about his black eye. From time to time he gives it a rub
and a little wince. The man's wired so tight he's zinging
like a guitar string about to snap.

My eyes feel like a boxer's bollocks. I've been tossing
and turning most of the night: lying on my right side
cursing myself for my less-than-professional behaviour

in Molly's kitchen, then on my left wondering what was wrong with me that I'd walked away from her.

Mitch is jabbering in my ear but he's all static today, like a poorly tuned radio, and I can't make him out. Needless to say, I'm not in the mood for Billy's drinking and scrapping stories. I ignore him and drive in determined silence.

'Caught some heat last night,' he says eventually, as we clear Sherriffhall roundabout and accelerate onto the bypass.

'So I see.'

'Darren Armstrong, ye ken him, aye?'

'No.'

'Ye must ken him. Boab Armstrong's laddie. Ponces aboot like David fucking Beckham, really thinks he's something. The Oak last night, he's fuckin' starin at us, laughin and that. Had tae get him telt, like. Ye must ken him. Really no?'

I shake my head, but it's not quite the truth. Darren Armstrong was a lean, swaggering kid a year below me at school, good on the football pitch and popular. He really thought he was something at school too, and maintained his hard man status by picking fights with bigger guys on a regular basis. I wasn't much of a fighter at school, but being big and good at rugby, I could bring down most people who tried it on with me. I flattened Darren on more than one occasion, but I don't let on. Instead, I think he can't be too much of anything if he's still here, drinking in The Oak. Not a person I care to invest time in remembering. There aren't many. My life here before the Marines is like a film I watched once a long time ago and never wanted to see again.

'Anyway, I goes up tae him and asks him whit's so funny, and he willnae say. So I turns around, and as I'm

36

walkin' away, I hear him tellin' his mate that he shagged Linda once, when she worked in the Waverley and he was like nineteen or something. So I go back and tell him to shut his hole, and he goes for me.'

He pauses, gives a manic laugh which turns into a raw cough. 'Fucking stuck the heid in, man, laid me oot. Ma heid's killin me the day. I think he's fuckin' fractured ma cheekbone. Wee bastard, man, I'm tellin' ye. I need someone tae sort him for me.' He glances at me again, waits.

'What?'

'You could do him nae bother, Sean.' His eye twitches and his hand snaps to it, fingernails digging.

'Probably.'

'Would ye, though?'

'Why the hell would I want to do that?'

He shrugs. 'Thought you squaddie types liked a scrap.'

'Not me.'

'Bet you blew the arseholes out of a few ragheads in Helmand though. Fuckin' Al Qaeda bastards. How many?'

'Jesus Christ.'

Billy shifts around in his seat, clears his throat harshly and gobs out the window. 'My mate Tam's brother, he was in the army. Said he kent a boy who cut an ear off every raghead he shot and hung them on a necklace.'

'That's not funny.'

'How? Whit's wrang wi' ye? How many terrorists did ye send back tae Allah, then? Go on, tell us. You're a hero, man.'

'JESUS MOTHERFUCKING CHRIST, IF YOU DON'T SHUT UP I WILL PULL OVER AND LEAVE YOU AT THE SIDE OF THIS ROAD WITH THE REST OF THE SHITE. DO YOU HEAR ME?'

I've learned to shout from the best of them. The stale air in the van seems to reverberate with it for several seconds afterwards.

Billy stares at me, mouth half open, breath rasping in his throat. The vapour it produces makes my eyes water.

'Don't call me a hero, Billy. You don't know anything about it.'

He holds up a nicotine-stained hand. 'Awright, awright, man, keep yer hair on, Ah wis only askin. Sorry.'

Take a chill pill, Nic. The angsty veteran act is SO American.

I nearly laugh; bloody Mitch. I bite my lip, pull in a deep breath and release it slowly, relax my grip on the wheel and let my gaze wander momentarily to a buzzard rising on an updraft at the side of the road.

'Forget it,' I mutter, pulling my eyes back to the road in front of me.

Billy clears his throat. 'So this bird up the road, she's a bit of alright.'

'Sorry, what was that?'

He raises his voice. 'Yon wifie whae's hoose yer clearin. She's no bad tae look at. I thought ye was gonnae take me up wi' ye tae shift the gear.'

'Only if you have a shower first, ye mingin wee soap-dodger.'

'Oh come oan, eh? That's below the belt.'

I glance at him, one eyebrow raised. 'Truth hurts, eh? Personal administration isn't your strong point, is it?'

His brows knit together and his lips go thin and bloodless. 'Ah'd fuckin hammer ye, son, if ye wernae drivin this van.'

I laugh, slowing as we reach the roundabout at Old Craighall and head left onto the A1 toward Porty. Billy sits there fizzing, then fishes his tobacco pouch out of his back pocket and with thin, deft fingers arranges some sticky, blackish hash onto fag paper. He doesn't light it though, just sits there fingering it gently as we find our way down to the address on John Street.

I bring the van to a halt in front of a sandstone Victorian villa, turn off the engine and stare at him. I don't know why I should care whether he gets high on the job; it's not like he's behind the wheel and it's hard to imagine him being much greater cope straight than he is stoned. But I do.

'If you light that, I'll report you.'

He looks at the spliff, shifts uncomfortably in his seat, seems to shrivel into himself. His eyes dart around with the familiar haunted panic of an addict denied his fix. 'Never pegged ye as a narc, like.'

I reach across and slide the joint out of his fingers, insert it gently into my shirt pocket. 'Give me the rest of it, man. You can have it back when you clock off tonight.'

'Get tae fuck.'

'Can you afford to lose your job? I bloody can't.'

A ferocious little flame kindles momentarily, then dies. Poor wee bastard, he'd be unemployable anywhere else. Looking utterly defeated, he hands over the full pouch. I stuff it into the glove box and lock it.

'It's gonnae be a long day for both of us,' he mutters as he shoves open his door.

'You make it till lunchtime without moaning, I'll buy you a black pudding roll.'

'I make it till lunchtime wi'oot stickin' ma fist in yer pus, ye'll be lucky.'

I slide out of the van and stretch my arms, enjoying the six or seven inches I've got on him. 'Feel free to try it anytime.'

He stretches his neck upward, which only succeeds in making him look scrawnier. 'I'll come at ye from the left and ye'll no hear me.'

'Pardon?'

Billy laughs, the first genuine belly laugh I've managed to get out of him, and it changes his whole face. I've never seen anything but ugliness in him until now, but with that laugh I get the tiniest flash of the man he might have been.

We step up to a grand, black front door and pull the old-fashioned bell, wait several minutes while some shuffling footsteps make their slow way toward us. A hunched wee woman opens the door, hair tied up in a loose white bun and a pair of gold-framed glasses on a chain perched on her nose.

'Good morning, Mrs Burns, we're from Once Loved,' says Billy in his best Cheeky Chappy voice. 'We're here to collect the settee.'

'Yes, come in,' she says, and we follow her along a tiled lobby into a corniced room full of books and musical instruments. A faded and particularly heavy looking sofa, upholstered in something like medieval tapestry, is partly pulled out from the wall, revealing at least half an inch of dust on the floorboards behind it. I stare at it, wondering how we are going to manoeuvre the monster out of the room.

'Is this the one?' I ask.

'That's never a real Steinway,' Billy says behind me. I turn, to see him approaching an upright piano against the far wall, Mrs Burns tottering behind him.

'My husband's wedding present to me,' she says. The proud, clear tones of an educated Edinburgh lady. 'I can't play anymore, my hands are too bad.' She holds up arthritic fingers.

Billy lifts the keyboard cover and glances at her. 'Mind if I have a shot?'

Cringe time. 'Billy . . .'

He and Mrs Burns ignore me. She nods at him, and he tinkles a couple of keys, then settles both hands over the keys and launches into a bluesy rock number.

Knock me down with a toothpick, he can actually play that thing.

Mitch is right. Close your eyes and you might be listening to Jerry Lee Lewis. Billy plays for a couple of minutes, grinning from ear to ear, then stops abruptly in the middle of the tune and clears his throat.

Mrs Burns claps, eyes alight with pleasure. 'Oh wonderful. Wonderful. Don't stop there.'

'Ach,' Billy grunts, turning back toward us. 'I've no played in years. Always wanted a wee shot of a Steinway. Ta for that.'

'No, thank *you*,' she says. 'I miss hearing it.'

Then he juts his chin toward the sofa. 'That it, aye?'

'Yes, that's it. I'm sorry to part with it, but I can't get out of it anymore. These blasted hips and knees. Hamish used to have to hoist me up. He could lift me with me with one hand, just up until the day before he died. He passed away four months ago.'

'I'm very sorry,' I offer.

She smiles at me kindly, without sentimentality. 'I do hope it will go to a family who needs it. It's a wonderful sofa for reading.'

I smile back. 'I'm sure it will. Right, Bill, how are we going to do this?'

With great effort, and no small amount of grunting and muttering, we angle the sofa through the door and down the hallway. As usual, I have to take the weight of it down the front steps and then up into the van, as Billy curses and wobbles and breaks wind with the effort.

At last, it slides into the van like a coffin sliding away into the flames of the crematorium. I glance back at Mrs Burns, who has followed us out into the street. Her lips are quivering ever so slightly.

'That's us,' I say, dusting my hands on my trousers.

'Thank you, gentlemen,' says Mrs Burns graciously. Then she turns to Billy and places a hand on each of his arms. 'Your little bit of music has brought a smile to my day.' She lingers there, fading eyes taking in the details of his face, and for just a moment I think she's either going to kiss him or offer him the piano.

It's not easy to silence Billy, but she's done it. 'Ach, well,' he says after an embarrassed moment, 'we aim to please, eh?'

We climb back into the van and are halfway to our next job in Craigmillar before he speaks again. He leans his head back against the headrest and releases a long sigh. 'Braw piany.'

'Where'd you learn to play like that?'

'My ma. She was a rare musician. Used tae sing in the jazz clubs and that in toon. Hard tae feed a family o' six on it though. Aifter the pit shut, that was the only money we had comin' in.'

'So why don't you play anymore?'

'Other things on ma mind.' He shrugs, then glances at me. 'Yer ma was Diana, eh?'

'What about her?'

'Nothin.' He shakes his head, laughs softly. 'She was a local institution, that's all.'

'What you saying?'

'Forget it.'

'Do me a favour and don't talk about her, right? Not to me.'

42

'Fine.' He holds up a hand. Then he snorts. 'A fucking institution though. Mair men in and oot her than all the pubs in Eskbridge put together.'

'D'you know what, Billy? I was just beginning to think you weren't the obnoxious little tosser I pegged you for at first. But I was fucking right the first time. You are. An obnoxious, foul mouthed little tosspot. Dinnae speak to me. Just sit there and keep your disgusting gob shut.'

He sniffs and crosses his arms, stares out the window and says nothing further.

We drive on, from leafy Victorian Portobello to the post-apocalyptic wasteland of Niddrie, where we collect a fridge and freezer that have been dumped in the rain to wait for us. Although there's little chance they'll be working, we take them to be broken down for parts and recycling. One final job in Morningside: a baby's cot that is in such pristine condition it might never have been used.

After this, Billy glances at his watch and slaps me on the arm. 'Reckon you owe me that black puddin' roll, Sunshine.'

VI

Molly meets me at the door on Sunday morning, eyes veiled and embarrassed. An icy rain splatters onto the gravel.

She stands aside to let me in, clocks the bags under my eyes. 'You haven't slept.'

'I'm fine.'

I've been awake most of the night, watching shadows on my bedroom ceiling and listening to the wind wailing around the eves like dogs howling over a rotting corpse. I've got a headache rumbling behind my eyes and I'm starting to feel dizzy in a jetlaggy kind of way, but buggered I'm going to admit it to her.

She doesn't believe me anyway. 'Well, I didn't sleep. It sounded like the roof was going to lift off. I had to get up and clean things. Better?'

The scree of old dishes and baskets has been cleared and the kitchen has been scrubbed clean. Years of burnt-on food splatters have been scoured from the surfaces, and the sticky coating of dust and grease removed from the shelves. It is now a functional farmhouse kitchen. There should be a pot of homemade soup bubbling on the range, a pile of green wellies next to the door and a collie sleeping on the warm flagstones.

I run my fingers through damp hair and then hold them in front of the Aga, which is putting out an intense, shimmering heat.

'Much better.'

'I . . .' She opens her mouth, then hesitates.

'What?'

'I wasn't sure you'd come back today. I . . . came on a bit strong, I guess.'

Of course he was going to come back today, sweetheart, it's been so long since he had a fuck, his bollocks are like hand grenades. Not that he hasn't had offers, mind, he's just choosy. Thinks he's above all this. Sordid little affairs behind hubby's back. Chicken, that's what he is.

'Don't worry about it.'

She doesn't look worried to me, son. She's about as subtle as a Bangkok whore.

'I'll . . . ehm . . . make some coffee.'

'I'll make a start.'

Her head bobs like a nervous little sparrow and I hurry along the corridor, past the now bare library to the sitting room. It is equally dusty, but there is less clutter and the room is cold, damp and musty smelling as an old stone church, as though it hasn't been occupied or heated in a very long time. A room reserved for guests in a house which never had them. On the mantelpiece is a largish vase painted with green and red Chinese dragons, and when I lift it carefully I find that it is tethered to the wood by a thick net of cobwebs.

Something clunks inside the vase as I begin to wrap it in newspaper, so I tip it upside down. Two dead spiders and a small parcel fall out. I examine the latter. It's a bundle of folded paper, crumbly yellow, tied together with a black ribbon. Letters, all written in the same decorative hand, addressed to a Mr George Finlayson from H.B. Starling, 195 West 135th Street, New York, NY, USA.

I flick my thumb over the brittle edges of maybe thirty

envelopes, then bring them to my nose and inhale. Dust, pipe smoke, and possibly the faintest suggestion of perfume- though I could be imagining this. I glance quickly over my shoulder, then untie the ribbon and slide the top letter out of its envelope and read:

15 October, 1947,

Dearest George,

Do you remember making love under the cherry trees in Central Park? I can't go there anymore. The city hurts me now, the places we went together can only remind me now that you are gone.

'Jesus,' I mutter, and stop reading. I'm alone but my face feels hot with the embarrassment of having peeked too far inside. Examining a person's objects are one thing, but reading their words – or in this case, those written to them by a heartbroken lover – is something else entirely. Quickly I fold the letter back into its envelope, tie the bundle back together and set this to one side.

So. Old Man Finlayson screwed some poor girl under the cherry trees in Central Park and left her pining. The image I had of a soulless old toff with a rod of iron up his arse crumbles a little bit.

As I work, I wonder who she was and whether the old teapot might contain letters from a woman in Rio and the piano bench a bundle from a girl in Hong Kong. I met an American Marine once who kept two wives on the go in different cities. We used to ask him what would happen if he got killed and they both turned up at his funeral. He would laugh and hold his hands wide. *I'll be dead*, he would say, *so who the fuck cares?*

'Coffee's ready,' Molly says from the doorway behind me, in a voice that is louder than it needs to be. This bugs the hell out of me, but I turn around and mind my manners.

'Thanks.'

'Let's sit in the kitchen. This room feels like a crypt.'

'I found this, Molly.' I hand her the little bundle of letters, which she examines as we return along the corridor. In the kitchen she drops the letters carelessly onto a pile of paper at the far end of the long table, sits quietly and pours frothy coffee from a cafetiere, then splashes in milk from a little silver jug.

'Have a croissant,' she says distantly, pushing a plate toward me. Face like sour milk.

I help myself and we sit there for a couple of minutes. She sips her coffee, pretends to read a newspaper, doesn't eat. I create little explosions of flaky crumbs with each bite into the warm croissant and wonder if it would be exceptionally greedy to reach for a second. There are three on the plate.

'The letters appear to be from a woman.' This is my retribution for her invasion of my privacy the other day.

'Oh, they would be.' She sighs. 'One of many.'

'In New York?'

'He lived there for a little while, after the war.'

'So . . . are you going to read them?'

A shrug. 'I don't know.'

'What was he doing in New York?'

'Spending his parents' money, by all accounts. Celebrating his survival in style.' She puts down her mug and looks at me, and I guess she's decided she's had enough questions. 'Have you done that? Celebrated your survival?'

'Not so you'd notice.'

'I think you should. Crack open the champagne and get drunk for a year. It might make you appreciate the fact.'

I feel my eyebrows lift. 'What fact?'

'That you're still alive.'

'I don't drink.'

This clearly surprises her. It surprises most people. 'Not at all?'

'No.'

'Why not?'

I sit back in my seat and narrow my eyes at her, enjoying the way her lipstick smears onto her cheeks when I let my vision go out of focus. Her features melt and shift and she looks someone painted by Picasso. I've opened the door too wide, I know that; she's got a foot wedged inside and I'm not sure I'll be able to shut it out again.

Instead of answering, I tear off a piece of croissant, then lean across the table and raise the buttery pastry to her mouth. She hesitates just for a moment, then opens and lets me place it on her tongue like a communion wafer.

'My turn,' I say, my face very close to hers as she chews. When she swallows, I break off another piece and feed it to her the same way. 'So . . . why are you distracting me with breakfast when I should be working?'

'You looked hungry,' she almost whispers.

I run my finger along the fine ridge of her lower jaw, and she doesn't flinch away. 'And why are you asking me so many questions? I'm just the removal man.'

'Maybe I'm just nosy. Maybe I'm like this with everyone.'

'You offer to sleep with every workman who comes to the house?'

Now she raises her hand to my cheek and worms her fingers into my beard. 'No, just you. Because I know you.'

'You don't know me, Molly.'

48

'I feel like I do. I fancied you at school. Did you know that?'

I let my hand slide down to hers and run my thumb over her ring. 'What about him?'

One shoulder rises and her hair falls over it. 'I'm not marriage material.'

I laugh softly, and curl a lock of her hair around my finger. 'Don't you think you should at least try? For the sake of honour, if nothing else.'

'I've been trying for six years, and honour has nothing to do with it. That's the Royal Marine talking.'

'I cannae help it, that's who I am.'

'*Were.* You're a free man now.'

I stare at her and move my fingers around to the back of her head, pull her close. Our lips meet, and gently I explore the soft moistness of her mouth, tasting coffee and pastry and toothpaste and a little of last night's wine. This could put me off if I let myself think about it, so I close my eyes and let her take over. She does, fiercely, opening her mouth and cupping both of my cheeks with her hands so I can't pull back even if I wanted to.

'I haven't shown you upstairs yet,' she murmurs into my ear, and then clasps my hand and stands. Like a blind man I allow her to lead me up one short flight, around a landing and up again, then to lower me onto a bed with a fluffy, cream downy. She gives me no more time to assess the lie of the land. Her scent billows up around me as I lie back and her hands press me down into the bed, start peeling off my clothes.

I close my eyes, lie there passively and let her run her lips down my chest and toward my groin. She plays around for a few minutes, flickering her tongue here and there, moving her hand around between my legs until I'm just about bursting. Then she slides her leg over

49

me and arches her back as she guides me into her. She doesn't leave much for me to do but lie back and think of . . .

Fucksake, man, she might as well be riding a sack of spuds. Get your mitts on her titties at the very least.

Bugger won't even leave me alone now. It's no good closing my eyes, so I stare at Molly's face and watch it contort with effort and pleasure. Short-lived pleasure. I can't help it. He's there, hanging over me like Adam on the ceiling of the Sistine Chapel, except there is just a formless, bloody pulp where his legs should be. I feel myself go soft inside her and slide out.

'Sorry,' I manage to say. Possibly the emptiest word in the English language.

She slithers off of me, leaving her own dampness on my legs, then props herself on one elbow, gazing at my face and running her fingers around my nipples. I can see all the questions in her eyes, but to her credit, she doesn't give them voice.

'What do you like?' she whispers.

I look up at the dirty ceiling, dust-choked cobwebs hanging from the cornices and lamp fixture, and my chest feels like an over-inflated tyre. What man in his right mind could lie here and fail to come up with an answer to that question? All I can do is shake my head and pull in a deep breath to try to calm the tide of nausea. It doesn't work.

I clamp my hand over my mouth and bolt out of bed bare-arsed naked. Thankfully I make it to the toilet next door before the coffee and croissants come spewing out into a porcelain pan stained brown by years of the old guy's concentrated, alcoholic piss. Three waves pass over me, until I am dripping sweat and retching up yellow bile, and when it stops I sit on the lino and thump

50

my head back against the wall. Tears burn my cheeks like hot acid.

This is your fucking fault.

I'm working on the daisies. Worm food, remember? You haven't learned to check your equipment's in working order before going into action by now, that's your own bloody fault.

'I need to get out of here,' I say, only realising afterwards that I've said it aloud.

Ha! Ha hahaha. Your kit's in a heap at the bottom of her bed. You and Mr Floppy will have to walk back in there. Hold your head high, boy!

'Sean?' A gentle knock on the door.

I scramble to my feet and pull a damp towel around my waist. 'Yeah.'

'Are you alright?'

'Just coming.' I splash some water on my face and rinse my mouth, glance tentatively into the mirror. I've humiliated myself enough without emerging with puke stuck in my facial hair.

The picture there isn't pretty. Hair too long, too greasy. Sandy brown with a shitload of grey ones in there. The beard is even worse; give me a year or two, I'm going to look like Kenny Rogers. The grey happened more or less overnight. One morning I was a young man, and by sunset I was old. Thirty-three, the age most men are just about growing up, and I'm bitter and deaf and impotent. A twisted old bastard with chunks in his beard.

I hold the towel around myself and open the door. Molly is standing in the corridor with a quilt around her, shivering. For the first time I realise how cold it is; apart from the range in the kitchen, the house is unheated and smells damp. Through the cloudy bathroom window, I see snow falling on the daffodils.

'Are you alright?'

I don't answer, and she follows me back to the bedroom.

I sit down on the bed and pull on my boxers. It's a moment before I can meet her eyes. 'It's not your fault. I'm just . . .'

I break off. There are very few that adequately describe what I am.

Molly sits beside me and rubs my back. Just the feel of her skin begins to stir my guts again, and I have to move away. 'Molly, I . . . can't. I cannae do this, I'm sorry.'

'Can't you tell me why? I thought you liked me. You were the one who started it this morning.'

I pull the sleeves of my shirt the right way out and stick my arms into them, stare at the floor while buttoning it. 'I know I did. It was a mistake. I'm an arse.'

'No you're not, Sean.'

I grab my jeans and stand up to put them on, then sit down again and pull on my socks. 'The snow's getting worse. I'd better get the van back up the road or I'll be stuck here.'

'And would that really be such a bad thing?' This girl really doesn't want to give up. She squeezes my hand and holds it. 'Maybe all you need is someone to show you that life goes on. It has to.'

'I don't need you to show me that.'

It's the truth. Of course life goes on. I watch it going on in all its sad and pointless little varieties, all around me every day. It's like sitting on a platform watching every train roll by except the one you need. And you can sit there forever, because the train you need – the one that will take you back in time – will never come.

'Maybe you'd better find someone else to do the house.'

52

Her eyes open wide. 'Oh no, come on. We made a deal.'

'But the deal didn't include this.' I double tie my boots and stand up again. 'I'll see you later, right?'

'But you're saying you won't!'

I hold my hands wide, let them drop again without saying anything, and leave her sitting on the edge of the bed.

There are a couple of inches of snow on the ground by the time I get home, and my fingers are clenched so tight to the steering wheel it's painful to pull them off. Janet is in the bathroom in an old t-shirt, trackies and gloves, massaging ammonia-smelling dye into her hair. She pokes her reddish, lathered head out as I march past, brows drawn together.

'What's up, kid?'

'Feeling sick. Going to bed.' I can't look at her, walk straight past, close my bedroom door. I strip down to my pants and curl into bed, pulling the quilt up over my ear and drawing my knees up toward my chest. At this moment, it's hard to imagine any reason to ever get up again. Sleep doesn't come quickly at the best of times, and after a while, Janet comes in and sits on the edge of my bed, hair in a towel.

'Will you live?'

'I expect so.'

'Want to talk?'

'No.'

'Will I bring you a bucket?'

'No.'

She strokes my hair, then bends down and kisses my cheek. 'Sleep then, wee man. I'll be here when you get up.'

I want to tell her to go away and leave me to it, but the best I can manage is a grunt into the pillow. I close my eyes, pretend to be on the verge of sleep. The mattress straightens as she stands up, and I lie still until she pulls the door shut behind her.

VII

Janet salvages me from a gore-splattered dream with a gentle hand on my cheek. Waking up sometimes feels like fighting my way to the surface from deep underwater. I gulp air and push my face out of the pillow.

'Are you okay?'

I groan, flop onto my back and press my palms into my eyes. My chest is still pumping and it takes a moment for the panic to subside.

'What were you dreaming about?'

I try to focus but my eyes are sticky with sleep. 'I was . . . attacking somebody with an axe. Except I wasn't me, I was a bear.'

'A bear with an axe?'

'Mmm. In a tent.'

'Sean, that's . . .'

'Don't analyse, Janet.'

'I brought you some breakfast. Do you think you can eat?'

I hear the clink of dishes and open my eyes to find a tray with cornflakes, toast and tea on the bed beside me. The blinds are drawn but I can hear the windows rattling with a ferocious wind.

'What time is it?' My limbs feel like anchor lines.

'Seven.'

I sit up slowly, becoming aware of the hollow ache of hunger in my belly. 'AM or PM?'

She smiles. 'AM. Monday morning.'

'Bloody hell.'

I've been in bed for almost twenty hours and have no recollection of having woken up once, even for a pee.

'How did you let me sleep so long?'

'You said you were ill, I figured was just as well to let you sleep it off. Anyway, no wonder. You hardly sleep most nights. How are you now?'

I lift the tray carefully into my lap and consider the question as I chew on a spoonful of cereal. The food feels like it will stay down, so I shrug. 'Okay.'

Janet watches me eat. She knows I'm avoiding her gaze.

'So . . . what happened yesterday?'

'Nothing. Honestly, I just . . . I don't know. Tummy bug or something.'

'I don't believe you.'

'Fine.'

'You didn't have an accident or anything?'

'No.'

'Sean . . .'

'Nothing happened. It's just me, Janet, alright? Just whatever this crap is that happens in my head. Just leave it, for fucksake.'

She huffs. 'It's snowed about six inches. You won't be surprised to know the street hasn't been cleared. Maybe you shouldn't be in the van.'

'I might ask for a day off. You going in?'

'Have to.' She works in the council's housing department, sorting out emergency accommodation for homeless wasters like me. Apparently we're both destined to spend our lives surrounded by Saddos.

'I'll walk to the bus.' She glances at her watch, then

56

places her hand on my arm. 'I'd better go. Don't try to do too much today.'

'Aye . . . okay. Thanks for breakfast.'

She raises her eyebrows – a maternal, disbelieving kind of a look – gives me a smile with half of her mouth, and leaves me to wolf my breakfast.

I scrape the bowl of cornflakes clean, polish off the toast and tea, then haul myself out of bed and shuffle down to the kitchen, pop another piece of Hovis brown into the toaster and stand gazing out the window at a world of grey and white. Fat flakes are swirling in the wind, blowing in thick clouds from the trees and making drifts against the parked cars.

After my toast and a second cup of tea, I ring Harry's mobile and ask for a day off in lieu for all of the extra hours I've been putting in at the farm. I can't bring myself to confess that I've walked out on the job.

'Of course,' he says in a voice so kind it withers me. 'I wouldn't want you on the road today anyway.'

Most likely he'll turf me out on my ear when he finds out what went on yesterday, but I bite my lip and tell him I'll see him tomorrow. Then I hang up and check for voicemails.

One from Molly. I hold my breath as I listen.

Sean . . . if you get this, would you ring me? A pause. *Please? I know what you think of me, and I guess I can't change that. I just want to know if you're coming back to finish the house.*

I hang up and stare out the window at a dirty water-colour of grey, brown and white.

And what do you think of her, anyway, Nic?

'She's a lonely, unhappy woman. She's no more inter-ested in me than she'd be in any man who came through her door.'

57

No, it's just you. She's turned on by the idea of saving a wounded soldier with her love.

'It's not love, it's sex, and that never saved anyone.'

Of course it has. Don't cast up, just because you couldn't manage.

'Fuck off, Mitch. Just leave me the fuck alone. Let me forget about you.'

That's not going to happen.

These quiet times are the worst: still, lonely hours when my mind has nothing else to occupy it. Mitch chatters incessantly when he's bored, just like he always did. Strange, rambling conversations that bounce from one topic to the next according to some rationale that makes sense to him and no-one else. He was a reader, like me, except instead of pulp crime novels, he read literature and philosophy and history. Sometimes on patrol he would quote from Shakespeare or Dante. More often, he would sing: everything from Welsh hymns to Radiohead, but his particular favourite was Hank Williams.

He had started a degree in history, but dropped out after a disastrous first year spent mainly in the pub or in someone else's bed. He used to say he joined the Royal Marines because it felt more honest to be part of a war than to read about it, and for all his intelligence, he was the most idiotically fearless man I ever met. He got up to all manner of crazy shit, maybe to prove he was a man, or prove he was alive or maybe just because he could. He was always first into minefields and hostile compounds. He swam in the North Sea in winter in just his trunks. His favourite sport was free climbing: no ropes, dangling by toes and wiry, horny fingers from sheer, wet rock. One time in the Cairngorms he fell thirty feet off a rock face, landed in a drift of soft snow, laughed and dusted himself off and walked away unscathed.

Maybe we all thought we were superheroes for a while, but Mitch had a kind of golden, bullet-proof radiance about him that made you almost believe he was immortal. Sometimes I think even he believed it, and maybe that's why now he won't give in and accept that he's dead.

I shower, then clear a patch on the steamed up mirror and stare at my pink skin and wet, shaggy hair. Sometimes you just have to face up to the ugliness of a situation; it's time for the beard to go. It's hard to remember exactly what my face looks like underneath, but it's got to be better than this. I trim it as short as I can with Janet's nail scissors, then set to work with the razor, watching the sink fill with foamy, slimy bits of scruff. I have to go carefully around the flack scars in front of my ear and down the side of my jaw, but the redness has mostly gone out of them. They don't look like much now, considering how they got there.

Ten minutes later I'm shovelling snow from the path at the front of the house, creating a dense bank at the edge of the lawn. The wind pushes at me, raw across my bare face, and the sky hangs heavy and smoke-smudged over the rooftops, thick with the smells of coal and snow. There aren't many people about; the usual scurry of old women with their shopping bags and young mums with their buggies and clicky-heeled boots has been replaced by the careful trudge of boots on ice. In the distance, I hear the scrape of shovels and the rev of engines, the chatter of crows and the raking cough of some old bugger with a chest full of black dust.

I reach the end of our path and keep going along the pavement that wraps round our gable-end and onto the street. The work feels good and soon I am sweating enough to pull off my jumper. The wind has subsided, I realise, and a weak sun is filtering through the cloud.

Four houses along, a door opens and a petite woman with bobbed dark hair emerges, steps carefully over the icy ground, then hesitates as she notices me.

I straighten up and run my fingers through my hair as she approaches me. Paula Fairbairn was as good a friend as I had as a kid, until the age of fourteen and a bout of childish fumbling under her duvet one day while her parents were at work. Things became too uncomfortable after that and we retreated to a position of polite civility, as though the years we had spent mucking about in the field, making dens of branches and leaves or hunting fictional lions, had never existed.

The last time I saw her was at Mum's funeral five years ago, but we never exchanged more than pleasantries.

She raises her hand and smiles, and as she approaches I notice that she is pregnant and quite heavily so. Her belly is round as a plum under a woolly tunic, her long coat hanging unbuttoned at her sides. Immediately I envy the man who planted that seed in her. I know she married some university boyfriend, but that was years ago now.

'Oh my God,' she says softly, little creases forming around the corners of her eyes as her smile widens. 'Hiya stranger.' She steps right up to me and places her hands on my arms, raises herself onto her toes and kisses my cheek in that cosmopolitan way I've never really got used to. 'Mum told me you were back.'

I clear my throat. 'Ehm . . . yeah . . . for a while. So . . . wow . . . how are you?'

She laughs and looks down at her bump, gives it a wee rub. 'I'm jammy. Fit to burst, but.'

'So I see. Congratulations.'

Her cheeks are flushed and her eyes as rich and dark as I remember them. 'Thanks. Jesus, Sean, I heard what happened in Afghanistan. Are you alright?'

'A wee bit bruised and battered, that's all. Deaf in my left ear, but I'll live.'

Thankfully the shadow of pity doesn't cross her face. Instead, she laughs. 'Indestructible as ever, thank God. It's good to see you home. So, is that you back out on Civvy Street, then?'

'Yep.'

'You working?'

'In a manner of speaking. I've got a wee gig shifting furniture for the recycling project down the High Street.'

'It's a job, don't knock it.'

'No. It's taken me long enough to get one.'

'So, it's good, right? You playing rugby?'

'I played a bit in the Marines, but not for a while. You still teaching?'

'Aye. Just started my maternity leave.'

'Still in Edinburgh?'

'Ehm . . . yeah. Tollcross. But I've been staying with Mum the last couple of nights. Her hips are knackered and she needs bit of help sometimes. You know Dad died a couple of years ago.'

'Janet told me. I was just shipping out to Afghanistan or I'd have come to the funeral. I was sorry to hear it.'

'Thanks. I remember you sent a card.' Her eyes flicker away from me and she nods. 'I still haven't got used to him being gone.'

'Yeah . . . I know about that one.'

She pushes her hands down into her coat pockets. 'It's really fucking crap, isn't it?'

'Pretty crap.' The cold begins to bite again, so I plant

my shovel and untie my hoodie from around my waist, pull it over my head.

Paula steps past me and examines the snow around the wheels of a little purple Ford Fiesta. She kicks the icy drift against the front wheel, then stands there pressing her fingers into her lower back.

'I wanted to get the messages in for Mum.'

'I don't think I'd bother with the car today.'

She sniffs and rubs her hands together. 'Pain in the arse, this weather. Everything's a pain in the arse when you're the size of a beached whale, mind.'

'I'll walk down to the Co-op and pick some things up for you. And you're not, by the way.'

Paula turns back toward me. 'Sean, you're a diamond, you know that? Would you really?'

'Aye, sure. It's fine. What do you need?'

'Just some milk and bread and a few tins of soup to keep her going for a day or two. I'd go with you but this bloody baby's squashing my lungs; I can't walk the length of myself either just now. I just hope I don't have to make a dash to hospital before the snow's away.'

'You don't fancy giving birth in a blizzard at the side of the road?'

'Oh fuck, no.' She laughs. 'I don't fancy giving birth at all now you mention it, but seeing as I've got myself into this situation, I guess I'll have to go through with it.'

'Not much else for it,' I reply, feeling my eyes settling on the curve of her belly. I've never spent much time around pregnant women, so it surprises me how delicious she looks.

I clear my throat. 'So . . . ehm . . . give me a wee list and I'll nip down the road.'

'Are you absolutely sure?'

'Aye, I said so.'

'Thank you,' she says, earnestly. 'I'll just pop in and get Mum to write a list.'

'Sure,' I say, and watch her pick her way back along the icy path. While she's inside, I clear the path from her mother's front door out to the pavement and scrape away as much of the underlying ice as possible.

Several minutes later, the door opens again and Paula's mother Brenda peers out, leaning heavily on a stick. She has the same dark, bobbed hair as her daughter, but it's dyed and her once plump cheeks are ravaged by years of smoking. There is no chocolaty softness in her eyes, just something flinty and hard and disappointed. She's what Paula might have become if she hadn't made her escape.

Paula and I maintained our friendship as long as we could in pure defiance of Brenda, who disapproved of me without really knowing me. She knew my mother, and that was enough to convince her that I was destined for a life of drugs and criminal behaviour. She was one of the gaggle of mums who never bothered to lower their voices when they gossiped in the schoolyard. Warning me to stay away from their daughters without wanting to speak to me directly.

I wonder why Paula hasn't come back to the door, but I refuse to let my face advertise my disappointment. Instead, I summon a grin and offer a snappy 'Morning, Brenda.' A salute is tempting, just to rile the old cow.

It's safe to say the dislike is mutual. Her eyes flicker over me and she takes a long breath, as though the idea of actually speaking to me causes her pain. 'Sean, dinnae worry aboot the messages. I've got enough and it's dangerous goan oot in this. Yer no exactly fit yersel.'

I glance down at my boots, lifting one foot and then the other. 'All still in working order, as far as can tell.' Then I raise an eyebrow at her. 'Or did you mean something else?'

63

'I'm not saying *that*, son.'

'In that case, I think I can manage the Co-op and back.'

Another long pause as she assesses me, mouth crumpling into a tight, colourless line. Eventually she shrugs. 'Ach well, Paula's nae much cope in her condition, so I suppose I'll have tae let ye. I'll have tae pay ye back later though, I've no got any cash on me.'

'Nae bother, pop it in whenever. Did you write a list for me?' Evil woman probably thinks I'll nick it.

'Here.' She lifts her hand and holds out a small piece of white paper, arm outstretched as though offering a scrap of meat to an animal.

I take it and fold it into my pocket. 'Good news about the baby, eh?'

She sniffs. 'If you say so. Mind and get us the iceberg lettuce, eh, no that leafy kind. That's if it can be had in this weather.'

'Right.' I look up at a sky the colour of a week-old bruise. A single disorientated pigeon swirls across it. 'I'm not back in three days, send out a search party, eh?'

Her eyes are humourless. 'Aye.' She lights a cigarette and leans on her stick. 'See ye, Sean.'

'No bother, Brenda. You're welcome.'

She puts her bulk into reverse and shuts the door on me. Hackit auld bitch, as my Ma would no doubt have said. In general and usually unfairly, Mum hated other women. But in this particular case, her judgement was spot on; Brenda's only redeeming feature is that she produced Paula.

You're the one who offered.

'For Paula's sake, not hers,' I reply as I crunch through the snow on my way down the road. 'The poor girl's about to drop.'

The poor girl's about to drop and you want to bed her.

64

*I'm just a dead guy, Nic, so feel free to disregard me, but
. . . possibly not the best move, tactically speaking.*

'I do not want to bed her, Mitch, and I will disregard
you.'

Go on, then.

'How can I when you keep fucking talking?'

*Look around, buddy boy. You're the only one talking
here.*

VIII

There has been a thaw and a freeze again overnight. Cars skite drunkenly on black ice, mouths forming the shapes of curses behind closed windows. Harry grounds the van again and brings me into the shop to help Al with some of the repairs and refurbishment. He sets Emma and Dawn on cleaning detail and asks Billy to rotate some stock. The minute he disappears into his office, the girls flop onto sofas and start in on yet another of their epic bitch-fests, this time about one of Dawn's ex boyfriends. Billy brings a couple of settees out from the storeroom and leaves them in an unceremonious queue before sloping off somewhere to light up.

Al and I work well enough together. We sand out scratches and knife scores from table-tops, re-glue shoogly legs, stitch the torn undersides of sofas, stain and polish. Al watches me critically but doesn't talk much, and when he does it is usually only a word or two. A noun and a verb, enough to let me know where to put the glue or what type of sandpaper to use. It seems to cost him a huge effort to string a sentence together. But as I watch him, I begin to notice the fluency with which his hands grasp the tools and move over the wood, as though they understand their work without any real input from his brain.

'You're good at this,' I say to him after a couple of hours.

He shrugs. 'Doddle. Cabinet maker to trade. Had ma ain business before.'

Before what, I want to ask.

'You mairrit, son?' he asks me.

'No.'

'Girlfriend?'

'Nah.'

He laughs, nods. 'Keep it that way. Mair trouble than they're worth.'

'Ken what I think?' This is from Emma, on the sofa behind us. She nudges my backside with her toe. 'I think he's a poof. They're all faggots on they ships.'

'Unoriginal,' I say, then blow away a thin layer of sawdust and run my hand along the sleek, fresh surface.

'So why don't you have a girlfriend, then?' asks Dawn. Her voice is more capable of kindness, but I think all the more dangerous for it.

Why? You want to screw him, do you, darling? Knock yourself out, eh? You won't get very far. But then, maybe that's for the best. There's enough little bastards in this town already.

'Because I don't.'

Dawn crosses her arms and tilts her head at me. 'My ma kent yer ma, Sean. Diana McNicol. I mind her tae. Used tae drink down the Miners Club. Pisshead, aye? My ma said she was a tart an' all. Bet ye dinnae ken yer da, eh, Sean. I bet ye dinnae.'

Emma squeals. 'Oh my God, Dawn, that's a bit harsh.'

Al says nothing, but looks from me to Dawn and back again. I keep sanding and can't think of anything to say. Denying the truth in a town this size is a hide into nothing.

Well, you've got something in common with her boys then, Nic. You could always tell her that.

67

I could. Another crazy, freaked out guy might do more than that. Still kneeling, I spread my dusty hands on my thighs, stare at them and allow myself three or four seconds to think about what they could do to her. Then I wipe them on my trousers and stand up. 'Dawn, you've got the social skills of a fucking amoeba.'

Al gives a bark of laughter and Dawn looks to Emma for reassurance. She doesn't actually ask out loud what an amoeba is, but I can hear her think it.

'D'you think I'm caring?'

'Nah. That's your problem.'

I walk away and head into the staff room to make a coffee. I fill the kettle, then grab a carton of milk from the fridge. It splats into my cup in a congealed lump.

'For fucksake,' I mutter. I chuck the week-old carton into the bin and wash the rancid curds down the sink.

All the way through school I lived in terror of someone saying what Dawn has just said. And sometimes I think I joined the Marines so I could reinvent myself as a legitimate person: someone more than the cast off result of a drunken accident.

The kettle starts to rumble and steam, so I switch it off and pour the water into my mug, watching it swirl into the instant coffee crystals and begin to froth. Al shuffles in as I'm digging in the fridge for usable milk.

'Are ye alright?' he asks, laying a broad hand on my shoulder. 'That wis terrible. Wee bitch.'

'I'm fine. It's no big deal.'

He sits heavily and his lips move silently for a moment. 'I kent your ma as well, fae ma school days. And ma drinkin days. Bonny lassie, she was. Kind. Wasted wi' the drink, aye, but . . . kind. Tragic, really.'

'Please don't tell me you slept with her. I don't want to know.'

68

'Nah. Nah, I didnae.' He waves his hand in front of his chest. 'She came tae the hospital tae see me aifter ma accident. Ah wis . . .' he stumbles over the words and his lips work away silently for a moment, 'Ah wis . . . right sorry to hear she'd passed.'

I sit down across from him and stare into my mug for a moment. 'What happened to you?'

'Wrecked the car in Roslin Glen. Mornin' aifter a big session, ye ken. Lynn, ma wife, wis killed. Ah killed her, son, wi' ma drinkin. Only reason I didnae go to the jail was I spent near a year in hospital. Shouldae been me, eh?'

'I'm sorry, Al.'

His pink-stained blue eyes fill with tears so he looks away out the window. 'Dinnae ken what Ah'd dae wi'oot this place. Nae reason tae get up in the morn. See if it goes doon the pan . . .'

'Why? You think it will?'

He shrugs. 'Harry's worrit. Yon government cuts.'

'Yon government cuts,' I repeat slowly. Words that carry the whiff of shit travelling in the direction of a very large fan. 'Yon government cuts have a lot to answer for.'

'Aye . . . ach . . . it could pick up. They lazy bounders oot there dinnae help.' He pauses for a moment, mouth half open, then shakes his head sharply. 'Ah can see ye're a good lad. Stick in and make somethin' o'yersel. Dinnae let this stop you.' He pats his left ear. 'War wounds. Badge o' honour, son.'

'Badge of honour, aye?' I ask softly.

Al's eyes open with curiosity. 'You think it's no?'

'Not really.'

'How?'

How can a wound gained as an accessory to a muddled

69

and potentially never-ending war be a badge of honour? Maybe it's just evidence of your own stupidity for taking the bullshit they fed you to get you there in the first place.

People seem to need to say these things to you. You learn to let them because it makes them feel like they understand the significance of what's happened to you. But the joke's on them, because there is no significance. It's just an event, the logical outcome of putting yourself into a situation of violence. A situation no more honourable or significant than a rammy between opposing gangs of chavs after an Old Firm game, just scaled up a little.

It seems unkind to say this to him.

'I don't know, Al.' I drain my coffee, stand up.

'Stick in, Sean.'

'Aye,' I say without commitment, and leave him sitting there.

* * * *

At home, a warm foody smell envelops me as I kick snow off my boots and hang my coat on the hook. I find Janet in the kitchen in her trackies and slippers, listening the nightly litany of bad news on Radio 4 and crying as she chops carrots. There is a large glass of red wine beside her.

'Hey,' she says.

'Hey.' I turn the radio off without asking permission. 'You alright?'

She nods and dabs at her eyes with the tea towel. 'Onions. Good day?'

'Just another day in the madhouse. You?'

A one-shouldered shrug. 'Same. Peel some spuds?'

I pick up a hefty potato and slide the peeler over it, watching a strip of red skin separate from the creamy flesh. It takes a bit of concentration to keep the peeler at just the right angle, and I feel slow and clumsy as Janet bustles around me in the small kitchen. She dumps a package of mince into the pot and breaks it up with a wooden spoon, pushes it around to brown it. Her brows creep together as she chews on her thoughts, the straight, graceful line of her nose shadowed, lines etched at the bridge.

We look nothing alike, and we have both wasted a lot of time over the years wondering about our respective fathers. She at least knows the name of hers, and carries a few shadowy memories of the laughing young man who would throw her in the air until she puked and then leave Mum to clean up the mess.

Bobby Jamieson was an apprentice bricklayer, seventeen when Mum fell pregnant and left school. They made a go of it for a couple of years, until Bobby finished his time and succumbed to the call of more lucrative building work down south. He reappeared four or five years later, wormed his way back into Mum's bed and Janet's affections, and lasted a couple of months before the responsibilities of family life became too heavy.

Mum always used to say she was the way she was because Bobby broke her heart, but really it was all her: the crushing lack of confidence which undermined every attempt she made to kill her habits – men, booze, tranquilizers – and which ultimately turned into a one-way ticket down self-destruction road.

There were a lot of men after Bobby, one of whom managed to hit the target and father me. Mum always told me she couldn't pick him out in a line-up, but she would never look me in the eye when she said it.

I hand Janet a tattie and pick up another. 'D'you never think about moving away from here?'

She looks up at me, knife in hand, trying to read the intent behind the question. 'I used to but there's not much point now. Where would I go, anyway?'

'Somewhere you've got no history.'

She sighs. 'I was never ashamed of Mum, Sean. She was ill, that's all.' Then she raises her glass and takes a large draught of wine. 'It could happen to any of us.'

'Speak for yourself.'

She turns her hawkish gaze on me. 'When was the last time you drank?'

I look down at the battered toe-caps of my boots, and a shadowy memory crosses my mind, lingers for a moment: the sickly whisky afterburn, the smell of an unfamiliar bed and a nameless girl who might be young enough to accuse me of child abuse, the first squinty peek out at a street that could be anywhere in the country, sunlight like laser beams through my eyeballs. No other indication of where I was or how I got there. Blackout panic.

'I got rat-arsed on my twenty-fifth birthday and woke up somewhere I shouldn't have been. It was starting to get a bit . . . excessive. It was making me slow and mean. So I stopped.' I shrug. 'I've got the addict genes.'

'So you're saying it has to be all or nothing?'

'I think so, for me. I scare myself.' I shrug. 'Maybe that's hard to get. Mitch did. I couldn't have stopped without him, I don't think. When the guys were going ashore for a session, we used to just pack up and go climbing.'

She watches me peeling, then quietly reaches across and removes the peeler and spud from my hands and finishes the job off quickly herself.

I lean against the bunker, stare at the floor and say nothing.

'Do you still . . .' she breaks off, stares at me with a cocked head.

'What?'

'Does he still talk to you?'

I don't say anything. There is dried blood down the front of my trousers and for a moment I scrabble about to recall how it might have got there.

'Sean?'

'I heard you.' Now I remember: wood stain, mahogany brown. 'What do you want me to say, Janet? Yes, he still talks to me. That's Mitch . . . he talks a lot.'

She dumps the last sliced pieces of potato into the pot and chews on her lower lip. 'I thought it might have got better, now that you're working.'

'Why would that make a difference?'

'I don't know. Something else to occupy your mind.'

'I'm not making him up out of boredom.'

'I wish you'd go back to the psychiatrist.'

'So he can fill me up with drugs just like Mum? No fucking way. If it's a choice between crazy and wasted, I'll take crazy.' The steam from the potato pot is condensing on the window and the little kitchen is uncomfortably hot. I start to hear the pulse at my temples.

'You're not crazy, just . . . damaged.'

'Damaged goods, aye.' The balloon in my chest starts to inflate and my volume rises with it. 'Jesus fucking Christ, the only ones who aren't damaged by it are the psychopaths, and there are a few of those out there, I promise you.'

'Alright, Sean. Please lower your voice.'

'Lower my voice.' I laugh. 'Naebody wants to hear it, right? That's the fucking truth.'

73

'Oh for Christ's sake.'

I stare at her, waiting for her to say something else. 'What?'

She stands there breathing heavily for a moment, then reaches her hand toward my arm but stops short of actually touching me. 'You have to let Mitch go, sweetie. He's dead.'

'Not something I'm likely to forget, is it? What was left of the bottom half of him would have gone into that pot.' I glance in at the greasy mince and onions. 'Add about seven pints of blood and you get the idea.'

'That's not fucking necessary!' She slams down her spoon and leaves the room.

The tattie pot has started to boil furiously, a froth rising to the brim and quivering there. I turn it down and stir it with a fork to kill the froth, then open the back door and face the night. Clouds cross quick time in and out of the moon's glare, fleeing for the safety of darkness.

'I'm sorry.'

I turn and we face off from opposing doorways.

'Too much information, huh?'

She nods. 'I can't even begin to . . .' She breaks off, blinks, picks up her wine and takes three or four hard swallows. 'What are you going to do?'

I shrug. 'Live with it.'

'How can you?'

I think about this for a moment. A curling breath of wind carries memory over the frozen fields. Burrowed like lemmings into the snow, the Norwegian winter screaming above us. Both of us close to hypothermia, we borrow heat from each other's bodies, hands tucked under oxters. His beard twitches against my cheek as he shivers. No embarrassment, just knowledge that survival requires you to be greater than yourself. You share what you have to share to keep each other alive.

'You remember Jamie Laidlaw? He still feels pain in a leg he lost seven years ago. He says he wakes up at night and it feels like he's lying there with his leg broken and bent the wrong way. He has to look down and remind himself it's not there. Maybe that's what Mitch is. My phantom limb.'

'Losing a person isn't the same as losing a part of your body. It's different.'

I pull the kitchen door closed and feel the blood flood into my face with the sudden heat. 'Not really.'

'Sean . . .'

I hold up my hand. 'Leave it, Janet. I can't explain and I'm tired of trying.'

'I worry about you.'

'I never asked you to.'

IX

After a couple of days the roads are clear again and daffodils lift their white and yellow heads clear of the slushy layer of snow on the fields. I finish my round of deliveries and uplifts by early afternoon so before Harry has a chance to ask about it, I steel myself and take a drive out to Cauldhill Farm. The sight of Molly's Volvo in the drive brings on a flutter of butterflies in my gut. She could tell me to get stuffed or come at me with a knife, or even worse, try to get me into bed again.

A momentary notion to drive past brings on a mini-torrent of Welsh-accented abuse (*You miserable spineless piece of excrement, Nic, you little yellow chicken turd, etc),* and I would rather face the wrath of a living woman than a dead bootneck. Without further hesitation I park the van and jog up the steps, ring the bell and take a deep breath as I wait.

She opens the door and stands there looking at me, face passive. It seems to take her a moment to recognise me, a moment which spins out painfully while I stand there with a sheepish grin. Eventually she shakes her head, returns the smile.

'That's the face I remember.'

'I'll . . . ehm . . . finish the job if you haven't got anyone else.'

She steps aside to let me in, then turns away from me

and fills the kettle. 'I haven't. I haven't done anything about it. I've been in bed since the snow started.'

'Are you alright?'

'Yes.' A soft laugh. 'It just seemed the best place to be. Somewhere warm and dark, where I didn't have to think about anything.'

'Oh . . . right.'

'I'm fine, Sean. Are you?'

I shrug, pull out a chair and sit down at the kitchen table without having been invited to. She doesn't say anything so I clear my throat and spread my fingers on the wood. 'I'm sorry about the other day.'

She sits down across from me, face creased with uncertainty. 'Me too. I've made a fool of myself, haven't I?'

I shift uncomfortably on the creaky wooden chair. 'No, that was me. I shouldn't have let that happen. I haven't . . . you know . . . been with anyone for a long time. I've spent the last couple of years living mostly inside my own head, if that makes any sense.'

Her face softens and the lines flatten out a bit. 'It does. I suppose in a way, I've been doing the same. I guess I just needed someone to put their arms around me.'

'Can't your husband come up and help?'

'Can't . . . won't. Is it awful to admit that I wouldn't even want him to?'

'That's not really for me to say.'

She looks away. 'I suppose not.'

I stare at a spot somewhere on the far wall and a muscle in my cheek starts to twitch. I stand up abruptly. 'Look, don't bother with the coffee. Where do you want me to start?'

'Oh . . . ehm . . . just . . . wherever. Just pick a room.'

'Molly, I . . .' I hesitate for a minute, feeling uncomfortably implicated in yet another conflict that should have nothing do with me. She waits curiously, eyes wide, and I scratch my cheek.

'Whatever's going on with you and your man, I don't want to be named as the final straw.'

She laughs out loud. 'Honestly, Sean? This particular camel has so many straws on its back, you hardly rate a mention. Maybe if . . . well . . .'

'If I'd been able to finish the job? Is that you want to say?'

'No!' Her cheeks flush. 'I was going to say, maybe if you'd felt differently about me.'

'All the same, I don't want to be your excuse. Alright?'

Her face tightens with hurt. 'You're not, I promise. I am going home, anyway. I have no intention of staying in this horrid, freezing house with no furniture.'

'Right,' I say slowly, only half believing her. 'I'll get going then.'

She nods sharply. 'Sure.'

I head out to the van for a stack of flattened boxes, and carry them back through the kitchen without stopping to talk. Molly opens a drawer and withdraws a box of papers, obviously trying not to look at me as I pass her, and lets me go through toward the stairwell.

Upstairs, I avoid the bedroom she's been using and select the one at the far end of the long corridor: a dreary wee chamber with pink-painted woodchip and a flowery wallpaper dado strip. There is dust everywhere, lying in a thick layer on the furniture and along the tops of the heavy red curtains, as well as a slight whiff of damp. The single bed is covered by a thin quilt and the floorboards creak suspiciously under the stained carpet. This might have been Molly's room once, but now it's so cold and sad it seems like a little pink prison cell. The room seems half a rugby pitch away from the bedroom where her parents must have slept, and I catch a hazy glimpse of a little girl curled in this bed as the wind swept down off the moors and rattled the old sash windows. Not a nice place to be if you're troubled by ghosts.

Well, I certainly wouldn't want to hang around here for eternity. The wallpaper is godawful.

I can't imagine the décor inside my head is much better.

You're right about that, Sunshine. It's pretty black in here. You should try cleaning the place sometime.

No amount of bleach is going to get rid of you, though, is it? What do I have to do?

Ah now, that would be telling.

The wardrobe is empty apart from a few bent wire hangers. In the top drawer of the dresser I find a ratty cloth doll with a yellowed frilly apron and red yarn hair. I raise the doll to my nose; she smells of dust and mildew and sawdust. Then I place her on top of the chest of drawers and begin removing the covers from the bed and folding them into the boxes. When the bed is stripped, I pull the mattress off the bedframe, half hoping to find some long forgotten diary stashed there. But all I find are saggy metal springs, dust many years thick and a single grey sock.

Having cleared the room of everything except the furniture, I stack one box on top of another and carry them down the stairs again, back through the kitchen past Molly, who is sitting at the kitchen table reading something on brown paper with a pair of small dark-framed specs perched on her nose. I carry the boxes outside and load them into the van.

'That's the wee pink room done,' I say, kicking mud off my boots before re-entering.

She looks up. 'That was my room.'

79

'Aye . . . I found a little doll. Maybe you want it.'

A forceful reply. 'I don't want anything from that room.' Then she softens. 'I'm glad you've done that one. I've been avoiding it.'

'Why's that?'

She takes off her glasses and folds the bit of paper, then stands up and fills the kettle. 'My abiding memory of childhood is of lying in that little bed, listening to my parents argue and crying myself to sleep. Nights were really fucking long in that room.'

'It's funny, I . . .' I pause, rubbing my fingers over my chin, still surprised to find smooth skin there instead of coarse hair, 'I was imagining just that. Wee Molly curled in the bed, crying.'

'Oh, don't.' She laughs sadly. 'Fat ugly Molly, who thought everyone hated her. Don't remind me. I was such a freak.'

'You're talking to the king of the freaks.'

'You aren't. You weren't then either.'

'I was. Or I thought I was.'

'You were aloof. That's what I remember most about you. You never gave anything away.'

'I don't know about aloof. Scared and embarrassed, maybe.'

'Wasn't everybody though?'

'No.'

'Maybe not.' She smiles sadly, eyes flickering over my face. Then she clears her throat. 'So I . . . ehm . . . I've been reading those letters you found. You were right, they are from a woman.'

'H.B. Starling of New York City. So . . . who is she, then?'

The kettle boils and she pours the coffee. 'Harriet Belle Starling. A singer. A blues singer from Harlem.'

She hands me a steaming mug. 'He washed up over there after the war and took up with her for a while. They wrote to each other for a long time after he came back here.'

'Why'd he leave her?'

'She was black.' She says it like it's an entirely obvious and rational explanation. 'Anyway, he didn't exactly waste away for want of company. Mum was his third wife, and he had mistresses.'

'You're the only child?'

'No. I have two half sisters in Australia, and another half sister down south.' She pauses, shakes her head. 'I'm the only one who was still on speaking terms with Dad by the end. He fell out with more or less everybody. So . . . I guess I get this place as a reward for my perseverance.'

'What about your mum?'

'She lives in the south of France with her second husband, *Patrice*. They make wine and run holiday *gites*. We don't talk much. Happy families, eh?'

'Is there any such thing?'

'Yeah, there is. Just, not for me. I don't think I know how. Dad was a miserable, twisted old tyrant. He never said much, he couldn't stand noise, he never showed affection to anyone. He used to give Mum orders like she was a dog, and he ignored me as far as possible. Mum used to say it was the war. That doing what he did in the war made it impossible for him to be close to anyone.'

'Maybe she was right.'

'Maybe.' Her eyes move across my face. 'Have you ever been close to anyone?'

'Yes.'

'Who was she?'

'Not a woman.'

81

'Oh.'

'Just a mate, Molly.'

She clears her throat and smiles. 'It wouldn't have bothered me. I'm not like that.'

'Neither am I, in case you're wondering.'

'Well. It's not really my business. But you're not like him. He was just . . . cold. Arrogant and stone-faced. Quite honestly, I don't think he gave a second thought about the people of Dresden, or wherever. Brilliant with horses, absolutely shocking with humans.'

'You'd better hope he's not listening.'

She tilts her head slightly to one side. 'You don't strike me as the kind of person who believes in ghosts.'

'I believe in ghosts. Some of the places I've been . . . they're everywhere. Sometimes you'd walk into a ruined village and you'd feel them hanging about, watching you.'

She shudders. 'Awful.'

'Mmm.'

Molly stares at the floor for a moment, biting her lower lip, then takes a step closer to where I'm standing. 'You're not at all like I thought you were, Sean.'

'Meaning?' I want to back away, but stand my ground.

'I don't know.' She looks at me as if she's seeing something in my face she'd never noticed before. 'There's just . . . a bit more to you than I realised.'

I raise my eyebrows at this. 'He's smarter than the average bear, is he?'

'I beg your pardon?'

'What did you think, exactly? Nice set of pecs but not a lot going on between the lugs.'

'No! Oh God, I didn't mean . . .'

'Oh come on, Molly. Why are you people so fucking patronising?'

'You people?'

'Aye. Toffs.'

'I'm not a toff!'

I laugh at her. 'You are. That's exactly what you are. I won't hold it against you.'

'If I'm a toff, what are you?' A note of challenge creeps into her voice.

'Cannon fodder. Exactly what guys like me have always been.'

She stares at me for a moment, eyes wide, then takes a deep breath and turns away. 'I'm . . . sorry . . . honestly, Sean, I didn't mean to come over like that. I'm not a snob. I promise I never meant anything like that and I apologise if that's how it sounded. I like you. I know maybe I shouldn't say it, but I do. I can't help it.'

'I'm sorry, Molly. It's just not meant to be, okay?'

She nods, her lips pressed together, accepting this without wanting to. I wish could call the whole conversation back. I've exposed far too much of myself, and it feels dangerous. She needs something I can't give; desperation radiates from her like some kind of tractor beam. Suddenly I realise something about Molly: she's just like me. Under the sleek clothing and reformed accent, she's just another one of the Saddos.

X

A Lammergeier soars above the mountain and drops a human skull from three hundred feet. It hits dry earth and explodes with the force of a mortar. I inhale dust, and wake up coughing. My latest crappy library book lands in a fan of pages on the carpet.

'Jesus,' I mutter, running my fingers through my hair and letting my feet clunk down off the coffee table. A spasm of pain in my lower back pulls me upright.

The doorbell goes, possibly for the second time. I hurry to answer it, and find Paula Fairbairn, coatless and round, rubbing her hands over her arms.

'Hi.' She looks embarrassed. 'Bad time?'

'Sorry, no . . . I only dozed off.' I stand aside. 'Come in.'

'It's alright.' She holds out a twenty-pound note. 'For the messages. Mum says keep the change.'

'Ta.' I stuff the note into my back pocket. 'Come in anyway. Janet's out at her fitness class, so I'm on my own.'

'Ah . . . well, in that case . . .' She laughs, steps inside and follows me into the kitchen, stands there pressing her fingers into her lower back and looking around. 'Oh God. I haven't been in your house in fifteen years, at least. It hasn't changed.'

'A bit cleaner, maybe.'

Paula smiles. She was one of the few friends I ever let

into my house as a kid and she saw it all: Mum drunk as a monkey at three o'clock on a Monday afternoon, a week's worth of dishes in the sink, and Janet digging down the back of the couch for coppers to feed the electricity metre. Most folk only came to my house the once; after that, there was always some excuse.

I pull out a chair for her at the table. 'You've grown since last week.'

'Aye.' She winces and lowers herself onto the chair with a little grunt. 'Bursting at the seams. Some women seem to carry a wee football tucked under their jumpers, but not me. I'm like Cinderella's bloody pumpkin.'

'You're a very bonny pumpkin. It suits you.'

Her laugh is like joyful applause. 'That is such an incredibly sweet thing to say. It's full of shit, but it's very sweet.'

'Honestly, I meant it.' I fill the kettle and switch it on. 'I assume you're having a brew.'

'Yes please.'

I turn away and reach down mugs, a plate and the biscuit tin. Paula says something behind me, but over the hiss of the kettle, I don't catch it.

I turn around. 'Sorry, Paula, I missed that. It's useless talking to me when my back's turned.'

'That must be annoying.'

'Very. What did you say, anyway?'

Her eyes catch the overhead light as she smiles. 'I said *you* don't look like a pumpkin. You still look unbelievably fit. You must work hard at it.'

'I run a lot. And I shifted about four tonnes of furniture from an old farmhouse out by the Moorfoots today. My bloody back's killing me.'

'Just par for the course for me these days.' She gives a heavy sigh and rubs her tummy. 'How are you, otherwise?'

'Ach, you know. Living the quiet life.' The kettle lets out steam and switches itself off. I pour water into the teapot and carry everything to the table on a tray. 'Trying to get used to being *here*.'

'For good, you think?'

'No idea. I try not to think too far ahead.'

A gentle nod as she lifts the teapot, swills it twice and pours tea for both of us. Then she takes a chocolate digestive and dips it into her mug, bites delicately and sits there chewing and regarding me thoughtfully. The fingers of her right hand curl through the handle of her mug, and I notice that she isn't wearing a wedding ring.

'Are you glad to be home?'

'Ehm . . .' I cup my hand over my mouth and drag it down over two or three days' stubble. It was always impossible to maintain any kind of pretence around her, so I don't bother. 'I don't know what home is, Paula. A place other people go, I think.'

'I can believe that,' she says softly.

I stare into my tea.

Paula puts down her mug and rests her chin on folded fingers. 'I always thought about you, you know. Whenever the news was on and they started talking about the war somewhere or other. Sometimes I watched those documentaries about the soldiers in Afghanistan, thinking stupidly I might even see you, but I never did. It feels like we've been at war ever since you joined up.'

'Not far off it.'

'Did you like it? The Marines, I mean, not the actual combat.'

'Combat's the best buzz you'll ever get. It's even legal.'

'That's sick.'

I give her an eyebrow. 'True though. No . . . Honestly, you know what I liked? Being part of the Borg. They

86

make you forget who you are and where you come from. The fact that you're the bastard whelp of alcoholic tart doesn't make a blind bit of difference to your quality as a bootneck.'

'For fucksake, Sean, is that really how you see yourself?'

'That's how people here see me.'

'No they don't.'

'Aye they do. I'm past caring, really. I wasn't the only one, by any means. I had a C.O. who used to say Jocks made the best soldiers because no war could match the violence and sheer bloody squalor of your average Scottish town on a Friday night.'

I watch the tree branches outside the kitchen window bend like dry bony limbs.

'I *did* like it. I loved it for a long time but it goes for your head eventually. I lost it, Paula . . . one day, I just . . . couldn't do it anymore. I was done with fighting, even before Mitch died.'

'I remember him well. It must have been horrendous.'

'When did you meet him?'

'Your mum's funeral.'

'Oh Christ, yeah, I forgot about that. He chummed me just to make sure I actually turned up.'

'Sean.' She sighs. 'I spoke to him for ages. Or . . . well . . . he spent about an hour regaling me with tales of adventures on mountains and seas and jungles.'

'Only an hour? You got off light. He must have sussed you were married.'

She smiles. 'I could have listened to him all day, with that lovely accent.'

'Aye, typical. Every bloody woman who crossed his path. I . . .' My voice trips in my throat and I sit there for a moment feeling like I've just been winded. It's maybe

87

ten seconds before I can inhale, and when I do it comes in a big, ragged gulp. 'I'm sorry. I can control myself, I promise.'

'Oh God, don't apologise. I've seen you cry before, remember.'

'Aye, I guess you have. I . . . assume you heard what actually happened.'

'D'you know, I heard it on the news.'

'Oh Jesus Christ. You're joking.'

'No. It was on the radio, early in the morning when I was getting up for work. When they mentioned the names . . . it was like . . . I knew already. It was just like a confirmation of something that I always knew would happen. To make it worse, I had to teach about Afghanistan in my Modern Studies class that day, and I kept bursting into tears.'

'Maybe the wee shites'll remember that lesson, at least.'

She nods. 'Maybe. I am so, so sorry, Sean. I'm grateful to him, though. Very selfishly.' She reaches across and draws my hands toward her, folds her fingers over mine.

I sit here, my hands in hers and my pulse rushing in temples, and wish I could bring myself to agree with her. I've spent so many shameful months wishing Mitch hadn't made that decision to send me back here when I deserved to be vulture food, that now the words *me too* seem impossible. Even with Paula here, the only girl I've ever come anywhere near falling in love with, so close I can smell the fruity perfume of her hair and feel the heat radiating from her body, her fingers tightening around mine in a way that makes me want to pull her onto my lap, I can't say them.

'Ooh . . .' She says, before I can gather a muddled collection of thoughts into any kind of response. Her eyes widen and her hand goes to her side, her palm pressing into her ribs. 'Kicking practice in there. Here.'

She pushes her chair back from the table, reaches for my hand again and guides it to the firm, warm curve below her breast. For a moment all I feel is the steady lift and fall of her breath, but then a hard lump pushes against my hand, like a foot trying to break free of over-tight blankets. I can actually see a ripple of movement beneath her jumper.

'Oh wow,' I breathe, and I keep my hand there, waiting for more. After a moment, there are a few more gentle flutters, and another kick. It draws laughter from somewhere deep inside me. 'That's incredible.'

'It's magic, isn't it? Just don't think about *Alien*.'

'Oh thanks. Now I will.' I move my hands over her belly, feeling lumps and rounded curves here and there. The baby seems to respond to my touch, following the movements of my hands with little prods and bumps. 'Is it sore?'

'No.' Paula smiles and places her hand over mine. 'It's reassuring. I start to worry when she doesn't move for a while.'

'She?'

She shrugs. 'I think it's a she.'

Her grin is infectious, and we sit there for ages grinning like a pair of jokers, my hand magnetically attached to her belly, every little scuff or inquisitive prod from inside sending a shiver up my arm. I look up at her, and for just a moment our eyes hold each other, hovering like droplets of water just before they fall.

Then I catch my breath, pull my hand away and stand up. A repeat of the Molly fiasco is definitely not on the cards. 'What am I doing?'

She takes a deep breath and lets it out slowly, like a

89

drag on an imaginary cigarette. 'You know I'm not with Ewan anymore, don't you?'

My mouth opens a little and hangs there. 'No. Since when?'

'Oh God. I'm sorry, I thought everyone knew. We separated last year. Technically we're still married but I'm working on fixing that. Mum is completely disgusted with me. I thought she'd told more or less the whole town.'

'She doesn't really speak to me. So, the baby . . .'

She drains her mug and puts it in the sink. 'Is it okay to sit in the living room? I'm not very comfy in that chair.'

'Oh . . .' I say stupidly, still chewing slowly over the potential implications of what she's just said. 'Aye. Sorry. Come on.'

She follows me to the living room and sits on the sofa. I settle on a chair, safely on the other side of the coffee table.

'How open minded are you, Sean?'

'What do you mean?'

'I mean . . . you haven't gone all right wing and conservative on me, have you?'

I laugh. 'I haven't turned into a raving Tory if that's what you mean.'

'Okay.' She presses her hands into a praying gesture. 'Ewan . . . didn't want kids. He worked too much, he played guitar in a band, he liked his mountain biking and his snowboarding, and he was just too into himself. I hit my thirties and realised that I wanted to be a mum more than anything in the world. We just couldn't find a way around it, so . . .' A little shrug. 'That was that. We had fun together, but I guess I grew up and he didn't.'

'I'm sorry.'

'I'm not, Sean. Not at all. So . . . the baby . . . doesn't

have a dad. I went to a sperm bank. I know I'm going to have to explain it all to the kid one day, and it's always going to be a little weird, but I don't care. I'm happy. My mother isn't, as you might imagine. I'm sure she thinks I'm going to Hell, and she probably thinks I deserve it.' She looks at me pointedly. 'Do you agree with her?'

'You know where I come from, Paula. How could I agree with her?'

'I don't know. I've met a few guys who've been in the forces and they all seem pretty traditional about family life.'

I shrug. 'They like you to be married. Probably they think marriage makes men more . . . I don't know . . .'

'Compliant?' she suggests.

'Maybe. Something like that.' I get up, turn my back on her and say the first thing that comes to mind, speaking to her reflection in the window. 'I watched some Taliban beat a woman to death once.'

Oh here we go, listen to Mr Depressive here. Take your Prozac and get over it, Nic.

'Oh my God.'

A silence stretches behind me, heavy with unspoken questions.

'We were looking for a guy, a serious bad nut. If we'd given away our position, we would have been dead and the job would have been blown, so we just had to watch this evil thing happen.'

'What horrible sin had she committed?'

I turn and face her. 'I don't know. That's Hell, Paula. Hell created by men and their twisted ideas of morality. So to cut to the chase . . . no, I dinnae agree with your ma. In fact as far as I'm concerned, Brenda can take her judgement and her gossip and her miserable face and get to fuck.'

Paula covers her mouth with both hands and blinks rapidly. Then she pushes herself off the sofa and crosses over to me, her belly swaying in front of her. I open my arms and she slips into them, her bump pressing into me.

'Thank you,' she whispers.

'Does my opinion matter that much to you?'

'Yes. It always has.'

I close my eyes and rest my chin on her head, and we stand there for a little while. Her hair is warm and silky against my cheek.

Eventually she straightens and looks up at me. 'This is like trying to cuddle across a beach ball.'

I hesitate for a moment, then lift my fingers to her chin and bend my face down to hers. 'Let's see what else we can do across a beach ball.' We kiss in a way that would ordinarily lead to fumbling with buttons and getting tangled in trouser legs. But circumstances are far from ordinary, for either of us.

I pull back and look at her. There are tiny lines at the corners of her eyes, each suggesting the passage of time I know nothing about.

'Tell me what you're thinking,' she says.

'Ehm . . .'

'What is it?'

'Just that I think I've suddenly developed a fetish for pregnant women.'

She laughs, slides her hands down my arms and grasps my fingers. 'They say sex can bring on labour. Give me another week, I may be banging down your door.'

'I'm sure I'd be happy to oblige.'

You could try, Mr Floppy.

Peace evaporates from the room like water on hot sand.

Can't you just give me a fucking break, Mitch?

92

It's a trap, mate, can't you see that? You'll be up to your bollocks in nappies before you know it.

And what if I said I didn't care?

Oh Jesus Christ, when did you get so soft?

I turn my back on Paula and stare out the window again. Her hand rests on my back and she says something quietly.

'Pardon?'

'Are you okay?'

'Yep.' I press my palm hard over my left ear, as if I could squash the bugger into silence. 'I get this . . . ringing in my ear sometimes. It's a bloody annoyance.'

Ringing? The fucker's laughing at me. *Aren't you going to tell her about me?*

'Can't anyone do anything about it?'

'It's psychological, apparently. Some kind of Post Traumatic Stress thing.'

She nods and takes this in. Now would be about the time for a sharp exit.

'Mum says sometimes she sees you running at four or five am, when she's up for the toilet. Do you do that because you can't sleep?'

'Mmm . . . yeah. That final tour finished me, Paula. My nerves are ripped to shreds.'

'Whose wouldn't be?' She comes alongside me and slips her arm around my waist. 'My dad used to have nightmares about the pit. He dreamt about being buried alive, right up until he died, and he was too proud to do anything except suffer it. Mum never wanted to speak about it; she just pretended it didn't happen. I'm sure that's what did his heart in the end, you know.'

'So what are you saying?'

'I'm saying you can tell me things, if you want . . . the way you used to. I want us to be friends again.' She lifts

93

her hand to my cheek and brushes her fingertips over the scars on my cheek, brows drawing together.

I turn toward her. 'Just friends?'

'Are you offering more?'

My shoulders rise and fall. 'I'm an emotional car wreck. You don't need that in your life just now, and neither does this wee one.' I place my hand on her belly.

She takes my hand and brings it to her lips, kisses it. 'You won't always be.'

An unexpected laugh escapes me. 'Aye. I'm glad you have faith.'

Paula's chin tips upward, her jaw set stubbornly. 'I do. Absolutely. I know you, and I know you're tough as old boots. Are you listening to me?'

'I am, Paula, it's just . . .'

'It's just what?'

'Forget it. Aye . . . you're right. Meantime, can we be friends again? I'd like that.'

'Me too.'

She stiffens and glances over her shoulder at some sound that I've missed. 'Crap.'

'What is it?'

'That's Janet back.'

'I'm a big boy, I'm allowed girls over.'

Paula moves away from me, runs her fingers through her hair and straightens her top as well as she can over her bump. 'I should maybe go. She'll get the wrong idea.'

I want to tell her to stay and that it doesn't matter, but I can see she doesn't want to have to make strained conversation with my sister. So I head for the kitchen and find Janet brewing tea for herself and washing the cups we've left in the sink.

'Hey.'

Janet turns, reaching for the tea towel to dry her

hands, obviously struggling to suppress her instinctive reaction. 'Hey. Oh . . . hiya, Paula. You're fair comin' on now, eh? How long now?'

Paula's cheeks are a brilliant shade of scarlet. 'Two weeks, give or take.'

'Keeping well?'

'Aye, grand.'

'How's yer ma?'

'Same as ever.' There's a terse, silent moment as my sister stands there, glancing between the two of us as if trying to find an explanation for what we might have been doing in her absence.

I clear my throat and back out of the kitchen.

'See you later, Janet, eh?' Paula says.

'Oh . . . aye . . . okay then. Cheerio, hen.'

'I'll see you soon,' Paula says, squeezing past me in the cramped corridor and moving toward the front door. She grabs my hand. 'I'll call you.'

'Have you got someone to go in with you when the baby comes?' I blurt, before I have a chance to change my mind.

She turns, her back against the door. 'My pal Claire wants to come, but . . .' her voice trails off, and she stares at her feet for a moment, 'I'll call you.'

I swallow disappointment. 'You'd better.'

She raises her chin. 'I will.'

I lean in and kiss her cheek. 'Okay.'

'Okay.' She nods, then opens the door and steps out into the night. 'Bye.'

'Bye.' I watch her go, leaning in the doorway until she turns the corner and disappears.

'So . . . what's going on?' Janet asks from behind me.

I hear her clearly, but to buy time I reply with my usual, 'Sorry, what?'

'Are you two . . .'

'Are we . . . what?'

She cocks her head and lifts an eyebrow.

I mimic the expression. 'I don't know what this means.'

'Sean.' An exasperated snarl.

'I'm knackered. Away to my bed.' I about face sharply and march up the stairs, run a brush over my teeth, then strip and flop onto the bed. Paula's smell is still in my nose, and I lie there in the colourless little room, breathing it in. For the first time in longer than I can remember, I allow my thoughts to venture, cautiously as a foot patrol through the poppy fields, to a future beyond the next twenty-four hours.

XI

Billy doesn't turn up for work the next day, so I'm in the van on my own. Harry has been on the phone three times flapping about health and safety and insisting that we postpone deliveries, but I'm buggered if we're going to lose a day's business because that mucky little twat can't be bothered getting out of his pit. Promising not to sue if I put my back out, I carry on humping dining tables and beds as well as I can alone.

My fourth delivery of the day is a beast of a wardrobe, but thankfully the boy who meets me at the door is of equally monumental proportions: taller than me and built like the proverbial brick shitter. He easily hoists the front end and helps me manoeuvre the thing up the stairs to a grim, greasy-smelling flat above the bookies in the High Street.

'I ken you,' he says, straightening up after we place the wardrobe into the desired position against his bedroom wall. 'Sean McNicol, I mind you fae the rugby club.'

Being recognised always makes me cringe; mostly people remember me for the wrong reasons. *Sean McNicol, I mind you. You were the yin who never had a jaicket in the winter.* But he holds out his hand. 'Jack Wilson.'

'Oh aye,' I say slowly, shaking his hand, casting back to a dim memory of a chubby ginger-headed kid who ran in tries by the dozen through sheer, unwieldy bulk. He's almost completely bald now but the face is the same. 'How you doing?'

He shrugs. 'Ach, ye know. Me and the wife just split up, so . . .' he waves his hand around the cold, boxy bedroom. 'I'm a joiner and there's no much work goin' either. So I'm skint and pissed off, but hangin' in. A few wee jobs here and there, plenty of time for training.' He steps across the dark hallway into a kitchen with a sticky vinyl floor, nodding for me to follow. He opens the fridge door, revealing bottles of lager, a dried up lump of orange cheese, a packet of corned beef and a carton of milk. He pulls out a Stella. 'Fancy a beer, man?'

'Nah, thanks.'

'A cuppa then. Tea?' He laughs nervously. 'Kindae early for drinkin, I guess.'

I glance at my watch – it's just coming up for lunch-time – then back at him. He's sucking on his bottle like a kid goat at its mother's teat. 'A quick brew, if you're offering.'

'Nae bother,' he replies, grinning as though it's the best news he's had in days. He switches on the kettle and whacks a teabag enthusiastically into a stained white mug. 'You play any rugby lately?'

'Nah. You?'

'Aye, I'm still at the club, in the second team, like. Cannae get a game for the firsts anymair, it's all younger lads now.' He pauses to make the tea, sliding the mug and the milk across the bunker toward me. 'I heard you got hurt out in Helmand. All the guys at the club were talking about it.'

'You mean they actually remember me down there?'

'Aye, they do. Jesus, man, they were talking about a fundraiser for the local hero and all sorts. Charity run or something.'

'Christ, dinnae start all that bullshit. I've been out more than a year now. I'm working and I'm fine.'

'What's it like being back, then? I think I'd prefer fucking Afghanistan, like. At least the sun shines.'

'Ha,' I manage, mostly to fend off any potential commentary from Mitch. 'It was a bit of a shock to the system for a while, right enough, but I'm getting used to it.' I gulp my tea to avoid having to say more.

Jack's eyes crawl over my face like little blue ants. 'Fancy coming along to the club? We're toiling for numbers, especially big rangy runners like you. Training tonight, seven o'clock.'

'Ach, I don't know.'

'Go on, you know you want to. The lads would love to have you back.'

'I'll think about it.' I knock back the rest of the tea and leave the mug in the basin. 'Better make tracks. Ta for the brew, I needed that.' I head for the door and he follows me.

'Good tae see ye, Sean. Get yersel' doon the night.'

'Maybe. I'll see. I've got a lot going on just now.'

'I ken,' Jack says, and there's something like dejection in his voice, 'you'll be busy, eh? Anyway, good tae see ye.'

I trot down the stairs, and Mitch ambushes me on the urine-scented landing.

Fucking liar. You've got bugger all going on tonight except sitting on your arse waiting for a woman who probably won't phone.

I ignore this and carry on to my next job: a bed and a couple of armchairs to an address up in Mayfield. It's one of those weird back-to-front sixties era council houses where you have to go through the back garden to get to the front door. A snarling brindled bull terrier

99

meets me at the gate, followed by a lassie with a couple of missing teeth and skin so pale she might have spent her whole life in a cave. She barks at the dog. It cowers and settles into a pathetic whine.

Picking my way around piles of bull terrier crap – the bloody garden is more treacherous than your average Helmand cornfield – I shoulder the bed inside and deposit it in a downstairs bedroom according to the girl's instruction. The house reeks of fags and stale chip fat. Passing the living room, I notice the TV flickering and a guy staring at it, mouth half open and eyes half shut, cigarette drooping between his fingers.

It's only as I carry in a brown upholstered chair and dump it next to him that I notice that both of his legs end just below the knees. He's young, lucky if he's in his early twenties, and there are scars on his neck and face. It's the unmistakeable signature of my old friend, the improvised explosive device; I look at those same scars in the mirror far too often to confuse them for anything else. A knot ties up in my stomach and rises into my throat.

I straighten up slowly and offer a casual, 'Alright?'

'Alright,' he grunts, glancing at me only briefly, before his eyes move back to the telly and his fingers bring the cigarette to his mouth.

'You ex-army, mate?'

'Uh. How'd ye guess, like? Something to do wi' the missing legs, like?'

I smile. 'I came out of the Marines a wee while ago.'

He grunts. 'You wanting a medal, like?'

'Just showing a bit of solidarity, pal. Nae offence intended, eh? That's your bed in as well. You got some decent bargains, there.'

'Second hand shite. I get to sleep on someone else's cum stains.'

100

'The mattress is brand new.'

He sniffs, uninterested. 'So fuckin' what, eh? It's still shite.'

I shrug. Any words of support I might have been prepared to offer have dried up on my tongue. Coarse little army wanker. 'You want me to take it back to the shop, I will. You'll have to pay the return delivery though.'

He turns pale, needle-ish eyes on me; little fucker would knife you as soon as look at you, if he had legs to run away on. 'Nuh.'

'Fair enough. Cheerio, then.'

He sniffs and juts his chin at me. I leave him to his fag and his eighties American cop show and let myself out. The girlfriend is sitting on the back step, cigarette in one hand and phone pressed to her ear with the other, grunting in hoarse tones. The dog stalks me up the path. I half wish it would take a lunge at me so I could knock it into orbit with a size eleven steel toecap, but it stands stiff legged as I squeeze out the gate. Neither the dog nor the girl barks a goodbye.

I'm shaky as I get back into the van, my hands sweating so much that they are slippery on the steering wheel. There's a pressure on my chest as bad as any I used to get on operations. My arms and legs are heavy with it. I drive the van round the corner to get away from the house, then stop again in a parking bay and sit there, staring down at the view below me. All of Edinburgh and Midlothian are spread below me like a crumpled, grubby quilt; the little huddled towns, a dirty sky and the battleship grey water of the Forth, the Pentlands still in their winter browns with a few patches of leftover snow.

I turn off the engine and lean my head back against the seat, close my eyes and fade into another place. Dry, scrubby land, the scarred earth around the Kajaki Dam, cold thin early morning air. The noises we make as we move: the careful thunk of our boots in the dust, the little creaks and rustles of our equipment. The smells of dust and sweaty men. Then a shout from behind me, Mitch's voice breaking with panic, his bulk colliding into my side.

The memory of that day is like the monster of your childhood, breathing heavily under the bed as you lie on top, wrapped in your armour of quilts and blankets. It can't hurt you if you just stay wrapped up on the bed – not a single toe or a hand dangling naked over the side to be snapped off – but something makes you want to look. You're compelled by some irresistible force to lean over the edge and face it.

I finger the flack scars on my cheek.

I wasn't aware of them at the time. I was hardly even aware that my eardrum had blown out and that blood was pouring down the side of my face. I might have lost consciousness for a short time, I'm not sure, but what I remember is becoming aware of Mitch's weight on top of me and the hot moisture of blood seeping through my trousers, not knowing whether it was his or mine or both.

I pushed myself halfway up and he made a little cry, then a wet, drowning cough. There was only one pair of legs sticking out beneath him, and they were mine; peppered with superficial flack wounds but otherwise unharmed. I could see shapes moving around us, men running toward us, but I couldn't hear them. They stopped a short distance away, seemed to linger in suspended animation. They couldn't help and they knew it. It was as though a glass dome had descended over Mitch and me. I held him and sobbed into his hair, and there was only the faintest rattling breath in his body to tell me he was still alive. One heaving gulp, then a weak one, then nothing.

And then the dome lifted and the chaos resumed. I clung to him, heard myself screaming at him to hang on and then Nate Finlay, the medic, shouting at me to let him go. He sounded like he was at the other end of a tunnel.

Let me go, Sean. Fuck me if I'm going to live as a tree-stump on a chair. Look at the state of you, man, crying like a big girl's blouse. You're okay. You're alive.

Mitch's voice in my head, clear as though the body in my arms had just spoken. I collapsed back into the dirt and lay there staring at a perfect blue sky as they lifted what was left of Gareth Mitchell off of me. Except that he's still here, blethering in an ear that is completely useless for anything else.

I open my eyes and focus in again on the quiet, weary street, feeling strangely like I've just washed up here after being lost at sea. It's no tropical island, that's certain, but it's where I am, and as Mitch said, I'm alive.

****

After work I appease the clamour of a hungry belly with some toast and a banana, then change into my running gear and head out into a blue dusky evening. I run my usual route up to the railway line, but once I reach it I turn left and head in a loop back toward town rather than right toward the glen. The floodlights are on at the rugby club and from a distance I can see the big forms moving around the pitch, passing and catching. Barely breathing hard, I push myself on, intending to run past and do another couple of miles before heading home.

But I make the mistake of watching the guys as I run

past the pitch, and Jackie Wilson raises his hand and shouts my name. Some of the others look up at his shout.

'Shite,' I mutter, and drop to a walk, shaking my head as I step onto the spongy turf. Immediately a bunch of guys I used to know jog over to me and greet me with handshakes and slaps on the back. In my head I struggle to pin names on the faces around me. Lean, clean-cut, banker's son, Paul Jacobsen; I'm surprised he's still here and not in more select company at one of the Edinburgh clubs. Yellow haired and red-cheeked farmer, always laughing, Calum Gregg. Davie Blair, resolute tighthead prop, five- foot seven, bulging at every seam, eyes lost above puffy cheeks. Alan Noble is six-foot six at least, with shoulder-length black hair and a beard. A few others whose names I can't bring to mind, and one or two I don't know.

They're all just bigger, uglier versions of the boys I knew years ago. Most of them have cauliflower ears or noses that have been bashed into unnatural shapes, some have lost teeth, some have bandaged knees, there are a few stitches and scars around the eyebrows. Steam rises off their damp shoulders. Jack Wilson goes over to an oversized kit bag at the side of the pitch and starts rummaging inside.

Their voices all swirl into mud and I laugh. 'Lads, I just popped by to say hiya. I'm not playin'.'

'How no? The RMC turned you into a fuckin' girl or something?' This is from Davie Blair, who stands with the ball in his hands, squinty eyes laughing at me. Trust Davie; at least he won't treat me like I'm made of glass.

'I've got a bad ear, Davie, I won't be able to hear you shouting. That's probably a blessing, mind.'

He laughs heartily, then points at his right eye. On closer view, the pupil looks strangely hollow. If he can

104

see out if it at all, I'll be surprised. 'And I've got a bad eye. Long as ye've still got yin that works, ye'll be alright. But onyway,' he rubs his lower back and inflates his impressive chest, 'suit yersel.'

'Sean.' A hand lands on my back, and I turn. Jack is standing there with a pair of knackered old boots. He looks like an overgrown puppy with a pair of chewed-up slippers. 'Size eleven do you?'

'I said I wasn't playing.'

We stand there head to head for a minute, a pair of mud-caked studs hanging by their laces between us, and as the circle of bodies closes around me, I feel my resolve disintegrating. Mitch isn't saying anything, so I take his silence for approval and take the boots from Jackie.

'Bastard. These fuckin' boots look like someone's been sick over them.'

'Those were mines, they're good boots. But you can get yer ain for the game on Saturday if you're above wearin' hand me downs. Come on, put 'em on.'

Inevitably, I crack. 'All bloody right. Go easy on me, yeah?'

Jack's face glows with his minor victory. He leads the rest of the boys back onto the pitch, and I shake my head, then sit down on the wet grass and pull off my trainers.

XII

'God, what happened to you?'

I step past Molly into the kitchen, scoping several empty wine bottles lined up under the window. She's in a baggy jumper and old jeans tucked into woolly slippers, her hair tied up in a sloppy bun on top of her head.

The little line of butterfly bandages at my hairline itches as she draws my attention to it. Gingerly, I scratch the skin around the cut. 'Rugby. Someone caught me with a stud in the ruck. I'm fine.'

'You're limping. You call that fine?'

I laugh. 'I'm sore in muscles I didn't know I had but honestly, I'm fine.' And I am, for the moment. I'd be better than fine if Paula would phone as she promised, but I'm trying to push her to the back of my mind. We scraped a win yesterday. I put in a bunch of epic tackles and a couple of decent runs with the ball, and the endorphin rush carried me through until bedtime. A handful of painkillers and I was unconscious for nine hours.

'Barbaric sport.' She closes her eyes and takes a deep breath through her nose. 'I haven't even touched anything since you were last here. To be honest, I've got the mother of all hangovers. Dad kept some excellent wines, and I'm afraid I'm not willing to donate those. Where's your scruffy little mate?'

'Billy? AWOL at the moment. He hasn't been at work for a few days.'

'He's allowed to get away with that?'

I shrug. 'I'm not the boss.'

Molly pours me my now customary cup of coffee, refills her own cup and stands leaning against the work-top, her hands wrapped round her mug. She looks shaky and ill and her voice is weak. 'I'm sort of glad.'

'Sorry . . . did you say you're glad?'

She looks up, nods.

I swallow some coffee and pause to enjoy the feeling of it working its way into my blood. 'About what?'

Molly doesn't answer. Instead, she stands there staring at me with an odd little smile. 'I had an estate agent here on Friday. The minute he arrived he had a look on his face like someone had died. At the very least I'm going to have to get that road sorted and replace the roof and windows before I'll have any kind of chance at selling the place. He wasn't even sure it was worthwhile putting it on the market just now, the way things are.'

She takes another steadying breath and looks up at the ceiling, tears quivering in her eyes.

'Oh come on, that's only one guy's opinion. Find someone else.'

'That's the third one, Sean.'

'Ah.' There is an uncomfortable moment as we both try to figure out what comes next.

Molly presses her fingers into her eyes. 'There's some money left in my dad's estate, but I didn't want to blow it on fixing this place up just to sell it. Peter's business isn't doing well just now and he's after me to come home, and I . . .'

She pinches the bridge of her nose, then spills a stream of words that seem to have been crowding in her mouth, plotting their escape. 'I've got nothing of my own. No career, just a few miserably paid jobs raising funds for charities. I've been at the mercy of men my entire life. Cambridge degree in Literature, that's it. Completely useless. I married a man with big ideas and became his fucking housekeeper. I can't even have a baby, Sean. Even my body's incapable of producing anything good. Everything's just . . . fucked up.'

I set my mug down and cross over to her, open my arms and gather her in against my chest. She leans in stiffly at first, but then gives in and goes a bit limp as my arms come up around her back. Her breath is trembly and thick against my shirt. There is something so familiar about that self-hating vulnerability, it makes my brain hurt with memory.

'It'll be okay,' I say.

'How will it? I don't know what to do.'

'You'll figure it out.' I rub her back. 'Look, why don't you just go home for a bit and get away from here. Just lock it up and leave it for a while, give yourself some time to think. I'll keep an eye on the place for you if you like.'

'How much will that cost me?'

I laugh. 'Nothing. Call it a mate's favour.'

She lifts her chin up and looks at me. 'What if I don't want to go home to Peter? What if I said I didn't love him anymore?' She lifts her hand up and gently touches the cut on my forehead.

I stiffen and back away. 'Molly . . . don't.'

'Why not?'

'Because I don't want you to.' I worm out of her grasp.

'I don't get you, Sean,' she snaps.

'What don't you get, exactly? I'm not that complicated. I was giving you a hug to be kind, I wasn't coming on to you.'

She refills her coffee cup and pushes a lock of hair

108

away from her face. 'You really don't like me, do you?'

She's just declared checkmate and absolutely nothing I say next will get me out of this situation unscathed.

Mitch hums in my head and begins singing about Mrs Robinson.

I clear my throat. 'Not in that way.'

Her eyebrows arch upwards, drawing deep lines on her forehead. 'Oh. Okay.' She sniffs and unties her hair, twists it around her hand, then ties it up again. 'I see.'

'Please don't take it personally.'

She laughs, drags a chair over the flagstones and sits down heavily. 'Oh no, absolutely not.'

'Do you want me to get on with the job or not?'

She mutters something and her words disappear into her hands.

'Pardon?'

She says it again.

I kneel in front of her and place a hand on her shoulder. 'Molly, I'm sorry, I can't hear you. I didn't mean to upset you, alright?'

She looks up and shouts in my face. 'Alright Sean, get on with it! Is that loud enough? Jesus Christ, just take all of this shite away. That's what you're here for, isn't it?'

I hold up a hand and nod slowly. 'That's what I'm here for.' I stand up, take two steps backwards, then spin around and duck out of the kitchen before any more venom comes flying my way.

By late afternoon, I have cleared more or less everything I am capable of carrying on my own, leaving only the heaviest items of furniture, the bedding in Molly's room, and the kitchen. Gutted, the house smells of damp stone and dust, and I notice dozens of places where the wallpaper is peeling, the skirting boards have loosened from the walls, dampness has seeped through, or the

109

plaster has crumbled overhead. The wind whistles down from the treeless hillsides behind, and the name Cauldhill seems entirely appropriate for such a place.

I load in one final chair and slide the van door closed with a grimace; my head is pounding and there isn't a part of my body that isn't contracting with pain. Reaching into the glovebox, I pull out a packet of ibuprofen tablets and press two into my hand. Swallowing them with some lukewarm tea from my flask, I stand for a moment letting the sun ease some of the strain in my shoulders. The air is sweet with gorse blossom and Scots pine, and I close my eyes, leaning on the bonnet, absorbing the stillness.

After five minutes, I'm so stiff it's an effort just to pull myself upright. I hobble into the kitchen and find Molly asleep, curled in a stained old wing-back in front of the Aga, a novel in her lap. We've been avoiding each other all day, walking round each other in large circles, exchanging only necessary words.

'Molly,' I say softly to wake her, and she sits up with a sudden intake of breath.

'That's me. I'll need to leave the rest until I've got another pair of hands.'

'Oh . . .' she pushes her reading glasses up onto her head and rubs her eyes, 'okay. Wait.' She scrambles out of the chair, opens a drawer and pulls out a key ring, with three keys on it. 'Were you serious about keeping an eye on the place?'

I shrug. 'Sure, nae bother.'

'Then take these.' She holds out they keys and drops them into my hand. 'You can take the rest of the furniture whenever. No rush. You have my number, just call me if there's any problem.'

I pocket the keys. 'So I take it you're going?'

'For a while,' she says slowly. 'I've got decisions to make. Sean, I . . .' she stops, her brown eyes wide and her lips parted. 'I'm sorry. I haven't behaved very well. You must think I'm half mad.' She sighs. 'Maybe I am, I don't know. I can't seem to think clearly about anything.'

There are a lot of things I'm tempted to say, about her and me and our respective brands of insanity. But I settle for, 'I'm hardly one to cast judgement.'

She looks up at me. 'Thank you. And I'm sorry I shouted at you earlier. It was insensitive.'

'Forget about it.'

'I'll call you.'

'Right.' I peel myself slowly from my leaning position and move stiffly toward the door. 'I'll see you, Molly. Take care, eh?'

'You too.' She touches my arm as I step outside.

I glance down at her fingers, long and pale on my sleeve, but I don't look back at her face. I descend the steps as quickly as my seized muscles will allow me, holding my breath until I am safe in the van and can let it out with a long groan of pain. Molly is still standing on the steps as I turn out of the drive and disappear down the road.

* * * *

'Put your coat in the wardrobe, will you?' Janet shouts from the kitchen. The usual pile of shoes and coats in the lobby has been tidied and the house smells of spices, not dissimilar from the smell that wafted from the little mud brick or cinder block Afghan houses in the villages. They were the lucky ones, of course, the ones who could afford spices and meat; so many others lived on rice and meagre bits of bread.

111

'I'm making curry,' she shouts over the canned laughter of some television studio audience.

I poke my head into the kitchen and breathe in deeply. Hunger rises in my belly like a waking dragon. 'Smells braw.'

She smiles, pushing a mush of onions, garlic and spices around in a pan. Beside her on the worktop is enough chopped chicken breast to feed half a dozen, three fat red tomatoes and a verdant clump of fresh coriander. A pot of yellow dal is simmering on the back ring and basmati rice is soaking in cold water by the sink.

'You having company?'

She gives me a nervous smile and a pair of wide, excited eyes. 'Tim's coming round.'

'Tim from work?'

She's been on about Tim for months. I know exactly what music Tim likes (hairy 70s country rock), that he writes poetry, was a social worker for years before coming to work in housing and that he *really gets it*, whatever *it* is. He sounds like a pompous, middle-aged hippy to me and I'm sure the only thing he has in common with my sister is the middle-aged bit. But then, if you're in your forties and still single, maybe that's enough.

'He called me, he said he's been hillwalking in the Borders and he thought he might pop by on his way home. I said just stay for his tea . . . it didnae take much arm twisting.' She flutters her hands. 'He's just a friend. It's *not* a date.'

'What is it?'

'Just . . . you ken . . . You'll eat with us, won't you?'

I give her the *aye, right* eyebrow. Even if I believed her, the prospect of dinner with her and Tim wouldn't be appealing. No doubt there have been long office conversations about the dubious state of her ex-commando brother's mind, and I'm really not in the mood for the smug, social worky gleam in Tim's eyes as he tries to suss me out.

Didn't she meet enough of them, I wonder, when were kids?

'Do I have to? I'd rather just confine myself to my cell for the evening. You can open the flap and slide some curry through.'

She tuts. 'Sean. You okay?'

'I hurt.'

'Poor baby. You will play rugby. Where?'

'Everywhere. I'll have a bath.'

'Leave the bathroom in a fit state, please.'

'Aye, ma'am.' I give her a lazy salute and drag my complaining legs up the stairs.

Half an hour in the hottest water I can stand – I top it up when it starts to cool – followed by a smear of liniment on the worst offenders (shoulders, thighs, lower back and arse) and a couple of extra-strength paracetamols, and I'm starting to feel vaguely mobile again. I comb my hair and wipe the steam off the mirror to have a look at the damage. The butterfly bandages on my head have peeled off in the bath, leaving a scabby, inflamed red line: another scar for my collection, for certain.

Having ensured that there are no short curlies left in the plughole for Janet to berate me about later, I step out of the warm steam and into the cold air of the landing. A male voice rises up from below, followed by a rich crescendo of laughter from Janet, and again, I think *aye, right,* then scurry along to my room before he politely asks to use the toilet and comes up to catch me dangling here.

I pull on some clothes and am just plotting my sneaky route out the front door when Janet raps once and pokes her head into my room.

113

'You decent?'

'You're meant to ask that before you come in. I think I'll go out, catch a film or something.'

'Dinnae go out, Sean, come down and have something to eat.'

'I'd rather not, if it's all the same to you.'

'It isn't all the same to me,' she snaps. 'You stay here and be sociable, please.'

'I'm not a fucking teenager.'

'Then dinnae act like it. And dinnae spoil this for me, like . . .' She stops short, mouth open like she's just inhaled something deeply unpleasant, and we face each other silently.

Like I've spoiled the rest of your life. She hasn't said it, and because Social Work Tim is downstairs and the walls are thin, neither will I. But we're both thinking it.

I breathe deeply and drop my voice. 'I'm not spoiling anything. I'm giving you some privacy, which I thought you might appreciate.' Then I turn my deaf ear on her and squeeze past, jog down the steps and out, swiping her car keys from their little hook by the door on the way.

XIII

I don't go to the cinema. I've been once since my injury and reckon I missed at least half of the dialogue: a pointlessly expensive and annoying experience, not to be repeated anytime soon. Instead I drive down to Portobello and park at the Joppa end of the Promenade near the public toilets. A wee gang of teenage boys is bumping up and down the steps on stunt bikes and I pause to watch them for a minute or two. One of them hops the bike onto a metal bench, balances his front wheel on the back of the seat for a moment before whirling a full 180 degrees and bouncing smoothly onto the ground. Courage, hormones and boredom put to impressive use; better use than I ever found for them, anyway.

I walk past and head along the Promenade, thinking back on my teenage self: all humiliation, aggression and jealousy, cleverly packaged so nobody could tell one from the other. I would have been the kid balancing the bike on the bench or pulling wheelies on top of the sea wall if I'd had a bike capable of it. Every Christmas I asked for a new one and Mum never came up with the goods. The best I had was a rusty green clunker that had belonged to my granddad: an ugly, battered old thing that to me looked like a neon sign flashing out POVERTY CASE to the world. Sometimes I wonder how different my life might have been if she'd managed to give me just one thing I really wanted.

You joined the RMC because she never bought you a bike? You blame that poor woman for a hell of a lot.

I joined because it was my only way out.

You could have gone to uni and got a job in Civvy Street, if that's what you'd wanted.

I was a fuck up at school.

That's nobody's fault but your own, boyo. You had the brain for it.

'You try learning the periodic table of the elements when your ma's puking her guts out in the kitchen sink. It's a bit distracting.'

You're talking out loud again, Nic. And there's no point blaming the dead; they can't talk back.

You fucking do. Are you just here to break my balls or what?

Maybe, if that's what it takes.

'For what?'

Bloody hell, you figure it out.

And he switches himself off with a ghostly little *harumph*, leaving only the soft rumble and hiss of the waves on the beach, the rush of the city traffic and the now distant, crow-like laughter of the boys on the bikes.

I lift my eyes from the ground and watch little waves rolling under a heavy, darkening sky. It's not a cold night but a blanket of North Sea haar is creeping up the Forth, blurring the lights of Fife across the water, moistening the air. There aren't many people out now, just a few dog walkers and couples holding hands, and lights are coming on in the bay windows of the Victorian houses facing onto the Prom.

I walk along, pass the Porty swimming baths and fall into a kind of oblivious march, not thinking about where I'm going. From somewhere behind me, I hear a shout but don't register any meaning in it so don't turn. After

116

a moment, footsteps come thudding along the pavement and a hand lands on my back.

I jerk sharply out of my daze and duck away from the hand.

'Holy crap, it *is* you, Nic,' a breathless voice says, just comprehensible over my rushing pulse. A face I know but haven't seen in at least four years, waving brown hair and green eyes that dart back and forth in a manic kind of way, a head that bobs up and down emphatically with every word.

'Jesus,' I splutter, 'Tigger, you scared the crap out of me, mate.' I grin, slap his arm. 'What you doing here?'

Tommy Davidson was a Peterhead boy who came of age on his dad's trawler before joining up, a year or two before I did. We were together through two operations in Iraq and the first tour in Helmand. He was called Tigger because of his bouncing stride and irrepressible cheer. He was one of the most eager bootnecks I ever met, but had to leave after breaking a couple of vertebrae in his back on a winter warfare training exercise in Norway. We kept in touch for a year or so after that but inevitably lost touch. Last I knew he was living with his wife and kid in Aberdeen.

We take the measure of each other. A lot of his muscle tone has gone south, and his face has the puffy look of someone who drinks too much beer and eats too much salty food. His hair is wet and he is clutching a small holdall.

'I moved down to Edinburgh a couple of years ago, man,' he says, still trying to catch his breath. 'Bloody hell, I've been shouting on you since the swimming baths. You deaf or something?'

I laugh. 'Aye. You not heard?'

'Nae joke?'

I show him my cheek. 'Fell foul of an IED, Tig. I can't hear out this ear at all. But all in a day's work, eh?'

He nods slowly. 'Too right. I heard about Mitch.'

'It was the same device got us both. He saved my life.'

Hooray for Mitchell the Hero, I saved a miserable bastard's life. Did you tell him about my George Cross? Go on, tell him. You don't get one of those for falling off a rock in Norway.

'Ocht.' Tig hisses through his teeth. 'A heart of gold, that boy. You guys were like that, from the start.' He holds up crossed fingers. Then he grins broadly again, refusing to descend into melancholy. 'You look fucking great, though, man. Except for the hair. What's that about?'

'It's . . . I guess it's just my way of saying cheerio and fuck you to my former employers.'

He laughs heartily and seems to think I'm kidding. 'You working now?'

'In a manner of speaking. Shifting furniture.'

'It's keepin' you fit, anyway. I wish I could do something physical, Nic, I can't lift so much as a shopping bag anymore.'

'How's the back, anyway?'

'Sair. And it gies me chronic fuckin' sciatica which isnae a barrel o' laughs either. Threaders, you know? Was on incapacity benefit till some beak tells me I'm capable of workin' and stops my dosh. So I'm driving a taxi. It's dull as muck and doesna dae my back any good. Some days I canna sit still for the pain, like, but the money's alright.'

'A pretty shite state of affairs, Tig.'

'Aye well.' He pauses, looks away for a moment and runs his fingers through damp hair. 'Cheerfulness in the face of adversity. Remember?'

'Vaguely.'

'So where ye off tae?'

'Just walking. Clearing the head.'

'I've been for a swim and I could murder a pint. Fancy one doon the Espy?'

'I've come out without the wallet, Tig, I've nae dosh.' It's true but sounds like an excuse, and a pathetic one at that.

He slaps my shoulder. 'Come on, my shout.'

'Just a juice then. I'm a cheap date, anyway, you know that.'

He nods, smiles. 'You still teetotal, Nic? I'd forgotten that.'

'Yep.'

His eyebrows curve upward. 'Each to his own, eh?'

We continue walking along the Prom and fall into an easy banter, reminiscing about guys we knew: Android Bradley whose only vaguely individual feature was the ability to burp God Save the Queen, Paul Lucas with his enormous hairy feet (no prizes for guessing that he was christened Hobbit the moment he took his boots off), Roger Rabbit Arundel, so called because he and his wife had four bairns by the time he was twenty-five. He used to say with a proud grin that all he had to do was hang his trousers over the bedstead and she was pregnant.

'Last I heard, Droid and Hobbit were still in,' Tig says. 'In it to win it.'

'Might take a while.'

'Aye,' he laughs. 'Rabbit's oot. He's living on a fucking farm, doon in Cornwall. Couple mair bairns for the collection. They all run aboot the place naked, Rabbit and the Missus too.'

'You kidding?'

'Hell no, man. I stayed with them for the weekend

119

last year. They raise pigs and chickens and grow all their ain fruit and veg. They say they want to live off grid, whatever the fuck that means.'

'No mains electricity or gas. Self sufficient.'

'Fucking hippies. Dinnae ken what's got intae the man.'

'Sounds like a nice life.'

He stares at me.

I shrug. 'It does. Not the naked thing, necessarily, but the rest would be okay. I could do that. Mind you, depending what the wife looked like . . .'

Tig laughs, shakes his head. 'Anyway . . . that's all I ken. Not really in touch with anybody since then. You?'

'Nah. I haven't wanted to, mind.'

'How's that?'

'Dunno. Clean break, I guess.'

In the Espy, I nab a table by the window with a view of the broody Forth and Tig goes to the bar. I watch as the barman pours my orange juice, and a pint and a nip for Tig. The nip goes down the throat before he even pays for it, then he opens his wallet, slaps some money onto the bar and carries the pint and juice over.

He sits across from me and sinks his top lip into the frothy head of his pint, drinking deeply and closing his eyes.

'Fuck, I needed that.' Then he clinks his glass off my own. 'I admire your moral fortitude, my friend.'

I smile. 'Morality has nothing to do with it.'

He snorts, then digs into his pocket and pulls out a small packet of tablets, presses one out and pops it into his mouth, washes it down with more beer. I think he's embarrassed that I'm watching him because he shakes the packet, taps it on the table anxiously and shoves it back into his pocket.

'Heavy duty co-codamol.' He laughs too loudly. 'Mix it with a couple of pints and I'm just fine.'

'Comfortably numb.'

He nods with veiled eyes. 'That's the general idea.'

'How's Rhona and the bairn?'

'Nae bad, so I'm told. I'm away frae her. She . . . liked being mairrit tae a bootneck, Nic. Once I came oot . . . it was a different story. Wee Joe, he's braw. Seven noo. I have him one weekend a month and a couple of weeks over the school holidays, that's my lot. Rhona's shacked up wi' a fuckin' polisman. Big fat baldy bastard, barely fits his vest. The pair ae us come to grief once or twice, which is why I've moved doon here. He was aching tae get me done for something, and that would have been that for me seein' Joe, ken what I mean?'

'Sorry to hear that,' I say hollowly.

His hands splay out in front of him, and for the first time I notice the RMC dagger tattooed on the back of his left forearm. He must have had it done after he left. It looks brutal and coarse. 'There ye go. I'm a free agent again. It's good, mate. There's plenty lassies, ken, it's no exactly a drought. You?'

'I recently met up with a girl I knew years ago, but . . .' I shrug. 'It's kind of complicated.'

'Complicated.' He snorts. 'Why does it always have to be so bloody complicated, I'm askin ye. What you done to your forehead there? Been scrapping?'

'Bad tackle.'

'You playing rugby again?'

'Aye.'

'Outstanding, man. What position?'

'Second row; one of the heavy mob. Just for the seconds at the local club; most of the guys are in it for the beer and the craic. There's only a couple of weeks left in the season.'

He nods but doesn't ask anything further about rugby, or much else for that matter. He blethers a relentless stream of bullshit about himself, interspersed by hyena-like laughter and deep draughts of beer: Rhona's crimes of passion with the baldy fat copper, girls he's bagged in nightclub toilets, the psychos he's transported in the taxi, the getaways he's made from the drug barons and small time gangsters, hammering the Hackney through the streets of Broomhouse, the time a guy stuck a knife up the back of his head and asked him to hand over all the cash. *Fuckin disarmed him from the front seat, one hand still on the wheel, wee chavvy bastard didn't know who he was messin' with till I showed him the tat. Then he crapped it and ran.*

The pub begins to fill with Sunday night drinkers. A gaggle of female forty-somethings settles at the table next to us and Tig's words quickly lose their meaning. I lean forward and try to watch his lips. He goes on and bloody on. I sit there, nursing my watery orange juice, chortling from time to time to show some token appreciation, my hollow belly grumbling at me like a bored child.

He breaks off mid-flow, drains his pint and points at my empty glass. 'You want another juice, mate?'

'I haven't had my tea and I'm fucking Hank Marvin. I should probably get off home.'

'Naw,' he says, almost desperately, 'dinna. I'll get you a plate of chips. It's too early for home time.'

I can see he's out for a proper session, and I can't think of anything more soul destroying than sitting here watching him drown his sorrows.

'To be honest, Tigger mate, I can't hear a bloody thing in here. It's a proper pain in the arse.' I stand

122

up abruptly. 'I'll let you get me something from the chippy. Coming?'

I half hope he elects to stay in the pub, but he snatches his holdall from under the table scurries to follow me out the door.

'I said something to piss you off, Nic?' he asks when we get outside.

I pause and look at him. He's still smiling, but his eyes are full of something else. He always did have that slightly needy way about him, like the kid who is so desperate to fit in with the popular gang that he'll do anything to win their respect.

I sigh and press my fingertips into my eyes, feeling the beginnings of a hunger headache as well as a chorus of aches from elsewhere in my body, chiming up to remind me what a long bloody day it's been. 'No. Sorry. I'm just wabbit and hungry, and I cannae hear half of what you're saying. I'm not so good in crowds.'

'Aye, I know what you mean. Normally I like to sit with my back to the wall. Just in case, you know?' A strange, strangled little laugh.

I nod vaguely and wander in the direction of the chippy. Tig bounces along beside me and buys us both some food, waving away my offer to get him one the next time. Probably he makes more money than I do, and probably the company (such as my surly presence may be) is worth the cost of a portion of haddock and chips. He even splashes out on smoked sausages as well as the fish suppers, Coke for me and a can of lager for himself.

We sit on the wall overlooking the tawny sand and fill ourselves with grease and God knows what: Scottish comfort food of the sort that will put you out of your misery a little more slowly but just as surely as any suicide method known to man. It sends its cloying, delicious smell out into the moist, salty air: a little whiff of the homely British seaside disappearing into the lonely haar. A ship's horn bellows in return from somewhere unseen.

That sound used to make me fantasize about going to sea, about sunnier shores, shabby cantinas lit by candles in waxy bottles, women with skin like milk chocolate, drunken sailors in hammocks. Not long after passing out we were pulled off exercise in the Caribbean to help with the rescue effort in Honduras following Hurricane Mitch. We spent our time up to our knees in mud, digging chocolate-skinned bodies out of the ruins of cantinas and schools and homes. The water was soupy with mosquitoes and disease and I carried the smell of rotting flesh in my nose for months afterwards. I doubt I'll ever be able to use the words tropical and paradise in the same sentence again.

'D'you know what I miss?' Tig says, waving toward the sea with his sausage. 'Foghorns.'

At least that's what I think he says. I glance at him. He's staring straight ahead, almost studiously avoiding my gaze, chewing with his mouth open and banging his heels against the wall.

'Think I might head up the toon,' he says after a moment, swallowing a mouthful of lager. 'Catch a band or something. Fancy it?'

'Nah. I'm cream crackered, mate.'

'I got something'll cure you of that.'

I stand up, crumple my chippy wrappers into a ball and toss them into the bin beside me. 'You're a veritable medicine man these days, eh, Tig? Watch yourself, yeah? Face down in a puddle of your own puke isn't a very noble way to go.'

124

He shrugs. 'I can think of worse.'

We face each other. 'So can I, but that's not the point. Thanks for the scran, I appreciate it.'

'Hey, swap numbers, eh?'

'Sure.'

We enter each other's numbers into our phones and promise to meet up again soon.

Then he spreads his hands wide and low and grins. 'Brilliant to see you, Sean. It's been too long.'

'Yep.'

He looks like he wants a hug but I leave him with a slap on the shoulder and head back along to the end of the Promenade.

It's nearly nine o'clock by the time I get back to the car, and I reckon by now Janet and Tim will be settled in the living room, having coffee or progressing on to after-dinner relations. It's not that I'm not pleased for her; the poor woman deserves a bit of romance and she's pretty taken with Social Work Tim.

I drive around for an hour: a big sweeping loop through Musselburgh and the coast road to Aberlady, then inland and over the hill to Haddington and the back road to Dalkeith. At home I pause momentarily at the base of the stairs and catch the murmur of voices in the living room, then poke my head round the corner at them. They're side by side on the sofa, drinking red wine in their socks, and I wonder if he's planning to stay the night.

Tim looks up at me and smiles, and to my surprise looks nothing like the kind of guy who would wear red shoes and carry a man bag. He's wiry, silver-haired and bearded, and looks more like a naval officer than a dithery social worker; my estimation of him increases cautiously.

'Hey,' I say.

Janet sighs, a frustrated noise that indicates I've been Subject of Discussion Number One. 'Tim, this is Sean.'

Tim gets up and shakes my hand. 'Pleased to meet you, Sean.' To his credit, he doesn't say he's heard a lot about me.

'Yep, you too.'

'I saved you some curry,' Janet offers. 'You want to join us?'

'I've eaten.' I nod at the pair of them. 'My bed's calling me. See you again, Tim.'

'I hope so,' he says kindly.

I back out of the room and head upstairs. I have a quick wash, then pull my clothes off and slip into the safety of my bed, lights out to indicate that visiting hours are definitely over. For a while I lie there thinking of Tigger, drinking pints and nips in some student bar up town, eyeing up the 20 year-old honeys in hot pants, hoping his war stories and dagger tattoo will somehow obscure his puffy eyes and dog breath.

'Poor old Tig,' I whisper up toward the ceiling, my head resting on my arms.

I bet he's saying the same thing about you, says Mitch.

'Fuck off Mitch,' I mutter, and swipe my mobile from the bedside table, check for messages.

Nothing. I scroll through my contacts and pull up the number Paula gave me, ring it and lie there. After six rings, I get her voicemail.

'Hey . . . it's Sean.' I pause, grapple with disappointment and uncertainty. 'Just . . . you know. Wondering how it's going. Baby should be here any day now, huh? I guess you've got a lot on your mind. Anyway, ring me whenever. Okay? Talk soon.'

126

I click the phone off and drop it back onto the table, blow a long breath out between closed lips and lie there feeling far from sleep.

Poor old Sean, says Mitch.

'Fuck off, Mitch.'

XIV

'So the situation is this. Sales have gone up over the last couple of weeks, thanks to the new shop layout, and we've had some extra income due to Sean's house clearance.'

Harry Boyle looks around at us, gathered on the sofas in the shop at 9:30 on a Monday morning. His hair is standing on end and his fingers are buried deep into his beard, grey tufts of hair sprouting between his fingers. He rubs his face and draws in a long breath.

'However, unfortunately, I have noticed some . . . financial irregularities. There have been a number of bank transactions over the past couple of weeks that don't match the till receipts. We also appear to have lost some items of stock.'

I'm half listening, trying not to fret about the fact that Paula still hasn't phoned. Emma and Dawn are sulking opposite me like schoolgirls caught smoking in the toilets, Dawn digging a bitten pinky nail into a pluke on her chin. Al is beside me chewing on his tongue and Linda is hunched and quivery as a little owl. The smell of last night's booze, or maybe this morning's, shimmers off her like the smell of rot from a corpse in the sun. Nobody speaks.

'Obviously I'm going to have to investigate this,' he continues, letting his gaze settle on each of us in turn. There are bags under his eyes.

'I also have to let you know that the Board has been made aware and that they are prepared to involve the police. You will each be formally interviewed as part of the investigation process, so that we can identify the person responsible.'

'It's really fuckin' obvious, innit?' Dawn says to her lap. 'It's fuckin' Billy, eh?'

Harry holds up a hand. 'Let's not make random accusations. If anyone has information, please share it with me in private. In the meantime,' he pauses, puffs his cheeks and pushes out a long breath. 'I'll be honest with you, stealing from a charity is about the lowest of the low. Things like this can put us under.'

He stands slowly, rubbing his lower back. 'That's all. Let's try and make the best of things. Thanks for listening, folks.' Then his eyes land on me. 'Sean, can I speak to you for a minute?'

'Ha ha,' Dawn crows behind me as I follow Harry to his office, 'you're nicked, mate.' Harry and I ignore her, but Mitch doesn't.

Ha ha, you're nicked, mate, he parrots, his laughter echoing in some hollow chamber in my brain. *Ha ha. Ha hahahaha.*

Fuck off!

For a split second, I think I've said it aloud and I glance around to check whether anyone is looking at me.

It's nothing to do with me and you know it.

You start work and things start going missing. It doesn't look coincidental.

'Close the door,' Harry says as we step into his office, and I feel as though he's just woken me out of a short but deep sleep. He smiles and pulls out a chair for me. 'Are you alright?'

'Pardon?'

129

'You look upset.'

I clear my throat. 'I was away with the fairies just there. Look, Harry, I don't know anything about . . .'

He holds up his hand again, cutting me off. 'I know you don't, Sean. There are only three of us who do the banking, including me, and it has to be one of us. No, it was just a couple of things. First, I thought you'd like to know that we've made more than two grand over our forecast income for this month, even in spite of things, and that's down to your antiques. Also, this came through the door this morning.'

He passes over a short, handwritten note, addressed to The Manager, Once Loved Furniture.

Dear Sir/Madam

I am writing to express my profound gratitude to you for allowing Sean McNicol the time to clear the house of my late father at Cauldhill Farm. Sean has been kind, gentlemanly and efficient, and he has spared me what would have been a long and traumatic job. He also provided a good listening ear when I needed to talk, which was over and above the call of duty. I hope you will pass my deepest thanks on to him.

Yours sincerely,
Molly Wells

I look up from the letter. 'A good listening ear. I would have offered two, but . . .'

Is that a sense of humour I detect, Nic? Are you sure you're feeling alright, son?

Right enough, Harry laughs.

'That was nice of her,' I say, wondering about her motive. Either she's trying to keep me sweet so I look after the house well, or she's still trying to bed me from afar.

130

'Yes, it was. If you don't mind, I'll share this with the board. They'll be delighted to know that someone is doing a good job in this place.'

'Why . . . do they think we're not?'

He presses the switch on the kettle on top of the filing cabinet. 'Let's just say they've questioned my capacity to manage *challenging* employees. But never mind. You're doing a stellar job. You want some coffee?'

'Okay.'

He spoons fresh coffee into a cafetiere, falling into a contemplative silence as he pours in the water and waits until the grounds have risen into a thick, black layer. The smell of coffee fills the stale little office.

Harry never speaks loudly, but around me he is always very careful not to talk with his back turned. I've noticed this and am grateful that he does it without having to say anything about it. Eventually he hands me a mug and sits down again, leans back in his chair and crosses his ankles in front of him.

'So yesterday I went round to try to talk to Billy. He wouldn't let me in the door.'

'He was at home?'

'Oh aye. He didn't look in any fit state to go anywhere.'

'Is he ill, or . . .'

'Fleein'.'

'Ah.'

He swallows coffee, then clears his throat. 'He's not well, though, you know that. He's been seriously depressed for a long, long time.'

At least he doesn't hear voices, I think, and stare resolutely into my coffee.

'He self medicates with hash, among other things.'

'So I've noticed.'

'To be honest, in the three years he's been here he's

131

managed alright. He's disappeared for the odd day here and there, but never anything like this. The thing is, Sean, he's tried to kill himself in the past. Somebody needs to go and talk to him. He likes you, I wondered if you would.'

'He *likes* me?'

'You're surprised by that?'

'He threatens to welly me on a fairly regular basis.'

'Aye, I know what he's like. But he does like you. He told me. He respects you. I know it's a lot to ask, so please tell me if you don't feel able.'

'One mad bugger to another.'

Harry puts down his cup and folds his hands together, presses them against his lips and studies me intently. 'Is that honestly what you think you are?'

I shrug.

'Some people describe Post Traumatic Stress as a natural response to an unnatural situation. Does that make any kind of sense to you?'

'Maybe,' I pause, waiting for him to respond. He just sits there, thoroughly happy in counselling mode, hands in a ball and any comprehensible thought well concealed behind the beard.

'Fuck, Harry, I *know* that. I know I'm not mad, it's more like . . . this probably sounds wrong . . . sometimes I feel like I'm the only person in the world who sees what's actually happening.'

'And what do you see?'

I take a deep breath, lean my elbows on my knees, and it all comes spewing out like semi-digested chunks of kebab out of the guts of a drunk on a Saturday night.

'That we're puppets on a string. That none of the wars I've ever played my tiny part in has ever been about freedom – ours or anyone else's – because freedom's a myth they've cooked up to keep us in line. That it doesn't matter if you're Scottish or English or American or Afghan, whether you swear on the Bible or the Koran, because we're all bent over the same barrel being fucked by the same forces.

'That ... that there's a tiny group of men in this world – the ones who control the banks and the corporations – who are holding the rest of us by the ball hairs and we don't even know it, and the more we fight amongst ourselves, the richer and more powerful they get, and I ... I just feel so fucking angry all the time. Everything that happened to us, every mate I saw die, every person I killed ... it's all for nothing. That's it, Harry. That's what I see.'

I sit up again and retreat into my coffee.

The slightest deepening of the creases around Harry's eyes indicate a smile. 'That view of the world isn't exactly compatible with service in Her Majesty's armed forces, Sean.'

'I know. They were quite happy to see the back of me after I told them that. It's easier to tell one twitchy, blown up Jock that he's nuts than to question their own motives.'

He chuckles. 'Then welcome to the resistance, Comrade. We'll lead the revolution one three-piece suite at a time.'

Relief swirls around me like a warm wave. I close my eyes and swallow the urge to weep. 'Sorry for going off on one.'

'Dinnae be. Believe me, I wouldn't be working here if I didn't feel the same. That's what keeps me here, you know? The thought that every ugly old settee we divert from landfill and sell to some poor person who needs it is a strike against The Man.' He bends forward and

133

refuses to let me break from his gaze. 'You know what I'm saying?'

This bloody guy thinks he's Tom Joad, Mitch observes, then goes quiet again. He agrees with Harry too, I know he does, but he wouldn't like to admit being on the same side as a wee fat hippy in a Fair Isle jumper and Clarks loafers.

Then I nod slowly and push the hair away from my eyes. 'So then . . . back to Billy. What about Linda? Why can't she talk to him?'

'They've fallen out. She won't speak to him. That's what started all this.'

I sigh. 'I'll go see him.'

So half an hour later I'm climbing the outdoor stair to Billy's flat above Sheena's Cafe in Pentland Street, to a long row of doors and a landing strewn with black rubbish bags and pigeon shit. The yellowish harling is flaking off to reveal the brick beneath, and telephone cabling hangs loose, catching the wind and tapping against the wall. A woman with pale, spotty skin and dyed black hair passes me, dragging a folded buggy with one hand and clinging to a scrawny, drool-soaked baby with the other. She eyes me coldly as we pass each other, suspicion oozing out of every pore.

It's not the kind of place many strangers would venture, except cops and social workers, and automatically my eyes begin scanning for shadows, right and left. A pigeon startles out of a recessed doorway and my whole body seizes. For five seconds I am down a back alley in Basra, completely rigid except for my heart, which is banging so hard it might be visible from the outside. When I take another step forward, my legs feel like they might give under me. Feeling a complete arsehole, I speed along to

134

Billy's door at the far end and bang soundly with a fist.

Receiving no response, I bang again and press my good ear against the door. Vaguely I can make out voices, then a creak and footsteps. They seem to approach, then stop.

'Billy!'

'Whae's that?' he demands.

'Sean. Let us in, eh?'

'Whit ye wantin?'

'Billy, I cannae speak to you through the door.'

The lace curtains of next door's window twitch and the drawn, frightened face of an elderly woman peers out. I raise my hand and offer what is meant to be a reassuring smile, though I think it's closer to a grimace.

'I'll kick this door in if you dinnae open up.'

Eventually he cracks the door. He's standing there in a stained blue dressing gown and greyish underpants, the skin of his face and bare chest pale and falling into loose, dehydrated creases. He's emaciated and the smell of piss wafts off him. His appearance is shocking even to me; the depth to which he has descended in a short space of time, albeit from a pretty low starting point, seems terminal.

A man steps out into the corridor behind him, pencil legs in skinny jeans, a black Super Dry jacket, pale hair gelled into a quiff. Darren Armstrong hasn't changed since school: he's still an arrogant, scrawny thug wrapped in poncy labels.

He sniffs. 'Well, look who it is. Alright Sean? I thought you got fucking blown up in Afghanistan or something.'

'But miraculously, here I am. The wonders of modern medicine. Long time no see, Derek.'

'Darren.'

'Darren, of course. How could I forget? What you doing here?'

'My mate Bill and I were just havin' a wee chat, weren't we, Billy? A wee cup of tea and a natter.'

'Aye, ye prick,' Billy growls, 'Now get oot.'

Darren laughs and slaps Billy on the shoulder. 'He's a good laugh, isn't he? If you can put up wi' the stench.'

Billy winces and huddles into himself.

I step past Billy and pause in front of Darren, not right in his face but three or four inches closer than most people are comfortable with. 'You were just going?'

Sure enough, he takes a step backwards. 'Maybe.'

'I think you were.'

He faces up to me but his eyes flicker about, doing the maths and obviously not liking the answer. Then he turns to Billy. 'One week. You fucking pay up.'

Billy's voice actually breaks. 'I bloody telt ye, that's it Daz. I cannae gie ye anymair. That's all there is.'

Armstrong places a spindly finger on Billy's chest. 'That's not my problem.'

I clear my throat and place my hand on the back of his jacket, fingers gripping the fabric lightly. 'Come on Dapper Daz. I'll get you to the door.'

'Get your hand off me, McNicol.'

He tries to duck away but I grip harder and steer him in the direction of the front door. 'Whatever he owes you, why don't you just forget it? A little charity between neighbours, eh?'

'This is nane o' your business.'

'Then give me a reason to make it my business.' I let go of his jacket and shove him hard toward the door.

He stumbles, catches himself and spins quickly, faces me. 'I dinnae want bother wi' ye, Sean.'

'No, you don't.' I smile personally and close the distance between us again, effectively pinning him to the

136

door. 'And your business with Billy is done and dusted. Understood?'

His lips work silently and his chest heaves up and down. 'Aye, whatever. I dinnae need the fuckin' dosh anyway. I'm no fuckin' beggar.' Cautiously, he leans around me and juts his chin toward Billy. 'See you around, Bill, yeah?'

'Piss off, ya cunt.'

I open the door and hold it open. 'Nice bumping into you, Daz. Cheerio, eh?'

He glances briefly at me, then scurries away.

I pull the door shut again and lock it, then turn around. My hands are shaking so I shove them into my pockets and take a deep breath. 'Well then.'

Billy sags against the corridor wall. 'What was that? Some kind of fucking Jedi mind trick or something?'

'He's a playground bully. Just called his bluff, that's all.'

'He's no fucking bluffing.'

'Neither am I.'

Billy grunts and turns away from me. I follow him into a dark sitting room littered with chip wrappers, beer cans that have been flattened into makeshift bongs, dirty socks, cups of week-old tea with mould floating on the top. The blue and white striped wallpaper hangs off in strips in some places. There are a couple of detached wires protruding from the wall in the corner, but no telly. It looks like someone has taken away everything of value.

'I see I'm a wee bit late.'

'It doesnae matter. Thanks anyway.' He drops heavily onto a stained grey settee and lifts his feet onto it, then closes his eyes. 'Harry sent ye, eh?'

'We're worried about you, mate. We just wanted to see how you're doing.'

137

His eyelids flutter. 'Well, see for yersel'.'

'I don't like what I see, Bill. I've been in some shitholes in my time, but this takes some beating. You want to tell me what the fuck's going on?'

'Nothing, I just dinnae feel like comin' tae work.'

'What happened with Linda?'

He opens his eyes and stares woozily at me. 'She got a better offer.'

Is it just me, or is that hard to believe?

I bite my lip until I'm sure Mitch isn't going to say anything else; three-way conversations involving a dead guy and a strung out hash-head are definitely to be avoided.

'Sorry to hear that.'

He gives a disdainful sniff and stares blankly at the nicotine-yellowed ceiling. 'Doesnae matter. You want a cup of tea?'

'Aye, sure.'

'Help yersel'.'

I sigh, then get up and go into the kitchen and stand there for a couple of minutes, eyes closed, breathing in for a count of ten and then out, until my pulse slows. I splash some cold water onto my face, but there is nothing to dry with except the hem of my shirt. Even if there was a tea towel, you probably wouldn't want to let it anywhere near your face. There are dead flies on the bunker and black mould creeping up the wall behind the sink, a few crusty dishes in the sink. I boil the kettle and locate a packet of powdery teabags, wash a couple of mugs and make tea. Unsurprisingly, the milk in the fridge is rock hard.

I bring the black tea back into the living room and nudge Billy with my toe. 'Here.'

'Dinnae want it.'

'Sit up, you lazy piece of shit and take the fucking tea.'

His body jerks and he pushes himself upright, takes the mug and sits there holding it between trembling hands, not looking at me.

I sit down on a sticky faux-leather chair opposite him. 'Drink it.'

He dips his upper lip into the tea and shudders. 'So . . . what's the story?'

'Someone's had their hand in the till. But you know that already.'

He opens his eyes properly for the first time since I got here; his pupils are huge and the whites are laced with pink. 'How would I ken that? Whae is it, like?'

'Why don't you tell me?'

His mouth opens and closes silently like a landed cod, and then a sheen comes over his eyes. I sit back and wait for perhaps two full minutes, drinking my tea and eyeballing him. From my position I can see across the hall into a bedroom that contains nothing but a mattress on the floor and a pile of clothes in the corner.

'What happened to you, Billy? How did you get this way?'

His laughter sounds like a cat trying to bring up a hairball. 'Nothing happened tae me. Nothing except whit ye see around ye. I was just tryin' tae get oot, that's all. I bought a motor off Daz. Like I said tae ye, he really thinks he's something. Thinks he owns this fuckin' toon.'

'Uh huh.' The story spills open in front of me, inevitable as black ink tipped over white paper.

'And I couldn't pay him, so he took the fuckin' thing back, and the interest.'

'Your telly and all your gear. You let him?'

'Look at the state o' me. He came wi' his mates. First class thugs, man, even if he's not.'

'So why's he back now?'

'He says I still owe him for the damage.'

'Damage?'

'Fuckin' door and wing are all scraped tae hell.'

I take a sip of tea to swallow a snort. 'I may be stating the obvious here, but you're not exactly in a fit state for driving.'

'It wasnae bloody me, I telt him that!'

'Aye, okay. But because you're such a big man, you stole from the shop to pay him back for damage you didn't cause.'

He puts the mug down and sits with his hands shaking between his knees. There is something almost transparent about him, as though he has already started to fade out of the world of the living. He's not solid enough anymore to harbour a lie.

'Linda did it for me.' The confession comes out of him like the final hiss of air out of a deflated balloon. 'She didn't want to, but the whole motor thing was her idea. She wanted us to pack up and go away, find a better life somewhere else. A fucking pipe dream, that's all.'

I feel Mitch warming up for a Hank Williams chorus and try to head him off at the pass by sliding my fingers into my hair and concentrating my gaze on a crusty, grey patch on the carpet between my feet.

'You can't run away from your habits, though.'

'Nuh. You're right about that, at least. What are ye gonnae dae? Tell Harry? Get us the sack?'

'That's not my job. You're gonnae go tell him yourself. Maybe instead of sacking you, he'll let you resign with some dignity. Go get dressed.'

'What if I say no?'

'I phone the cops.'

140

'You're a self-righteous bastard, ye ken that, Mister Green fucking Beret.' He hauls himself off the sofa and wobbles onto his feet. 'I ken who you really are. I kent yer ma.'

'So did every other waster in this town, Billy. Get some clothes on, unless you want to go like that.'

He shuffles into his bedroom and drops his dressing gown onto the floor, revealing the bowed ridge of his spine and the blue stain of an old tattoo on his left upper arm.

Take a good look, boyo. That could be you in a year or two.

Fuck off, Mitch.

That's what you turn into if you sit about feeling sorry for yourself. Gollum's body double.

I go to the window and look out at desolation of the sort we Scots are so good at: slimy paper in the corners, flaking roughcast walls and graffiti.

Look at this place. This is where you've left me.

Bollocks. This is what you chose.

You took the better part of me with you. Tell me what to do.

No.

Mitch . . .

'Tell me something, Sean, why do you fucking care, anyway?'

I turn around. Billy has propped himself in the doorway, chest rising and falling heavily with the effort of dressing himself. Sweat beads at his temples.

'Because for some reason I can't fathom, Harry's still paying you to sit on your scrawny arse and get high, we're losing money, and I'm not prepared to let you take the rest of us down with you. And at the end of the day, neither are you.'

A meek nod. He's too exhausted to be anything other than compliant.

'Come on, I'll get you to the shop.'

'I'll go myself.'

'No you won't. Let's go.'

We leave the flat and he walks up the road beside me, then stops at the door of the shop. Both hands come up toward my chest as if to push me away. 'Sean, just . . . let me go in myself. Dinnae frogmarch me in there.'

'Fine.' I step backwards. 'Do the right thing, Billy, yeah?'

'The right thing . . . aye.' He squints into the sun and shields his eyes. 'There's nae such thing, sunshine. Maybe the fucking Royal Marines'd have ye believe it, but oot here in the real world . . . nuh. But ye'll need tae figure that oot for yersel, eh? Been nice workin' wi' ye.'

He backs through the door and leaves me standing on the pavement outside. I pull in a long breath of sweet, spring air and take a walk up the street. My clothes and hair carry the sickly toilet smell of Billy's flat, and briefly I consider going home for a shower before heading back to work. Instead, I pause outside a new barbershop run by pair of smartly dressed Turkish brothers. One of them opens the door, releasing a waft of wet hair and aftershave, and holds his hand out in a gesture of welcome.

'Hello there, my friend. We got no queue, come in please.'

I smile and sweep hair away from my eyes. 'It looks that bad you had to drag me in off the street.'

He shrugs. 'You want to keep it long, I will just tidy it up for you.'

'No.' I sit on the chair and let him drape the cape around me. 'Chop it all off, mate. Short back and sides.'

142

'Ah, okay.' He pats my shoulder. 'I'll make you brand new. For your lady, eh?'

'I wish.'

He laughs and selects his scissors for a big job, then attacks the shoulder length mop with obvious relish. I watch the familiar old hard-edged version of myself emerge from the prison I sent him to a year and a half ago. He acquitted himself reasonably with Darren and Billy, but whether he's ready for release, whether he's penitent enough – whether he ever can be – is still to be established.

An idea floats into my head and lodges there. I pull my phone from my pocket and punch in a text to Jack Wilson:

Want to give us a hand shifting some furniture? Reckon you owe me one.

I send this off, and a couple of minutes later the reply comes. *Anything to get me oot the hoose, mate.*

The barber runs the clippers up the back of my neck and around my ears, then brushes the fallen hair off my shoulders. 'Alright. You want shave?'

'Eh . . . no. I'm alright.'

'Okay. Your lady will like you better now.'

'Insha'Allah.' I give him a little nod of prayer, then pull a tenner out of my wallet. 'Keep the change, mate.'

'Good man.' He laughs and holds the door for me a second time.

The Saddos are out as usual, smoking in front of the bookies and shuffling out of the Spar with their bottled provisions. One of them eyeballs me as I walk toward him, scoping me in a way that has my right hand sliding down my hip in search of a weapon. As I draw nearer, I recognise Duncan, the shepherd and would-be owner of Cauldhill Farm.

143

'Alright?' I say as I pass.

He gives me a single, curt nod. 'Aye. I ken you, by the way.'

'Cauldhill Farm. Helping Molly clear the house.'

He doesn't seem to register this, but smiles and repeats himself. 'Aye . . . I ken you, son.'

I nearly stop. For half a second, my foot hovers above the ground, mid-stride. But then it makes contact with the pavement and propels me another step away from the old man. I turn my eyes away and head back to the shop.

XV

'Elaine's fuckin' movin' in wi the new man. *Alister.*
He's some kind of biotech researcher up at Roslin, got
seventeen bloody letters after his name or whatever,
and a bungalow in Colinton. Fucking prick.' Jack
hawks and spits into the ditch at the side of the road.
'She's not his type. I mean, I dinnae ken what he can
see in her, like.'

We're running past Rosewell toward Cauldhill Farm
after work. Harry has agreed to take Jack on a casual
basis in between his bits of building work, and we've
managed to clear the day's jobs by mid afternoon. He's
been silent and distracted all day, chewing over some
gristly piece of news, eyes fixed on a different view
entirely to the one in front of him.

'You alright today, Jackie?' I made the mistake of asking him a moment ago, and unleashed a torrent.

'I mean, Elaine's rough as anything. She'd have you
believe she's no, like, she spends a fucking fortune on
herself. Racked up thousands on the credit cards, which
I'm *still* paying back. She knows how to dress classy, and
when she puts on the phone voice you'd think she was
yin o' they Morningside lassies, ken. It's all *sweetie* and
luvvy and *honey bunny*. A fucking scientist, ken? I mean,
what does she bloody know about stem cell research and
that? She's a bloody secretary oot there, that's it. She
types up the minutes of their meetings, so she thinks she

145

kens. She thinks she's clever, that's her problem. Thinks she's better than us.'

His voice breaks and he falls back, stops, stands there at the side of the road staring at a discarded beer can under a gorse bush. His big square shoulders start to shake. I lean on the stone dyke, watch a couple of magpies tussling over a dead rabbit and let him cry it out.

After a couple of minutes, he wipes his face on his shirt. 'You must think I'm pretty fuckin' soft, eh? After everywhere you've been and that.'

'I dinnae. I've seen some of the meanest bastards in 45 Commando reduced to blubbering wrecks by Dear John letters.'

'Never happened to you?'

'I never had anyone to cry over, mate.'

He turns back toward me with a doubtful look in his watery eyes. 'Sorry.'

'What for? Come on.' I resume running. He falls in beside me again and carries on blethering, except now he's on my deaf side and over the sounds of our footsteps and my own breath I don't manage to take in very much of what he says. Also, somewhere in the background, Mitch is singing *Ring of Fire*.

Eventually we reach the rutted drive at Cauldhill Farm and fall down to a walk. Everything is quiet and still except a few seagulls overhead and the gravel grinding under our shoes.

He looks around, at the big house with its shutters like closed eyelids, the tumbledown outbuildings, the trees and the hills behind.

'Nice spot, eh?'

'Aye.'

'D'you ken, I always wanted to buy a broken doon pile like this and fix it up. I only ever wanted to be a

146

joiner like my Da. Elaine never fucking got it, Sean. She just didnae get it. She thinks a man who works wi' his hands is a failure. But look at these.' He holds up massive, scarred mitts the size of bear paws. 'Too big for a computer keyboard, eh? What the fuck else am I meant to dae?'

I'm relieved he's not crying again. 'Find yourself a woman who likes real men, brother. There's bound to be a few of them around. I want to show you something.'

He follows me to the barn. The door creaks as I pull it open, and we step to the damp, stony interior and wait for our eyes to adjust before I crane up into the beams.

'There he is, look.' I point at the little white cylinder above us. The owl watches us calmly and Jack stares up like an entranced kid.

'Braw,' he whispers.

'Aye.'

We watch the owl for a minute or two, until it opens its eyes more widely and stretches on its perch, craning its neck in the direction of the door. Its sudden alertness sets my heart going and I turn and walk slowly toward the door, eyes scanning for movement or shadows.

'Whit is it?' Jack says, following me, and I hold up a hand to silence him. The wide barn door is sticking out into the yard, a barrier I can't see around, and I curse my carelessness for leaving it like that.

The first real sign that there is someone hiding behind it is the smell of whisky fumes, strong even outside in the breeze. Then the shuffle of an unsteady gait in the gravel.

'Duncan, is that you?'

The shepherd comes barrelling around the door, more falling than running, growling incomprehensible syllables. I restrain him and pin him face first against the wall with his hands behind his back. Although he's a big

147

bugger, there isn't much resistance in him and I hold him gently so he doesn't tear his face up on the stone.

'Fucking kids comin' oot here wi' yer drugs, this is breakin' an' enterin'. Yer trespassin' on private property.' His voice is slurred, muffled.

I speak to him in the clearest voice I can summon. 'Duncan, I'm Sean. You've seen me before. I'm just looking after the place for Molly. I'm going to let go of you now, mate. I promise I'm not going to hurt you. Just calm down, eh?'

I release him, and he turns around and leans heavily against the wall, his knees bent like he's about to slide down and sit on the ground. His face is a mess of grey stubble and there is a sheen of drool on his chin. My eyes are enough to pin him there, and he makes no attempt to move.

'Who the hell is this, Sean?' Jack says behind me.

'Duncan lives in the cottage up the hill,' I say, without removing my eyes from the man's face. A shadow crosses my mind: a memory from so long ago it's possible I didn't even have language to give it substance. Somewhere back in the murky ooze of my early childhood, I have met this man before.

'He's a bit worse for wear. Duncan, mate, why don't you let us take you home to sleep it off, eh?'

'Ah dinnae need ye tae tak me hame. This is ma fuckin' hoose, and ah'm the yin lookin' aifter it. The auld man telt me tae because he kent she wouldnae.'

'What old man? George Finlayson?'

'Aye. Yon wee bitch whae thinks it's hers, she disnae ken anything. I'll get this hoose, ye'll see. It's mines.'

'Alright, Duncan. Molly asked me to pop up from time to time just to make sure everything is okay. Do you understand?'

148

He narrows his eyes and considers this, obviously working out whether I'm trying to trick him. Then he raises a finger and pokes it toward me.

'Whit's yer name?'

'I told you, I'm Sean. Sean McNicol.'

His eyes widen. 'Ah ken you.'

'So you've said. You've seen me here before.'

'Naw, I ken you fae . . . fae before. I ken yer ma'

'No you don't, Duncan,' I hear myself saying but even as I do I feel the blood rushing to my face. I feel a tic in my cheek and press my fingers over it.

'Aye, I dae. Diana McNicol. I ken her. And I met ye . . . yince or twice. Yer . . . her . . . yer . . . the wee laddie she . . .' He's trying his damndest to focus on me. 'Ask her. She'll mind me.' He laughs. 'Aye, she'll mind me awright.'

I take a deep breath and let it out slowly. It shakes. 'I'm afraid she won't. She's dead. How'd you know her, Duncan?'

He's staring at me with a mixture of malevolence and curiosity. He'll be seeing the same thing I'm seeing, if he's coherent enough to notice it. The fumes coming off him make my eyes water.

'Duncan, how did you know Diana McNicol?'

'Dinnae ken where I met her. In a pub, maist like. Aye . . . it wis . . . the Scotsman bar up the toon. It was a long time ago. Thirty-odd year. How'd she die, like?'

I clear my throat. 'In intensive care, with tubes coming in and out of her and skin as yellow as fresh piss. That's how she died, and that's how you'll die as well, if anybody bothers enough about you to take you to hospital.' I back away from him. 'Go on home.'

He doesn't move. I grab him by the front of his jacket and manhandle him toward the gate. He stumbles but

149

comes with me, nowhere near strong enough to refuse even if he wanted to. I bawl at him, 'Get the fuck out of my sight now, or I'll kick your sorry arse from here to Peebles!'

Duncan trips out onto the road and wobbles there, but manages to save himself from collapsing. He pauses for a moment, staring at me, then growls, 'Ach, fuck ye,' and hirples away, two steps forward one step back, toward the road's end.

I stand there watching him until I'm sure he's not going to come back, only after several minutes remembering that Jack is standing behind me.

'What the bloody hell was that all about?' he asks when I turn around.

I shake my head and walk past. 'Nothing.' I've lost the heart to go into the house now, so push the barn door shut and dust my hands on my shorts. 'Let's go.' I start running, stretching my legs, desperate to be away. It feels like I could run full tilt all the way home.

Jack comes pounding up behind me. 'Sean, what the fuck? Who was that? What was all that business about yer ma?'

'Do you remember my mother?'

'Once met, never forgotten.'

'Duncan's just another guy who fucked her in a pub toilet. Jack, just do me a favour and don't ask, alright?'

'Okay . . .' his breathing is coming in sharp gasps. 'Whatever you say. Jesus Christ man, you gonnae fucking slow doon or what?'

I stop dead, then deliver a swift kick to the stone wall at the side of the road. Pain explodes up my leg.

Jack grabs my shoulder before I can do it again. 'You break your foot, I'm not carrying you back up this road.'

150

The weight of his enormous paw grounds me, and I close my eyes for a moment, my chest heaving up and down until I catch my breath. I feel calmer after a moment, but I can't turn and look at him.

'Don't ask me, Jack. Okay?'

'I willnae, I swear.'

I nod, then push myself into a jog although my body is starting to feel cold and stiff. The run home feels longer than normal and neither of us says much. My foot aches every time it meets the ground and I force my mind to focus on the pain so it doesn't keep turning over a set of highly unpleasant possibilities. It's getting dark by the time we pass the field behind my house, and I can see our kitchen light on.

Jack pauses outside my door, looking weary and cautious. 'I'll see you tomorrow, yeah?'

'Yeah. Listen . . . that carry on back there . . . don't mention it to anyone, right? I'll tell you what it's about sometime, if I figure it out myself.'

'Sure. Dinnae worry, Sean, Ah'm no yin for gossip.'

He jogs off and I do some stretches, then go into the house. Janet's in the living room watching *Place in the Sun* with her tea on her lap. I poke my head in, and she sets down her glass of wine on the coffee table and looks up.

'Hi. You alright?'

I open my mouth to say yes, but nothing comes out.

I can see her face fall at the prospect of one my tantrums. 'What's up?' Her teeth are purple from the wine.

Whether she knows anything or not, or whether she'll be willing to impart any broken shards of memory or understanding, I can't face her purple teeth. I swallow hard and back away. 'Nothing.'

'Sean!'

I'm already halfway up the stairs. 'I'm having a shower.'

In the shower I turn my face full into the water and stand there, wishing the spray could get into my head and clear it of memory. I wish brains had delete buttons. I wish I could rewrite myself as a braver person. I get out of the shower only when the steam becomes so thick it's hard to breathe and I dry off, go into my room and pull on a pair of trackies. I search the crumpled pile at the bottom of the wardrobe for a t-shirt and pull out an old green one with the word COMMANDO in plain black letters across the shoulders and the dagger below it. I don't like wearing it anymore. I wish when they'd given me that label they'd taken away the part of my brain that had a conscience.

I lean on the windowsill and stare out at the street. There is no movement except a black and white cat on night patrol. The moon is bright above the field, with Jupiter and Venus in line beneath it. I open the window and suck in a deep breath; the air smells of manure and the sea.

'Mitch?' I say aloud. 'What do I do, mate?'

He doesn't reply. I close the window, sit on my bed and stare at the photograph of the two of us that I keep on my bedside table. We're sitting outside our tent in the shade of a scrubby little tree, our faces brown as old leather shoes, and his hair catches the sun like ripe wheat. He's got his guitar on his lap: a little narrow bodied Gibson he bought off an American at Bastion. He used to sit there and pick out melodies or sing softly to himself, hillbilly songs in his lyrical Welsh tenor. The minute he started playing, we'd all stop whatever we were doing and gather around him and listen.

I have his guitar in my wardrobe. Somehow it ended

up among my possessions when we were both shipped home, and I haven't had the balls to bring it back to his parents. I remove the case from behind a pile of clothes and set it on the bed, sit with the instrument on my lap. I finger a G, a C and a D – the only chords he ever taught me. They sound dull and unmusical. The strings are choked with Afghan dust.

'Talk to me, bud,' I say, and wait.

Nothing.

I set the guitar back in its case and bring my knees up, hug them against my chest, huddling against a sudden, panicky emptiness. After all the times I've told him to fuck off, maybe he's actually done it.

'I need you to give me a sign,' I say into my knees. 'Come on Mitch, just . . . please help me.'

Just then, my mobile phone beeps from inside the pocket of the running shorts I've left on the floor. It actually startles me enough to make my heart jump. I unfold myself, fish it out and read the text.

Hey you. The craziest thing has happened: I've had a baby! Eva Mairead. Born by c-section on the 13th. I'm home now and ok but hurting a bit. Please come see us as soon as you can. 53C Gilmour Place, Tollcross. I'm sorry I didn't call sooner. P.

XVI

I drive too fast through the still busy streets, up Causewayside and onto Melville Place, past the Meadows toward Tollcross. Her building is a typical dirty yellow Edinburgh sandstone tenement with window boxes and a red door. I press the buzzer labelled Fairbairn and wait, only now beginning to wish I'd phoned first; she'll get the idea I'm desperate. But then, maybe I am.

After a few seconds I raise my finger to buzz again, then hesitate. I stand there, finger touching the button, feeling as stupid as I look, and I nearly turn back to the car. But then there is a bit of static and Paula's voice sounds through the tinny intercom.

'Hello?'

'It's Sean.'

'Hey you.' The door clicks open and I enter a wide, clean stair which smells of lemons and damp stone. A door opens above me and Paula peers over the black iron railing as I jog up the stairs. 'Wow . . . short.'

'What? Oh . . .' I rub my hand up the back of my head. 'Better?'

'Much.'

Her lovely round belly has deflated and she looks pale in a baggy white blouse and leggings. I open my arms when I reach her and we hug each other tightly. 'Congratulations.'

'Thank you. God, I'm glad you're here.' Her smile

flickers as she takes me by the hand and leads me into her warm living room. It's just as I imagined her living room would be: walls painted a calm creamy white and hung with framed art prints, plush red Persian rug covering the wooden floor, potted plants, a high ceiling and Victorian cornicing. The gas fire is puttering gently and there are seven or eight candles burning on the mantelpiece, giving the room a soft, yellowish light. There is a Moses basket on a stand beside the sofa.

'Come see her, quietly. She's just gone down. See if that buzzer had woken her up, I'd have had to strangle you.'

'Sorry,' I whisper, then peer into the basket at the wee bundle, tightly wrapped in a white blanket. The tiny face is pink and plump, with a dimpled chin and a crop of spiky black hair. The eyes are closed and the rosebud mouth makes a sucking motion, as though working at an invisible breast.

'She's beautiful,' I say. Paula stands close next to me. I let my hand fall onto her back and rub the flat place between her shoulder blades. 'Like her mum. How are you?'

'I'm tired, Sean.' Her eyes are liquid and she looks as if she might cry. She presses her fingers into them. 'Come into the kitchen.'

I follow her, and she pulls out a chair for me at the table that sits in a recessed window, overlooking the back green and the little squares of light from the surrounding tenement windows. An old fashioned pulley hangs from the ceiling, draped with white and pink baby clothes and blankets.

Paula fills the kettle, then leans her bum against the bunker and looks at me. 'I'm so sorry I didn't phone you, I just . . . freaked out a bit.'

'It's fine, don't worry. Are you okay?'

'I'm just fucking knackered.' She closes her eyes. 'The birth was horrific. Forty hours of labour and an emergency section, and I don't think I've slept more than three hours in a row since. I'm sore, it's a nightmare getting the pram up and down the stairs and I'm not allowed to drive. My tits feel like someone's sticking hot needles in them when she feeds. Nobody tells you *that* before they're born. I'm starting to think my ma was right, you know, about how hard this is going to be on my own. I don't know if I'm up to it. Tell me this is going to get easier.'

'Come here,' I say, pushing the chair away and crossing over to her. I wrap her up and hold her against my chest. She cries for a minute and I hold her until her breathing stops shaking and she goes a bit limp. She smells of fabric softener and something that might be baby sick.

'Have I done the right thing, Sean?'

'You're asking the wrong man.'

She looks up at me. A lock of hair falls over her eye and I want to move it aside and feel it glide over my fingers.

'I'm being a jessie, huh?'

'Major surgery, sleep deprivation and another wee person sookin' the life out of you. I think possibly jessie is too strong a description. Have you had your tea?'

'No. She was crying for an hour before you got here.'

'Neither have I. Why don't you go close your eyes and I'll make us something.'

'I'll make it, Sean. What do you want? There isn't much in the fridge.'

I pull away from her and point toward the door. 'Go lie down. That's an order.'

'I'd like to have a bath.'

'Then go have a bath.'

'If she wakes up . . .'

'Don't worry about her. Go on.'

She stands there looking at me for a moment. 'Sorry, Sean.'

'Shut it and go have a bath, woman.' Turning my back on her, I open the fridge. She's right, there isn't much in. I hear her leave the room and the squeak of the bath taps across the hall, the water splattering into the tub.

There are eggs and bacon in the fridge, so I take these out along with a slightly wrinkled green pepper and a lump of cheddar cheese. Before starting the food I make two cups of tea and bring one in to her. She takes it from me without a word, sets it down on the shelf beside the bath and kisses me on the cheek.

It takes me a few minutes of rummaging in her cupboards to find everything I need, and I try to do this with a minimum of banging. Once I have set out the required pans and dishes, I peek in at the baby. She has worked her arms out of the blanket and laid her tiny wrinkled hands up next to her ears, but her eyes are still firmly glued shut and her little mouth working away.

Her cheek looks soft as a peach and I want to touch it but don't dare. So I go back to the kitchen and click the gas on, peel open the bacon and lay six strips into the pan. Then I mix up a bunch of eggs and chop the green pepper for an omelette.

Although I've never been in Paula's kitchen it feels good to be here, prodding the bacon with a fork and grating cheese. I think about Duncan, alone in his bothy with the wind sweeping over Cauldhill. I think back on what happened and what I saw on his malt-cured face. Little genetic signposts: a nose that was straight and slightly too long for the face, a small indentation on the chin, eyes that couldn't decide whether they were grey or green or blue, skin that has a tendency to freckle. Common enough Scottish features, but put together in such a familiar arrangement that I can't believe no-one else has noticed.

I also saw the way the drunken belligerence became something frightened and more damaged at the mention of my name.

Everything clicks, maybe too neatly. Maybe I'm forcing things. Further recon will be required, for my own peace of mind at the very least. I'm don't know how I'm going to do it without going up and trying to tease some information out of the man himself, and the prospect of that makes me queasy.

And what the fuck do I do if it turns out to be true?

A voice behind my back startles me, and I turn sharply. Paula's behind me, pink-faced and wet haired, in silky green jammies and a white dressing gown.

'Sorry, I didn't hear you.'

'I said penny for 'em.'

'They're not worth that much. Feel better?'

'Aye.' She comes up behind me and slips her arms around my waist, then looks at the omelette in the pan. 'Jesus, that looks good. I'm starving.'

'Me too, I ran miles today after work. I think this is ready.' I pull away and dish up the omelettes and bacon, with toast and a pot of tea to refill our mugs. Paula carries the plates to the table, and we sit across from each other.

I begin eating at double time as I always do, until I notice that she's watching me with a funny smile on her face. Mouth full, I pause and look up.

'What?'

She shakes her head. 'Thank you.'

'What for?'

'For being a good guy.'

I raise my eyebrows and swallow. 'That's a funny thing to say.'

'No it's not. You are. You might not have been, after the kind of life you've had, but you are.'

'How do you know, Paula? You've hardly seen me in years.'

'Because you haven't complained that I didn't ring you when I said I would, and you've come here tonight and cooked my tea.'

'Maybe I have a selfish motive. Maybe I think I'm going to get a shag.'

'You're not. I plan never to have sex again.'

I half rise from my chair. 'Okay, I'm off.' Then I laugh and sit down again. 'No, really I just came for the food. Are you going to eat that? Because if it's not up to your usual standards, I'll be happy to have it.'

She picks up her cutlery and begins to eat. 'It's good. It's fucking brilliant, in fact.'

'Why are you surprised?'

'I guess I never thought cooking would be high on the list of essential skills for you guys.'

'It *is*. Mind, if it isn't boil in the bag, it generally involves foraging or hunting something vaguely edible and doing your best over a fire or primus stove. Rabbits, birds, fish, worms . . .'

'You've eaten worms?' she says through a mouthful. 'You haven't really.'

'I have. Mountain Leader training. It's amazing what you'll eat when you have to.'

'Oh my God.'

I laugh. 'There was this guy on the course who was a

159

bit of an expert on wild mushrooms. In the dark, after hours or days on exercise, he could pick a helmet-load of mushrooms and fry them up with some salt and wild herbs. Then he'd sit there eating what looked like a gourmet French stew while the rest of us scrabbled around in the mud for blaeberries and worms.'

'I guess it can't be much worse than Gaz's Supper Van. Remember that?'

'Oh Jesus, I'd forgotten the van. Properly minging. I'm sure Gaz used to cook with a fag hangin' oot his mooth . . . ash all over the fish.'

Paula laughs heartily. 'Salt, sauce and fag ash. Sprinkle of dandruff and a pickled onion. It's a wonder we survived it.'

'So it is. I haven't seen him since I came back.'

'Nah, he died . . . four or five years ago. One black pudding sausage too many. Poor old Gaz.'

'Aye . . . he was alright though. Used to give me and Janet the leftovers at the end of the night . . . sweets and things, you know.'

'Us too. During the strike when we were so skint. I'll always remember that. I think he must have about bankrupted himself giving out free food.'

I polish my plate with a last corner of toast, and just as I lean back in my chair and bring my mug to my lips, a little high- pitched cry comes from the living room.

Paula's face falls. 'Bollocks. The wee bissum, she hasn't been asleep an hour.'

'I'll get her.' I stand up for real this time. 'Just you get that eaten.'

'She'll want feeding.'

'You want feeding. She won't starve in the time it takes you to finish that.' I leave her there and go back to the living room. Eva has managed to work her legs loose

160

from the blanket and is now waving her arms about, fingers finding her face and then her mouth. She inserts her fist into her mouth and makes a snuffling noise, then pulls it out and starts to cry again.

'Hey,' I say, bending over her and presenting a finger. She grabs onto it with surprising strength, and I shake it gently. 'Hello, wee one. Come on then.' I get my hands under her back and lift her, supporting her neck with my fingers. Her little body feels like a hot water bottle as I lean her onto my shoulder, and she turns her head toward my face, mouth open, looking for something to suck. Determined to give Paula enough time to finish her meal, I walk her around the living room, muttering under my breath each time she snuffles and starts to rev up into a cry. We inspect the photographs on the mantelpiece: Paula in a cafe somewhere that looks like Paris, Paula with her arms around a girlfriend on top of a hill. An old one of Paula's dad in his pit helmet and donkey jacket: a handsome barrel-chested man with pork chop sideburns and quick eyes.

I lean down and examine the photo. Andrew Fairbairn was about the only man I knew as a kid who wasn't interested in screwing my mother. He had a big laugh and big opinions, a booming voice which by all accounts he used to great effect on the pickets during the miners' strike. Sometimes he would take me fishing down on the Esk and tell me about the coal face and the men he knew down there. He told me what it meant to work hard and to trust other men with your life. He told me those things because he knew nobody else would.

'There's your granddad, Eva. I wish you could have met him.'

'So do I.' Paula comes up behind me and stands next to me for a minute. I think she might be about to cry

161

again but she just stands there, teetering on the brink. 'It's the thing I wish more than anything else. This would have been a different story if he'd been around.'

I'm not sure what the appropriate response to this should be, so keep my mouth shut.

Then she holds out her arms and delicately I transfer Eva into them.

'Sean, I could fall in love with you right now. She's puked down your back. Sorry, I should have told you, she pukes. A lot. Baby sick trumps commando dagger.'

'Charming.' I laugh and crane my head around to peer at the cheesy white cascade down my shirt.

Paula swipes at my back with a muslin cloth and giggles. 'How very symbolic.' She lifts Eva up and kisses her cheeks. 'You can be our secret weapon, Eva-bean. Semi-automatic, just point and hurl.'

The baby opens her mouth, snuffles, then screws up her face. I duck away from her and cover my head with my hands. 'Incoming. Take cover!'

Paula snorts. 'Oh my God, that's so wrong. Poor child will be damaged for life.' Then she sighs, sits on the sofa and lays Eva on a cushion on her lap, fidgeting around into a comfortable position before lifting her top. She looks up at me, her cheeks flushed with laugher. 'Sit down.'

I sit beside her, and she leans into me. The baby slurps and makes little gulping noises, little fingers curling and uncurling. I stroke the top of her head, feeling the indentation where the bones have not yet fused. 'Fuelling up for another sortie.'

'Believe it. God, I feel like a cow. I don't know how men think boobs are sexy after they've seen this.'

'That's what they're meant for. Why should everything be about sex?'

162

'I don't know. Isn't it?'

'Is it fuck. Sex and booze. As far as I'm concerned, they cause more trouble than they're worth.'

Her body shakes against me. 'Are you considering taking holy orders or something?'

'Aye. Maybe I'll go live in a Tibetan monastery. D'you know what, after everything, that doesn't sound such a bad idea. I'll shave my head and raise yaks.'

She studies my face. 'I wish we'd written all this time. I have missed you.'

'Me too.' I look down and stroke Eva's head. 'It was . . . too hard, I guess. Thinking of you married to someone else. It was easier not to be in touch. I'm sorry.'

'What do you want, Sean?'

'What do you mean?'

'In your life? Now that it *is* your life?'

I rest my head against the back of the settee, close my eyes, think for a moment. It doesn't seem to matter what plans you make; you put your foot down in the wrong place and your world gets blown to pieces. A tremendous weariness presses me into the cushions, but right now there's no reason to be anywhere else.

'Nothing very much,' I say eventually.

'That's not a very good answer.' For the first time, she sounds like a teacher.

I sigh and wish Mitch would tell me what to say. But all I hear are the baby's little grunting noises and the traffic outside.

'A bit of peace, Paula. When I say nothing very much, that's what I mean. Just . . . a bit of peace. Is that better? Is that enough?'

She nods, eyes veiled, turned down toward the wee dark head at her breast. 'That's enough. Will you stay here tonight?'

'I've got Janet's car; she'll need it for work in the morning.'

'I'll probably be up at five feeding her. You can head off first thing.'

'Are you sure?'

'Yes. No shagging, mind.'

I kiss the top of her head. 'I thought we were just friends.'

'Oh yeah.' She grins and rests her cheek on my shoulder. 'I forgot.'

XVII

Davie Blair's monumental arse clenches in front of me and the scrum grinds like a tank, with an almost orchestrated harmony of groans and grunts and curses. The resistance is fierce at first, then eases and we begin to drive forward. The ball rolls about like an egg between the tangle of legs and I manage to catch it with my foot and pull it backwards.

'Connor!' I shout for the scrum half, and he fishes the ball out from between my feet and pops it out to the waiting line of backs. The scrum breaks up and Alan Noble heaves himself forward seven or eight metres before being felled like a giant redwood. I scoop the ball from his outstretched hands and run headlong into a wall of Gala men, Jackie and Callum clattering into my back and propelling me forward. Somebody comes in low from the other side, and I feel my feet swept out from under me. I release the ball to Callum as I fall, and my breath is forced violently from my lungs as the Gala loose-head lands on top of me. Sheltering down in the soft turf, I lie still until the pile of bodies above me untangles itself, then rise experimentally to my hands and knees, waiting for my lungs to re-inflate and feeling for anything that might be damaged.

The whistle goes for full time and I stay there on all fours, recovering my breath, until a hand lands between my shoulder blades. Davie Blair's swollen face appears beside mine.

'Alright, son?' He may only be two or three years older than me, but he always calls me son. I nod and he extends a hand, pulls me to my feet.

'Thanks Davie.'

'Well played, Sean. Nearly did it, eh?'

Our last game of the season has been a war of attrition, ending 10-13 to Gala. Already I can feel the tender places on my ribs, which by tomorrow will have turned purple. We line up for sweaty handshakes, then start off toward the clubhouse for icepacks and showers. A few spectators mill around, chatting in the soft sunshine, holding plastic cups of beer. I look around for anyone who might have bothered to come and watch me, but there isn't anyone.

It was that way when I was young too. For Mum, watching me play would have meant getting her stilettos dirty. She came down to the clubhouse one time, to the annual Ne'er Day Party, when I was ten or eleven. She was still pissed from the night before, and she just carried on knocking back vodka and coke until she passed out in the toilet and cracked her head open on the bog. I didn't know anything about it until the paramedics arrived and took her away on a stretcher.

I ended up being taken home by one of my coaches, fed, given some spare clothes and allowed to sleep on their son's bottom bunk. He was alright, big Gav, but his wife was a cold fish. I could tell she didn't want me there. Quite likely, she thought I would try to sneak away in the night with her silver under my jersey.

When Mum came home the next day and lay on the settee, smoking, her sunglasses on and a massive, stitched lump on her forehead, I told her I never wanted her to come to the club again. She never did. I threatened to batter anyone that gave me a hard time about her, so mostly people just pretended I didn't have any parents at all.

In the changing room I strip off my shirt and body armour, then press an icepack against my ribs and sit there with my head against the wall and my bare feet on the cold, concrete floor. The guys are whipping each other with towels and laughing, cursing loudly about their various injuries, and something about the acoustics of hard, bare room makes it hard for me to pick out anything they're saying. I am in my tunnel again, and I'm not sure whether I want to come out of it and be in the room with them or not.

'Oi, I ken ye can hear me, McNicol. Your captain is speaking.'

I open my eyes. Davie's standing in front of me with a towel stretched around his hips, gaping open down his left thigh like a prostitute's skirt. He's just out of the shower, standing with his legs apart and his fists on his hips, all fierce pink flesh and reddish, matted hair.

'It's all sorted. Clubhouse, The Oak, The Raj for a feed, then back here. You're in, aye?'

'Davie, I . . . mate, I dinnae drink.'

'Fucking result, lads,' he shouts over his shoulder. 'Sean's driving!'

I stand up. 'Nah . . . sorry, I've got stuff on.'

'Aye, you've got a night oot wi' yer pals. Captain's orders.'

'Next time, yeah?' I turn my back on him and rummage in my bag for shower gel.

'Sean, ye dinnae get away wi' all that depressive nonsense here, right?' he bellows, to avoid any possibility that I could claim not to have heard him.

167

'Leave him, Davie, aye?' Jack slots his shoulder in between Davie and me and puts a hand on my back. 'You alright?'

'Fine. Just . . . got other stuff on, Jack.'

'Nae bother, Sean. Dinnae worry aboot it.'

Maybe it has finally dawned on them that I am truly an antisocial bastard, because nobody says anything else as I step past them and get into the shower. I stand there for a few minutes, letting the water pound onto my shoulders before attacking my mud-encrusted knees with the soap.

Dried and dressed, I hoist my kitbag onto my shoulder and head outside. The ground has mostly emptied now, but movement at the far end of the pitch catches my eye and I look up. A man stands between the end of the pitch and the copse of trees beyond it, a little stooped, with a black and white dog by his knee. He's just standing, very still, staring towards us.

From this distance, I can't say for sure that it's Duncan but my heart speeds up and I walk toward him. He waits for a moment, then turns away from me and moves into the woods.

I break into a jog, my bag bumping against my thigh, but by the time I get to where the man had been, he's gone.

'Duncan,' I shout into the woods, then listen intently. No voice in reply, no twigs cracking, nothing except the hush of the wind and the birds. I scan the ground and find both human and dog footprints, but this wood is a popular spot for walking so they could belong to anyone.

I follow a set of tracks a little way through the trees. If he was here, he must have moved quickly to get so far ahead of me, and eventually I give up.

There's no one here, mate.

'Mitch? I saw him.'

Did you?

'Didn't I?'

I don't know. You hear me, and I'm not here.

'I thought you'd gone. Where have you been?'

Nowhere. How could I be anywhere, technically speaking?

'Don't fuck with me.'

You're fucking with yourself. You sure you didn't take a knock on the head back there? Tough game.

'I saw him, Mitch, I'm not mad.'

If you say so. Did you know you're talking out loud?

I snap my mouth shut and look around me, seeing only packed earth, pale spring leaves and dappled sunlight. Shaking my head, I walk back out of the woods and make my way home. Janet's car is in the drive but she's not home, so I dump my bag at the bottom of the stairs and rummage in the fridge for some leftover pasta and bread. I drink milk from the jug while the pasta is heating in the microwave, then shovel the food down without really tasting it.

After eating, I leave my bowl in the sink and grab Janet's car keys before I have a chance to think twice. I drive out to Cauldhill Farm and park in front of the house, go straight inside and snoop around, upstairs and down. It is cold as a mausoleum but quiet and undisturbed, mostly empty just as Molly left it. I'll need to bring Jack and the van up soon and shift the rest of the furniture.

I lock up and have a good prowl around the grounds and outbuildings. A worry had crossed my mind that Duncan might try to stake his claim on the place for real by breaking in and squatting, but there's no sign of that.

The late afternoon sunshine filters in beams through the clouds, and somewhere in the distance a cuckoo calls.

169

Cauldhill Farm isn't so bleak on a day like this, and in the suntrap of the yard, it's verging on pleasant. I imagine horses and dogs and kids playing on rope swings, and the smell of freshly cut hay. Rabbit and his wife digging the garden in the buff. Then over that ridiculous image, I superimpose myself and Paula. Clothed, naked, it hardly matters, just here.

I walk out the gate and up the road, toward the end of the tarmac and the little track leading up the hill toward Duncan's cottage. The road becomes increasingly broken until eventually it gives way to mud, and then a cattle grid and a rutted Land Rover track between two barbed wire fences festooned with bits of blown wool. The track leads up toward the ridge of the hills, which itself slopes upward for a couple of kilometres to the west. Duncan's cottage sits on the left side of the track. It's grey and shabby, with dirty windows and weeds growing in the guttering; you would be forgiven for thinking it derelict. The place smells of wet wool and sheep shit.

I peer through the front window into what looks like a lounge, though the glass is so clouded it's hard to see more than silhouettes. There is no motion inside or any noise to give away a man's presence, so I bang on the door and wait a moment, listening as well as I can. There is no response after a second bang, so I try the door and am almost surprised to find that he's bothered to lock it.

Turning my back on the door, I scan up and down the track and up along the ridge of hills. Surely, if it was him I saw at the rugby club, he'll be on his way back here now. But then, I don't have any idea how he gets himself about; it's a long walk for an old guy in his condition and it seems impossible that he would be driving. The wind stirs some dried leaves in a little spiral against the corner of the house and a buzzard cries overhead.

170

Satisfied that we aren't going to pass each other on the road, I head back down the hill toward the farm. Reaching the gate, I shove my hand into my pocket for the car key, then pause and turn around. The trunk is still in the barn; the trunk containing the old veterinary equipment and the little box with the photographs.

I go into the barn, open the lid and remove the little box. Once again, I pick the lock and remove the photos, take them outside and sit in the car with the door open. I focus on the soldier at Edinburgh Castle, and this time I know who he is. Or at least, I know his name. The photo in my hand, I replace the box in the trunk and leave the barn.

I look back up toward Duncan's house. A cloud has moved across the sun the trees cast long shadows over the yard. The air has cooled and once again Cauldhill Farm feels like a haunted place, where stories are never told but just whispered on the wind.

'What do you see here, Mitch?'

I see what you see.

'Are you a ghost?'

If it makes you feel better to think of me that way.

'Are there others?'

One or two. But you know that.

'She doesn't talk to me.'

You don't talk to her.

'Oh for fucksake, you're no help.'

I'll leave you to it then.

I sigh, kick a stone and watch it bump over the cobbles and splash into a little puddle, then get into the car and drive down the road, the photographs on the seat beside me.

XVIII

I park the van behind the shop after a long shift and head inside to make a cup of tea and check out tomorrow's jobs. Harry is in the kitchen waiting on something heating in the microwave, looking weary with his arms folded over his chest and his face turned toward the window.

'Is this your tea?' I ask. It's mid-May now and the early evening sun is still high, beaming in through dirty glass, illuminating grease and sticky patches on the table. The light makes the place look even more squalid, if that could be possible.

'Aye. I've got a couple more hours tonight.' He massages his eyelids. 'Grant evaluation report due tomorrow. Fucking bureaucracy gets worse every year and I always leave it till the last minute.'

'Anything I can help with?'

'It's a one-man job, really. Thank you, though.' A smile flickers, fades. 'Ach, I'd better tell you, Sean. Billy's in hospital. The Royal Ed. I went to see him this afternoon.'

'How is he?'

He shrugs. 'He's where he needs to be just now, I think.'

'Bloody hell.' I mutter and look out the grimy window at the van in the car park.

Harry looks at me. 'I think possibly you saved his life.'

'I doubt that.' I stare at the floor. 'Maybe just prolonged the inevitable. What about Linda?'

'Wasted. She'll never work again, I'm sure.'

I sigh and run my hand over my cheek.

'Sean, Al told me about your mum. If I'd known, I wouldn't have asked you to go see Billy. It must have been very hard, and I'm sorry.'

'No, it wasn't hard, just . . .' I look up at him. His eyes are full on my face. 'Some battles are lost before they start, you know? Some people can't be saved. Mum couldn't face life straight. She was in hospital a few times, this or that detox programme. I always wondered how much money they spent trying to fix her when she didn't want it. She never believed she could stop. She had no intention of it.'

I pull a teabag out of a little canister and drop it into the mug, then switch on the kettle. 'You know, the thing about it was, Harry, I was relieved when she finally popped off. I'd spent my life trying to get free of her. My sister about killed herself trying to look after us when I was little, and all I could ever think about was leaving.'

'And so you left.'

I nod. 'Yeah . . . I certainly did.' The kettle boils and I pour the water, stir and then press my teabag against the side of the mug and watch the brown liquid slide over white china. 'And now I'm back here. How the fuck did that happen?'

Harry chuckles. 'You didn't *have* to come back.'

'The Marines wanted to keep me. You know . . . at first. I could have stayed in as an instructor, spent my time climbing mountains and playing in the snow. I could have got a commission eventually and had a bloody good life, but I was finished. I couldn't have stayed in to train other guys to do something I couldn't justify anymore.'

'No . . . no. Absolutely not. Sean, if there's any training you'd like or if you'd like to go back to college or university, we'll find a way to help you.'

'I . . . well . . . I appreciate the offer. I've been thinking lately I might like to move up north. Start a business as a mountaineering guide. I think possibly I'd be a bit saner if I could get out in the hills more.'

Harry smiles. 'Good therapy, huh?'

'Something like that. You don't have time to be depressed when you're trying to keep yourself alive on the side of a mountain. It's always where I've been happiest.'

'Then you should do it.' He opens the microwave and stirs the contents of his bowl, takes an experimental taste of what looks like beef stew out of a tin. 'We'd be sorry to lose you.'

'I'm not going anywhere yet, I'm too skint.' I sit down with my tea and the order book for tomorrow. My eyes flick over the notes on the page, but I don't really read, and I realise that it's not so much money that's holding me back as a reluctance to walk away from the unfinished business I have with this town.

Harry looks over my shoulder. 'Another big day tomorrow.'

'Aye.'

He nods. 'Good.' Then he pauses and tilts his head to one side, mouth half open. For a second he looks as if he's not sure whether to speak, but then he says, 'You've got your life ahead of you still. Don't slip in to thinking this is all there is.'

'I feel a hundred years old sometimes. But . . . I will try, Harry. I promise you, I'll try.'

I finish my tea, close the book and rinse my cup, then change into running clothes and leave my work gear in a holdall on a shelf in the staff room. I say a quick cheerio to Harry, leave him hunched over his stew and his paperwork, then stretch out and run along the High Street in hazy sunshine. Dodging pensioners, stout, bristly dogs and weedy boys in hoodies, I eventually clear the small-town rush hour and turn into one of the new housing estates on the eastern edge of the village.

The estate is made up of one wide crescent, curving through what used to be a dairy farm, with little cul-de-sacs off it, treeless pavements with small islands of newly-laid turf, cookie-cutter houses alternating brick and cream roughcast. The tiny gardens are trimmed, the windows are respectably dressed with venetian blinds, the flat screens flicker from inside as women with artificially straightened hair and spray-on tans make tea. Kids play on scooters or bikes, or sit on patches of grass huddled over their iPods and phones.

It's only a few hundred metres from the centre of Esk-bridge but you could be anywhere, any cozy, amnesiac estate in any town in Britain, totally disconnected from the history that has brought you to this place.

Here and there are little fenced-in ponds, choked with weeds and bits of rubbish, and I know these are probably sinkholes from the old mines underneath. The whole bloody place is undermined and I can't believe they've found a way to build houses here and guarantee that one day the earth won't just devour them. I wonder whether if you were to dive into one of the ponds, you could swim down into the flooded tunnels and hear the ghostly shouts of the men with their shovels and picks. I wonder if the orange women wake up at night and hear the sounds of phantom coal cutters rumbling beneath them.

175

I run faster, reaching the other end of the crescent and turning back up toward the village again, over the main road and out past the rugby club, then toward home. Brenda Fairbairn is shuffling up her path as I turn into our street, leaning on her stick, cigarette drooping from her lips. Her eyes follow me, her mouth turning down as she sucks on the fag.

'Alright?' I ask as I drop back to a walk.

'You're aye runnin, Sean,' she says, as if this was yet more evidence of my undesirable quality.

I grin at her, challenging her to lift her cheeks out of that perpetual scowl. 'Cheer up, Brenda, there's worse places in the world than this.'

A pang in my chest. We made it through the thirty miler across Dartmoor singing *Always Look on the Bright Side of Life*, still whistling as they handed us our green berets. Years later, pinned down behind a rapidly disintegrating mud wall with rockets screaming in from the far hillside, the falsetto voice: *Aw, cheer up, Brian*. Thinking it wouldn't be so bad to die laughing.

'I suppose ye think ye ken all aboot it, son.'

'I don't know much, but I know that.'

'Aye, well,' she concludes, and hoists herself up her front step, a surly badger growling into her den.

Just imagine, if you ever manage to get it together properly with Paula you could have that for a mother-in-law.

Aye, she'd love that.

You wouldn't.

Nae joke, Mitch.

Makes you think twice, doesn't it? All women turn into their mothers, that's their curse.

I stretch one leg back, then the other. Do they? There's an unpleasant pull in the tendons at the back of my right knee and a persistent ache in my lower back. What about fatherless men, who do we turn into?

Janet is in the kitchen with the back door open and the radio on. She's working on a glass of red and folding washing just gathered in from the line. She looks up at me as I come in, scanning me quietly for a moment to assess my mood.

'Good day?'

'Not too bad.'

She shakes out one of my tee shirts and folds it into a smooth square.

'I can do my own washing.'

'I know,' she replies in a tone that might be kindness or might be martyrdom. She swings between them at will and I've never quite mastered telling one from the other until all hell breaks loose.

I sit down on the back step, the evening sun warm on my face, and unlace my trainers. I peel off my socks and spread my toes on the pavement. 'There's something I want to ask you.'

She lays a stack of folded clothes into the basket. 'What?'

'So . . . there's this old shepherd who lives on the hill above Cauldhill Farm. Ex-squaddie, total jakey. Duncan, he's called. Mean anything to you?'

'Should it?'

I can almost hear the wheels of her mind grinding behind me. I stand up and turn to face her.

'He knew Mum.'

'A lot of jakeys knew Mum. Duncan who?'

'Don't know his second name, but he looks like me. Or maybe I should say look like him.'

Her eyebrows arch upwards and suspicion shades her face. 'Sean, don't leap to conclusions. Who is this guy?'

'He worked for Molly's old man. He sees himself as the self-appointed guardian of the place in Molly's absence.'

'So who mentioned Mum?'

'He did. He knew her. He said he'd met me before. Tell me, Janet. You remember him.'

Janet puts down a pair of socks and picks up her glass. She sips slowly, then chews on her upper lip. 'I don't remember anything from back then.'

'You were ten.'

'I don't remember, Sean. I don't remember very much from my childhood at all.' She closes her eyes, and tears form around her lashes. 'I remember feeling tired and scared, all the time. That's all. Your brain blocks things out for a reason. I don't know why you'd want to go digging around in ancient history. What does it achieve?'

I get up, close the back door, then sit at the kitchen table and run my fingers through my hair. 'I just want to know who I am.'

'You know who you are.' An obstructive statement of something neither of us believes. She knows it won't turn me so she bolsters it with a further plea. 'Why do you need to know more? Why can't you just accept things as they are?'

'Because this is my fucking life, not some top secret mission I've signed up to without knowing the facts.'

She aims a finger toward me. 'I'll tell you something about your father. He was an arsehole. And he's either still an arsehole or he's dead. One or the other, guaranteed. You're better off leaving it.'

'I'll decide that.' I sit back in my chair and watch her as she shakes out a pair of work trousers and folds them so they crease down the fronts of the legs. She tries to ignore me for a minute or two but her lips are pressed

178

together so hard the blood has drained from them. When she finishes folding, she puts the laundry back into the basket in a neat stack and places it at the base of the stairs. Then she comes back to the kitchen, refills her glass and exhales wine fumes and annoyance.

'What?'

I keep my eyes on her. 'You drink too much.'

'Oh, here we go again. Give me a small break, would you?'

'You do.'

'I'm not Mum.'

I can tell I've hit a sore one and I smile a little. 'I didn't say you were; I said you drink too much. You're strung out and anxious all the time. You can't relax until you've had at least half a bottle.'

'Well fuck you very much, Mr Sobriety. Strung out and anxious . . . that's good coming from you, isn't it? You're a fucking basket case.'

'Is that an official diagnosis?'

Then she sinks into her glass, eyes turned away from me. It's pretty obvious she regretted saying it the moment it was out of her mouth, but I'm not in a forgiving mood. I stand up, collect my trainers and socks and walk out of the kitchen.

'Sean . . .' she calls as I'm halfway up the stairs. 'Come down. I'm sorry.'

'I cannae hear you, Janet,' I shout back. As I say, sometimes being half deaf has its advantages.

I shower, then sit on my bed for a while, contemplating my next move. I need talk to Duncan, to somehow tease some sense out of his pickled brain. But I'm apprehensive. There's an edge to the man that makes me think he's capable of violence, and in his state he might not be able to restrain it. Worse than that, I have to admit,

Janet might be right. I might find out more than I want to know.

I need to know a bit more about him before I confront him. Before I lose my nerve, I grab my phone and scroll down for Molly's number.

It rings five times before she answers and the connection isn't great. There's a lot of background noise.

'Molly, it's Sean.'

'Oh. Is everything okay?'

'Ehm . . . yeah, the house is fine. Molly, I wanted to speak to you about something, is this a good time?'

'Not really, I'm . . .' she replies, and a wave of static interrupts her voice, '. . . tomorrow.'

'Sorry, you cut out there.'

'I said I'm on my way up there. You can come see me tomorrow night if you want.' She sounds annoyed.

'You're coming back?'

'Yes. I'm driving now, I can't stay on. What did you want to talk about, anyway?'

'Ehm . . . why don't we leave it until you get here, eh? I'm going to the gym after work, so it'll be after eight. Is that too late?'

'No, it's fine, Sean.' I hear her sigh and the rush of what sounds like motorway traffic. 'See you then, okay?'

'Okay,' I say. 'Bye then.'

'Bye.'

XIX

I wait on the doorstep for Molly, hair still wet from my post-training shower and a symphony of aches in the lower back and legs. From somewhere behind me, the screech of a barn owl, followed by a reply from somewhere in the distance. I turn, scan the sloping barn roof and the silhouettes of the trees behind it. A silent, pale figure glides from the gable peak, catching the moonlight before disappearing into the trees. The wind breathes in the grass.

The door creaks open and Molly stands there in her own baggy tracksuit bottoms, Ugg boots and a thick fleece. Her face is pale and her eyes slightly puffy, but she smiles and seems genuinely glad to see me.

'Come in. How are you?'

'Fine, thanks.' I step onto the tiled lobby floor and she backs against the wall to let me past, face turned away from mine, embarrassed. 'How are you, Molly?'

She pushes the door closed gently and locks it. 'I don't know how I am. Sean. Come through. It's just as well you never got round to moving the rest of the furniture out.'

I follow her to the kitchen and stand in front of the range in the vain hope that the heat will ease the tightness in my muscles. She turns her back on me to fill the kettle, then says something over the stream of water.

'Pardon?'

She turns toward me again, a look of apology on her face. 'Sorry. I just said thanks for looking after the place.'

'It's fine. So . . . I take it you've decided what you're going to do with it?'

Her lips press together for a moment. 'Not really. I've . . . ehm . . .' A small pause, as though she's not entirely sure she wants to tell me. 'I've left Peter.'

'Oh.'

She must hear panic in my voice because she smiles. 'Don't worry, it's nothing to do with you. But I can't stay with him anymore, he's . . .' Her voice trails off into nothing and she changes the subject. 'D'you want coffee or tea?'

'Tea,' I say meekly. 'What happened?'

'He's been seeing someone.' She shrugs. 'Apparently it's been going on for quite a while.'

Quick judgement call, but I reckon it's probably best not to say anything about double standards.

'Sorry to hear that.'

'Me too, believe it or not. It's funny. I didn't think I would be. I've been indifferent to him for so long, I think I must have driven him to it. Anyway . . .' She stretches her mouth into a stiff smile, 'keep calm and carry on, as they say. At least I had somewhere to run to.'

'So are you going to stay here?'

'Maybe.'

'What will you do?'

'I'll be alright for a while. And I've had an idea, but . . .' She pauses to make the tea, her lips pursed as she fills the teapot. 'It's probably mad.'

'What is it?'

'I told you I used to work as a fundraiser for charities. A couple of years ago, I did some work for a social enterprise farm down in Devon. They grew organic vegetables and raised chickens and ducks and things. They brought groups of young people out from the poor estates and taught them skills, set them challenges, helped them build their confidence. It was a beautiful, inspiring place.'

'They weren't naked, were they?'

'Pardon?' she giggles.

'Nothing. Just . . . forget it. Sorry.'

'Okay . . . I was driving up here yesterday and it just came into my head. I couldn't sleep last night, so I spent about four hours writing a business plan.'

She brings two mugs to the table and sits down, motions for me to sit down opposite her. 'A bit daft, I suppose.'

'Maybe not. I work for a social enterprise. That must have been somebody's mad idea once. You could turn the barn into a bunkhouse. Get the wee tearaways out here for weeks at a time, teach them outdoor skills, take them yomping up the hills, get their hands dirty.' I pull out a chair and sit. 'Aye, why not?'

Molly's jaded expression becomes a little more enthusiastic. 'You'd help me, wouldn't you?'

'Me? I don't know the first thing about farming. Or kids, for that matter.'

She leans forward and her face becomes more animated than I've ever seen it. 'You've got the outdoor skills, though, you'd be perfect. I could see you barking orders at the surly little Broomhouse chavs. You'd have them all up the hill in the winter, living in snow caves, hunting rabbits and stoats. That's your kind of thing, isn't it?'

'Is it?'

This confuses her. 'Of course it is. Bloody Mountain Leader, you, not just your average bootneck.'

183

'I never told you that.'

She winces. 'I Googled you.'

'Ah.' Heat moves up from my neck to my cheeks. 'Why?'

'Curious, I suppose. There's quite a lot about you guys and your exploits. Haven't you ever Googled yourself?'

'No.'

'I thought it was something everyone did.'

'I have no idea what other people do.'

She studies me. 'There was an impressive obituary of your friend Mitch. That was quite a thing he did.'

'Yeah. Quite a thing.' A mouthful of tea, swished slowly between my cheeks, swallowed carefully. The feeling of being distilled by this single event, as though I might never again be more than the salvageable remnants of that one explosion. If I spend the rest of my life running, I'll never escape the blast radius of this one.

'Not something I want to talk about tonight, if you don't mind.'

'That's okay. I'm sorry.'

I shrug. She says this, but she will look at me differently now, and forever. Everyone who knows the story will see me through the filter of this knowledge: I am alive because Mitch is dead, and he is dead because of me.

'What did you want to speak to me about, anyway, Sean?'

'Oh . . . ehm . . .' I swallow heavily. 'I wanted to ask you about Duncan.'

'Duncan?' A shadow crosses her face. 'Duncan up the road? What about him?'

'Where did he come from? Who is he? What's his connection with the farm?'

'Why do you ask?'

184

I stare into my tea, not sure what to say. 'He . . . spoke to me one day when I came up here and it appears he used to know my mother. Years ago. I just . . . wanted to know a bit more about him.'

Molly's eyes widen with surprise. She sips her tea and puts down the mug. 'Well . . . I don't know that much about him. He's lived in that wee house most of my life. He was in the army before that.'

I nod. 'The Royal Scots.'

'How'd you know that?'

'I found a photo of him while I was packing up. I mentioned it to you, remember? You were pretty vague. Purposely so, I think.'

'Oh.' Soft, careful voice. Then she sighs. 'There's a bit of history and I didn't want to have to go into it. He's . . . always had a drink problem. He got into trouble in the army for assaulting another soldier. Spent some time in Colchester for it.'

'Charming character. So how did he end up here?'

'I believe he used to hang about with some woman from Eskbridge when he came out of the army. I don't know where he came from before that . . . he didn't seem to have any other family anywhere. Dad met him in town, took a bit of a liking to him and offered him work and a place to live. He looked after the sheep and did odd jobs around the place, and my dad looked after him. Made sure he was okay, and gave him lifts places and things like that. Had to bail him out of jail once or twice for stupid stuff. Drunk driving, fighting, that kind of thing.'

'Why does he think this house should be his?'

'Dad must have said things to him . . . I don't know. I was actually surprised to find that the will doesn't mention Duncan at all.'

'So, if you sold up, he'd be forced out.'

185

'Technically, I guess so. That's another problem for me, isn't it. I don't have any desire to turn the man out. He's not doing anyone any harm up there, except to himself.' She stares at her nails and continues softly. 'Dad was . . . strange. I think Mum was right about the war . . . he was distant and angry. And he hated women.'

'He slept with enough of them.'

'Oh yeah, but as far as he was concerned that was all women were good for. He was like fucking Henry VIII or something . . . he just kept going through wives in hopes of getting a son, and he never got one. So Duncan became the son he never had. Mum hated Duncan.'

'Why?'

'She thought he was dangerous. There was rumour he'd had a kid that he wouldn't acknowledge, and she couldn't forgive him for that. He was good looking then, believe it or not, fit. We all fancied him.'

'Honestly?'

'You wouldn't think it now, would you?'

'When you say we . . . who do you mean?'

'My friends and me. Stupid pre-teen girls. We went giggling around after him all the time. Obviously he was far too old to really be interested in us, but it didn't stop us trying.'

'How old is he?'

'Oh . . . I guess he'd be late fifties now. Maybe sixty. I'm not sure, exactly. Younger than he looks. Why do you want to know all this?'

'Like I say, he knew my mum,' I reply vaguely, trying to process all of this without giving away too much.

She chews on her lip for a moment, then stands up and rinses her cup under the tap, staring at the ghost reflected in the window. 'He's alone up there. If he died in that cottage, nobody would notice.'

'Would you not look in on him from time to time?'

She turns around again. 'No. I don't like to have anything to do with him.'

'Why not?'

Molly closes her eyes and the colour rises in her cheeks. 'Just something that happened years ago.'

'What was it?'

'It's private, alright? I don't want to tell you.'

'So it's alright for you to play snoop, but not me?'

'I'm sorry, Sean, some things are ... painful. My life here was horrid, to be honest. Very lonely.' She sits back down on the chair and lifts her eyes to mine. 'When you say Duncan knew your mum, what do you mean?'

I focus on a patch of damp on the ceiling and wonder if there is a slow leak in the pipes above. 'I'm sure you remember what people at school used to say about my mum.'

'I ... no.'

'You do, Molly. They used to say she was a drunk and a whore. She's been dead for years and they still say it.'

A reluctant nod. 'I suppose I do. I'm sure it wasn't true.'

'It *was*, for the most part. She was a drunk and she slept with a lot of men. To my knowledge, she never took money, but quite honestly I wouldn't rule it out. She always told me she didn't know who my father was, and I never believed her. My sister knows more than she's telling me, and I'm pretty fucking tired of being lied to. Duncan knows.'

'Why would you think that?'

I chew my lip and consider keeping my cards close, but only for a moment. 'You know that rumour about the kid Duncan wouldn't acknowledge ...'

She leans back in her chair with a jerk of something

187

like fright, then forces out a high-pitched giggle. 'No way, Sean, that's just . . . stupid. It's ridiculous.'

'Take a close look at him.'

'You're nothing like him.'

'I am.'

'I don't see it. That's just . . .' She pushes back from table and stares out the window into the dark, eyes wide, blinking from time to time. Muffled, half-muttered words.

'Pardon?'

Her breasts inflate, then lower slowly. 'Nothing. Never mind. What are you going to do?'

I run my finger along the curving grain of the table top. 'I haven't decided yet.'

'Sean, be careful. I wish you'd just . . .'

'What? You're cutting out on me.'

Her eyes disappear behind crumpled lids, and she holds her fists up to them. 'Fucking hell.'

I get up and cross to the other side of the table, stand in front of her. 'Molly, what are you trying to tell me? Are you alright?'

'I am, Sean, honestly. I'm just tired and . . .' She takes a deep breath. 'Look, if Duncan says anything about me, please just know that I . . . didn't want to do it. Alright? It wasn't my idea.'

'What wasn't? Please tell me, whatever it is.'

'I can't.'

I want to push her, but she is so fragile she might crumble. I just shrug. 'It's up to you.'

'I think you should go now. I want to go to bed.'

'You can phone me if you need anything.'

She nods, her eyes looking past my shoulder. 'I hope you find what you're looking for.'

XX

'You given up shaving for Lent or something?' Tigger laughs, then shoves half a Lorne sausage roll into his gob and chases it with a slug of Red Bull.

We are in the cafe downstairs from his flat on Easter Road, having breakfast at lunchtime because he's had a heavy night and I've been out for a big run over the tops of the Pentlands, from Turnhouse to Scald Law and back along the Glencorse road. After four or five texts from him, I've finally caved and agreed to meet him, mainly as an excuse to get away from home on a Saturday afternoon.

I glance at my reflection in the window next to our booth. A bit navvyish, right enough, with four or five days' stubble and a shirt I pulled off the bottom of the wardrobe.

He *has* shaved, but his eyes are shot with pink and he's got dark circles under the arms of his blue polo shirt. There's a particular smell about him: sweat, stale booze and greasy food, disguised but not completely masked by spray-on deodorant.

I pour myself another mug of tea from the pot. 'Lent's past. Anyway, given the dubious circumstances of my birth, I figure the obligations of Catholicism never really applied to me. Nah, it's just that since I cut my hair off, I was in danger of looking too much like a fucking bootneck.'

'You a Catholic, Nic? I didna ken that.'

'No. My mother thought she was, and my Granny really was. Let's just say God and I have an arrangement: I deny he exists and he pisses on me from a great height every now and again, just to keep me in my place.'

Tigger chews with his mouth open and studies me, then says in all seriousness, 'You've got some anger issues going on there, my friend.'

I laugh out loud. 'You think so?'

'Aye.'

'What about you, then? Everything's hunky dory in your wee world, is it? You're actually okay with how your life has gone?'

I'm riled and he can tell. He stares down at his fingernails. 'What happened to me wasn't anybody's fault, Nic. My back's fuckin' agony every day o' my life, and it's hard enough to manage that without getting myself tied up in knots aboot it. Sometimes I canna, so I get high, I admit that. But on the whole, I'm pretty thankful to the Big Man.'

'Amen, brother.' I poke at my food, should be ravenous but feel slightly queasy. The tines of my fork pierce the flabby sausage on my plate and shiny grease trickles out, mixes with streaks of egg yolk and runny tinned tomato. The Full Scottish looks like a bomb blast on a plate. 'Look at this. Nae fuckin' wonder we're in the state we're in.'

'What d'you mean?'

'Look around.'

Tigger surveys the busy cafe, eyes passing over bloated arses oozing over the edges of chairs, bellies resting on thighs, man-tits gathering crumbs and blobs of chewed meat.

'No exactly the pillar o' health as a nation, are we.' He sighs and pops the last of his roll into his mouth. 'We're not all destined to be Mountain Leaders. Sometimes you just have to accept where you are. There's a reason for everything, ken?'

'No.'

He fixes his eyes on me, waiting for something else.

I wait a moment too, because now is about the time Mitch can be counted on to offer a honed one liner. When he doesn't, I shrug. 'Sorry, Tig, but I don't. There's no reason, and you don't have to accept anything. Just because you land in the shite doesn't mean you have to stay there.'

'Life's a lot bloody harder if you fight it all the time. It's all part of His plan.'

I push my plate toward the edge of the table. 'Where's all this sanctimonious crap coming from, anyway? Last time I saw you, it was all angst about Rhona and her new man, and now you're sounding like a proper devil dodger.'

He hesitates for a moment before speaking, which is unlike him, takes another slug from his tin of chemical pish and then wipes brown sauce from the corner of his mouth.

'The church up the road started up a wee support group for ex-servicemen,' He eyes the leftover sausage on my plate like a gull, but doesn't take it. 'Wednesday nights. There's a few of us now. Ten, sometimes fourteen, fifteen turning up. It's good, like. I've been talking to Ian, the Padre, quite a lot and he's ... you know. Helping me see things differently, eh?'

I open my mouth, but Mitch leaps in: *Don't say it.*

This surprises me a little, but I close my mouth again and try not to let it show on my face. My legs start to jitter. I glance at my watch, then take a deep breath and will myself to be still. 'Good for you, mate.'

'You should come along.'

'Ah, Tig . . . I dinnae think so.'

'How? You'd fit right in with all the guys, it's like . . . being home. Civvies just dinna get it, you know?'

'We *are* civvies.'

'Come on, Sean.'

'No, listen Tommy. I asked to leave the Corps, right? They wanted me to stay and I wrapped. I had . . . a moment back in Sangin, before Mitch died, when it all came clear to me. We were just tools in the war machine, and there's nothing honourable about it. You and I, mate . . .'

Here we go again. You'll be manning the barricades at Faslane next.

I press my fingers over my ear and ignore this. 'We were only ever clones sent out to do the dirty work of our corporate puppet masters. It's a total clusterfuck.'

Tig looks like I've just slapped him in the face. 'That's no true at all.'

'It is. It took me a while to get it but once I did, I couldn't see it any other way. The last thing I want to do is sit about swapping war stories with a bunch of twisted old Tobies and praying for the souls of the poor innocent lads who died for the cause. I'll tell you who they fucking died for. They died for the CEOs of BP and Monsanto and those motherfuckers at RBS. They died to maintain the global order, so fat-arsed Americans can keep getting fatter on their cheap, processed food . . . and looking around here, so that we can do the same. They didn't die for the rights of any poor Afghan woman, and they most certainly didn't die for the rights of that bugger in the doorway over there.'

I point with my thumb toward a beggar huddled under a blanket in the doorway of a boarded up shop. Tig glances about in case anyone is staring at us.

192

Cue thunderous applause for the great orator. Give that man keys to Number Ten. You're wasting your time, Nic.

'He's a dosser. He's there every day.'

I told you.

I close my eyes for a moment, press my fingers into them.

'You go ask him why, Tig.'

Tigger rubs his cheek and deep lines form above his eyebrows. His open, round face is lined with distress, whether for me or himself or the sanctity of his little world, it's hard to tell. He puffs out his cheeks and blows, then shifts and pulls his wallet out of his back pocket.

'Mitch didn't die for some corporation, Sean, he died for you.'

'Yeah.' I pull out my own wallet and drop a tenner onto the table. 'My shout. If there's any change, give it to him.' I point toward the homeless man again, then slide out of the booth. 'I'm gonna head up the road.'

'Nic, wait.' He leaves the tenner on the table and scurries after me.

I step out into moist air, heavy with the smell of the brewery and electricity from a passing thunder shower, then turn and face him. He looks frightened and apologetic.

'I didn't mean it that way, ken . . . aboot Mitch. Naebody blames you. All that other stuff back there . . . it's just grief talking.'

'No, it isn't.'

I can tell he doesn't believe me. 'Listen, dinna run off. Come up to the flat for a bit and chill out. Watch a film or something.'

'Nah, I . . .'

Mind your manners, Nic.

193

'Thanks for asking, Tommy. Next time, eh?'

He nods. 'You alright?'

'Aye, sure. See you later, okay?'

I leave him and walk up Easter Road, then turn right and head along Regent Road, the Old Town rising up from Holyrood on my left, golden gorse blossom on Salisbury Crags catching the filtered sunlight behind. I pause in the gardens halfway along the road and look out over the view. Far to the left, the water of the Forth looks like wrinkled blue leather, stretching out into the North Sea and beyond.

I sit down on a bench and look out for a few minutes, imagining myself into a kayak, cutting through the waves like a clean, sharp knife. It's a good picture – calming – and I keep it there for a little while. Then I get out my phone and bring up Paula's number.

She answers with a slightly frayed, 'Hey, you.' I can hear Eva crying next to the phone.

'I'm in town. I was going to ask if you wanted to meet up, but it sounds like a bad time? What you up to?'

'My eyeballs in slimy water and dirty washing, that's what. My fucking washing machine's just packed in and flooded my kitchen.'

'Ah. Want me to come round and have a look at it?'

'Do you know how to fix washing machines?'

'No, but how complicated can it be, right?'

She laughs and her voice brightens. 'At the very least, you can entertain Eva while I phone round and try to get an engineer. Aye, do come. I'll get this mopped up and make you some lunch.'

'Oh God, no food. I've just had the most bogging fry up. I may never eat again.' I get up and start walking. 'I'm just heading for Princes Street. See you in twenty or so.'

194

'Great.'

I lengthen my stride and dodge tourists, chattering clusters of European students and Saturday shoppers. Princes Street continues to be a building site, obstructed by barriers and fences and holes in the ground where the mythical tramline should be. The once beautiful street has become a cacophonous nightmare to walk along, and as soon as I've passed the Mound, I cut down into the gardens and jog along the path, over the railway line and below the castle.

'That was quick,' Paula says when I arrive, watching over the railing as I come up the stairs two at a time. She hugs me. 'Thanks for coming.'

I follow her in. Eva has stopped crying and is lying happily on a play mat, waving her arms and fingering the little toys dangling above her. I squat down beside her and she focuses on my face, squawks and gives me a slavery smile. I can't help but mirror the expression.

'Hiya, kiddo. Look how much you've grown,' I say to her, offering a finger for her to grab. She tries to pull it toward her mouth.

'No wonder,' Paula says beside me. 'The amount she eats. She's a wee piggy, aren't you, Eva Bean?' Then she rubs my back. 'You look weary, Sean.'

I sit back on my heels. 'A bit, I suppose. Did a monster run up the hills this morning.'

'You sleeping?'

'Ehm . . . yeah . . . sometimes.' My knees crack as I get to my feet. 'Let's have a look at this rebel washing machine of yours, eh?'

The kitchen smells of dampness and washing powder, and there is a heap of wet towels in the sink. Paula sets Eva in a bouncy chair beside the window.

'What's happened?'

195

She sighs, sweeps her hair back from her face. 'It jammed up and wouldn't drain. I opened the little hatch to see if there was something stuck in the filter, and all this bloody water just came pouring out. Not very clever, really.'

'I take it you didn't find anything.'

'No, that would have been too easy.'

I stare at the machine for a minute, rubbing my chin. 'Maybe the hose at the back. We'll have to pull it out. Have you got an old sheet or something?'

'Aye.' She goes away and comes back a moment later with a cream coloured bed sheet.

'Ta.' I spread the sheet on the floor at the base of the washing machine. 'If we can just get the wee feet onto the sheet, then we should be able to slide it out.'

'Good luck,' she says, standing back and watching me try to work my fingers into the tiny gaps between the machine and the kitchen units. 'So . . . what you doing in town?'

'I met up with a guy I knew in the Marines. We had breakfast in this grease pit below his flat, and honest to God, I feel like I've got a ball of congealed lard sitting in my stomach.' I tip the machine to the left and trap my fingers between it and the cabinet.

'Ow . . . f . . .' Then I remember Eva, bite my lip and tip it the other direction. It makes a cracking noise as the feet unstick themselves from the floor.

'I'm glad you've got a mate in town. Must be nice to see him.'

'He's never been my best mate. I don't think we parted company on the best terms today. I had a bit of a moment.'

'A moment?'

'Aye.' Once on the sheet, the washing machine slides

out over the floorboards, dragging streamers of dust and debris. I kneel and peer into the gap, tracing the grey drain hose to its connection with the pipework under the sink. 'I need a bucket and a wee Philips screwdriver. By the way, did you know you've got mice?'

'Aye. There was a fat one in the middle of the kitchen floor the other morning, gallous as anything. Hang on.'

Once more, she goes away and comes back with the things I need.

'What kind of a moment?' she asks, as I set about loosening off the jubilee clip from the hose. It pops off and I drop the end into the bucket. A dribble of soapy water trickles out. I sit back and watch it for a moment.

'He invited me along to some church group he's got himself involved in, some thing for ex-servicemen, and I just . . . you know. I guess we all deal with things in our own ways, and great if that works for him. I gave him a bit of political commentary and it rattled him.'

'It rattled you too, I think.'

I glance at her. 'Maybe. I've been a bit rattled lately in general. So . . . I think there's something in the hose. If I tip this forward and hold it, can you take the hose off?'

'Yep.'

'Right.' I get back to my feet, hand her the screwdriver, then tip the washing machine forward and balance its weight on its front edge so the rest of the water doesn't spill out the back.

She deftly detaches the hose, then laughs at the watery clunk of hard objects on the floor. She bends down to pick them up. 'Forty seven pence and the key to my mother's house. Trust her to be obstructive.'

'That's about right. Go and get that hose back on; this thing weighs a bleeding ton.'

'Put your back into it,' she says robustly, reconnecting

the hose and twisting the clip tightly back into place.

I ease the machine upright again. Grey, soapy water flows freely into the bucket for a few seconds, slows to a trickle, then a drip. I reconnect the pipe and push the machine halfway back into its slot, then switch it back on to complete its cycle. We both stand there for a minute or two, hopefully, as it begins to hum.

'I think that's it.' I shake my hands to unknot my arms, and Paula rubs my shoulders.

'*I'd* give you a medal. You're a fucking lifesaver.'

'Nobody ever died of a broken washing machine.'

Paula laughs and points at Eva. 'When you have a baby, you'll understand.'

A wave of fatigue spills over me and I sit down at the table and stretch my complaining legs out in front of me. 'Jesus, I'm buggered. I ran too hard today.'

'Cuppa for your efforts?'

'Aye, ta.' I close my eyes and lean my head back against the wall. 'Don't mind me.'

'I don't mind you at all,' she replies, voice loaded with suggestion.

I smile and listen to the washing machine going about its business, water filling the kettle, the crinkle of biscuit wrappers and Eva's little gurgles and squeals. Paula's kitchen is warm and filled with bright afternoon sunshine, which glows even through my closed eyelids. I feel myself drifting, but it feels safe here so I give in to it.

'You're snoring, Sleeping Beauty.'

My eyes pop open. Paula sets the tea and biscuits onto the table and sits down beside me, pats my knee.

'Mmm.' I rub my eyes and sit up. 'Sorry.'

'It's alright.' She fills two mugs, slides one toward me. Eva has conked out in her seat, a beam of sun falling across her cheeks. Her little lips work at an imaginary teat.

198

Paula's gauzy blue blouse falls low at the neck, showing off a teasing hint of breast. I allow my eyes to settle there for a few seconds, and I want to catch her hands and pull her onto my lap. I wonder how long Eva will sleep and whether Paula can have space in her mind or her heart for anyone else.

The line between appreciation and lechery is far too easily crossed, with dire consequences if you misjudge the timing of your crossing. So I pull my eyes away and grab my tea.

Paula leans back in her seat and crosses her legs at the ankles. 'So . . . are you okay? What's rattling you?'

I take a drink and a deep breath. 'Janet and I are at each other's throats, so home isn't the nicest place to be just now. I can't talk to her, she's . . . uptight. She can't handle anything that's the least bit scary or traumatic.'

'She's probably had enough trauma of her own to last a lifetime.'

'Mmm. Maybe. I'm grateful to her, even if she doesn't believe that. She didn't have to let me come back. She probably wishes she hadn't. But . . . I'll have to get out soon, get my own place.'

'Where will you go?'

'I don't know. Away from fucking Eskbridge. Too many ghosts there for my liking.'

'Ghosts?'

'Reminders of things I'd prefer to forget. You know what it was like for me, Paula. You're one of the few people in this world who does. I thought with Mum gone the place would be okay, but . . . I don't know if it can ever be.'

She draws her hand over her mouth. 'Is it Eskbridge, or is it you? Your life is your life, wherever you go.'

'Aye, but the place doesn't help. Face it, it's a dump. I'm thinking about moving up north.'

I don't know why I've said this, because it's only ever been a transitory notion, which progressed through my head and disappeared without any call to action. Maybe I've only said it to gauge Paula's reaction.

Her eyes widen fiercely. 'Oh no, don't move away!'

'Why not?'

'Because . . .' She checks herself. 'Well . . . because I'd miss you, Sean. But at the same time . . . maybe it's what you have to do. It sounds right for you. What about your job?'

'It's okay until I can come up with something better.' I sigh. 'It's just a thought.'

Her dark eyes flicker over my face, then she takes my hand and examines fingers that I trapped.

'You've taken the skin off your knuckles.'

'Ow,' I say, without really feeling it.

She gets up and dampens a bit of kitchen roll, then takes my hand again and cleans away the blood.

I watch her doing this, my throat crowded with things I want her to know but can't bring myself to say. Such a confusion of events and emotions and colours and smells – *a proper boorach*, my Granny would have said (the description she often bestowed upon Mum, hands on hips and head moving slowly from side to side) – that I can't follow a single thread long enough to tell her about it. I want to tell her about Mitch, and about Cauldhill Farm and Duncan and Tig and Harry and Billy, and I want to tell her about the things that I've swallowed – snow and mud and dust and blood and shite and lies – and that they're working on me like poison. I want to tell her that I have a black hole inside me, where the future disappears into the vortex of the past.

200

'That's better,' Paula says, then brings my knuckles to her lips and kisses them. 'You'll live.'

I swallow hard, sit there with my hand in hers and think about all the things I want to tell her.

'I want to go to bed,' is all I can manage.

'You want to go to bed.' She repeats, her voice low and careful.

I nod and pull her toward me and slide my hands around her hips. 'With you.'

She sits on my lap, her warm weight heavy against my groin and her breasts rising and falling with her breath. 'Oh you do, do you?'

'Aye.'

She tilts her head to one side and moves her hair away from her face. 'Okay, then. With any luck, Madam will give us half an hour.'

XXI

We explore each other's bodies, undressing piece by piece, revealing the places that might once have seemed ugly but which are now defining marks of who we have become: the scars on my face and legs, the stretch marks on the soft curve of her belly, the little red line of her Caesarean incision. Kissing hesitantly at first, with no urgency to reach the inevitable conclusion except the certainty that Eva will, at some point, wake up. I wait for Mitch to comment, but maybe he's learned his lesson after last time and gone away to a quiet corner to put his Hank Williams on. He'll be yodelling away to himself and pretending he can't hear us.

I move over her, then pause, circling one dark nipple with my fingertip. 'Are you sure about this?'

She kicks the covers out of the way and turns onto her back, pupils huge in the dark room, her hand running from my shoulder blade, down the small of my back and coming to rest on my arse for a moment before sliding around the front. Her fingers close around my cock and it stands eagerly to attention like a fresh recruit on the parade ground. It's tempting to let out a cheer.

'I am now,' she whispers, then grasps more firmly and guides me between her legs.

Her knees come up to either side of me as I slide into her, and she arches her back so that I can kiss the hollow at the base of her neck. After a few minutes, she moans softly, pulls me harder into her and nibbles my left ear.

It's a strange sensation, warm and wet but without sound, and it makes my breath catch in my chest. My knees shake as I come, with a wave of emotion I can't quite identify. Relief, maybe? Gratitude. Love? Something that will disappear if I try to name it.

We collapse in a sweaty tangle of limbs and covers, the air cooling our skin, pulse rushing in my temples. We lie there for several minutes without speaking, then she kisses me, rolls away and pulls on her knickers, steps lightly over the wooden floorboards and into the lobby. I hear her go into the kitchen to check on Eva, and then into the toilet, the water running in the pipes. She comes back after a minute or two, curls up beside me and draws the quilt over us, her arm sliding around to my front and her fingers spreading on my chest, her mouth against the back of my neck.

'That was worth waiting for,' she whispers.

'Mmm. I've been wondering what that would be like for twenty years.'

A giggle. 'I hope it wasn't an anti-climax.'

'I wouldn't use that word.'

'Oh good.' She pauses. 'My first time since having Eva. I'm glad it was with you.'

I glance back over my shoulder. 'I didn't hurt you . . .'

'No, you didn't hurt me. Just the opposite.' She kisses my shoulder, then sits up and pulls her shirt over her head. 'I need to feed her. Stay here as long as you like.'

'Don't say that.' I close my eyes. 'I might never go.'

'That might be okay with me.'

I wake sometime later, sweating and sticky under the duvet, the late afternoon sun beaming into the high window. My heart is hammering against my ribs as the

203

tail end of a dream recedes into a dark cave in my brain, like the final scene of some cinematic gore-fest. Paula is sitting on a white upholstered chair beside the window in her dressing gown, sunlight glinting on the crown of her head. Eva lies across her lap, legs kicking and little fingers kneading as she suckles.

'Hi.'

I catch my breath and sit up too quickly. Stars swim in front of my eyes. 'Hi.'

'You alright?'

'I was somewhere else there.'

'I could see that.'

My mouth is dry as cotton and it's difficult to swallow. I pull in a deep breath through my nose and let it out slowly, willing the monster back into its hole. My hands are shaking visibly.

I hold them up and watch them, as if they don't belong to me at all. 'Look at this.'

She nods slowly. 'Will you tell me what you were dreaming about?'

I swing my legs out of the bed, reach for my jeans and pause, looking at the two of them with the sun illuminating their faces. 'You look like Mary and Jesus sitting there. I wouldn't want to ruin it.'

'Kinda late for that, isn't it? After what we just did? Anyway, my arse is too big for a pedestal.'

'Your arse is just perfect.' I force a laugh and pull on my jeans. 'Do you mind if I have a shower?'

'Go ahead.'

She's in the kitchen when I come out. She pours tea from a pot with pink and green polka dots and hands it to me. Eva is lying on her back in the playpen, slavering and doing her best to get her toes into her mouth.

'Feel better?'

'Aye. Ta.'

I sit in the window seat beside the cooker and look out at the lines of washing stretched across the back greens, fluttering in the pinkish light. 'Do you really want to know what I was dreaming about?'

'Only if you want to tell me.'

'I have this recurring dream that I'm trying to kill a man with a knife, or sometimes an axe. I'm on top of him, covered in his blood, and no matter how many times I stab him, he doesn't die. He just sits there looking at me.'

'Jesus, Sean.' She sits down at the table.

'I have others, but that's the worst. Fucked up, huh?'

'A wee bit. Please tell me that never actually happened.'

'No. In reality, if I'm going to knife some bugger I'll get him first time. Slitting the throat from behind generally works better.'

'Right . . . it's a little scary how confident you are about that.'

'I was a reconnaissance specialist, Paula.'

'What does that mean?'

I sigh. 'It means it was my job to scout out positions ahead of operations. To locate targets and send back information. It means that I had to put myself into very dangerous places, very close to the enemy, very quietly. The knife comes into its own. So aye . . . yeah . . . two. Two men with the knife. More with the rifle or the side-arm . . . I don't know how many.'

'You haven't told anyone that before, have you.'

'Confessing to murder isn't very pleasant, strangely enough. I needed to say it but now . . . I feel like I don't deserve to be sitting here drinking tea with you and Eva, getting away with it.'

205

'Getting away with it? It isn't murder, Sean, it's war. It's different.'

'Murder on a mass scale. That's the only difference.'

'Why did you go, if that's how you see it?'

'I didn't see it that way then.'

'But you do now.'

I nod. 'I do now.'

'Oh Sean. You're too good, that's the trouble. I've always known that.' She crosses the kitchen, squeezes onto the seat beside me and places a warm hand on my back. 'What changed it for you?'

Her touch just about dissolves me and I can't speak. There is a hot stone in my throat. I draw my knees up toward my chest and stare out the window. The back greens blur through a sheen of tears. Paula watches me blink them away but doesn't ask any more. I know the precise moment it changed. I can still remember the substance of that day; its smells and sounds and particular terrors. I remember it all, but I can't tell her.

****

Monday's delivery round finished, Jack drops me at the shop and heads off for a more lucrative job fitting Davie Blair's new kitchen. I find Harry standing in the storeroom staring at a tangled jumble of bicycles that have been donated to us by the police. Some of them are partial: frames missing wheels and seats and handlebars.

Harry's fingers are twined in his beard and his breath whistles in his nose.

'They're all nicked or just . . . dumped places. Nobody claims them.' He surveys the collection, with something like despair across his face. 'The world we live in, eh? You any good at fixing bikes?'

206

I spend the afternoon straightening spokes, patching tires, oiling gears, salvaging useable parts from knackered frames and swapping them onto good frames where I can. The smells of mud, rubber and grease are reassuring, and the fiddly work fills the empty places in my mind where more disturbing preoccupations might otherwise creep in.

After a couple of hours a shadow falls across the floor in front of me and I look up. Dawn is leaning in the doorframe, arms crossed, jaws grinding on chewing gum. She's dyed her hair black, which makes her look even pastier than usual, and cheap perfume wafts off her in nose-tingling waves.

'Alright Sean?'

'Yep. What's up?'

'What ye daein tonight?' She gnaws the cuticle on her left little finger and seems very young.

'No plans. Why?'

'There's an Abba tribute band at the Miners. There's a few of us going. Fancy it?'

'Not really.' I spin the front wheel of the upturned bike in front of me and crouch down to check its alignment.

'How?'

'I don't go to bars and I fucking hate Abba.'

'Whit dae ye like? We could dae somehin else, like. If ye wanted. Pictures or somehin.'

I sit back on my heels and wipe my greasy hands on a cloth, clearing my throat to cover a laugh. She's trying to keep her cool, still scraping at her finger with her bottom teeth.

'I don't want to go out with you, Dawn. Sorry.'

Her expression shifts from baby doll to hard bitch, and I have a passing vision of her staring up the rope climb in Bottom Field at Lympstone: full webbing on, black hair hanging over her eyes, chewing on her finger.

'Whit's wrang wi' us, like?'

An under-fire appraisal of the situation suggests that honesty isn't the best policy for maintaining workplace relations, such as they are. 'There's nothing wrong with you. I'm seeing someone.'

Paula and I still haven't managed to articulate what our relationship is, if it's anything at all, so it's possible that the statement "seeing someone" is a little overcooked. But it's a useful defence at the moment.

Dawn looks doubtful. 'Who?'

'Paula Fairbairn.'

'Never heard of her.'

I shrug.

'She doesnae have tae ken.'

'I'm too old for you. Let's just leave it at that, eh?'

'I've got two bairns, I'm no a baby.'

'Dawn, what part of *I'm not interested* don't you understand?'

'Ye're a fucking wank bag,' she blurts. 'Ye think ye're all posh or somehin, the way ye talk an' that. Ye're nae better than us.'

I stand up. 'A bit of advice for you. You want a guy to like you, it's probably better not to slander his family in public or call him a wank bag. Just a thought. 'Scuse me.'

I push past her and head for the kitchen, hoping to hell she doesn't follow me. She doesn't, but instead stomps off through the shop, lets fly with the back of her hand and knocks over a glass table lamp. It shatters spectacularly on the concrete floor and Dawn flounces out the front door without looking back. Al looks up from the bookcase he's working on, eyes following her out the door then turning back to me.

'Fucking nutter,' I mutter under my breath. 'I'll get a brush.'

Harry comes out from behind the counter and follows me back to the storeroom. 'What was that about?'

'She asked me out. I said no.'

'Ah.'

'Sorry.'

'Not your fault. You alright?' He presses his fingertips into his eyelids and sits down on an old wooden chair.

'*I'm* fine, Harry. You look like you've had it.'

Harry leans his head back against the wall and laughs softly. 'I'm getting too old for this. I suppose I'd better go after her.'

'Why not just let her go?'

'You think?'

'That's what she wants. Someone to go running after her. Why should you?'

'Maybe she needs me to.'

'Or maybe she needs to learn the consequences.'

'Ach, fuck the consequences, Sean,' he says, uncharacteristically sharply for him. 'There are worse things than breaking a lamp.'

'What, like stealing money?'

He stands up, pats my shoulder. 'I'd better go find her.'

Sufficiently reprimanded, I take the brush and dustpan, then glance back over my shoulder at the blue mountain bike I've been working on. 'Harry, would it be alright if I buy that bike, before someone else does? Tell me how much you want for it.'

He gives a weary wave of his hand. 'Just have it. There aren't many perks in this job but I reckon we could stretch to that. Is it functional?'

'Oh aye. It's a good bike, actually. You sure?'

He nods. 'It's my pleasure.'

By closing time I've conjured another four saleable

bicycles from the heap, and arranged them in the window display. I wheel mine out into a fine soft afternoon. A gentle breeze comes from the west carrying the smell of rain and gorse blossom, a flotilla of silver clouds moving across the sky from behind the hills. I glide home in a couple of minutes, decide to change out of my work clothes and head out for a proper ride.

'Where'd you get the bike?' Janet says from the kitchen sink. She looks pale and apprehensive, and my chest begins to tighten again. I'm beginning to wonder how much longer she and I will be able to put up with each other.

'Harry gave it to me. I'm going out for a spin just now.'

She huffs, lips drawn. 'You don't have a helmet.'

'I'll get one.'

'Please.'

'Aye, ma'am.' I turn to head upstairs.

'Sean, before you go up . . .'

I pause. Janet dries her hands and stares at me for a moment, then takes a deep breath, picks up a large brown envelope from the kitchen table and hands it to me.

'I lied to you the other night. I'm sorry.'

XXII

I glance at Janet, then slide my hand into the envelope, close my fingers on smooth photographic paper and withdraw them again. My hands shake a little as I stare at two faded colour prints. The first is of a soldier leaning on the wall of Edinburgh Castle Esplanade. It is not exactly the same as the photo I found in George Finlayson's trunk, but must have been taken at the same time. The second picture is of the same man, this time dressed in dirty jeans and a jumper, smoking a cigarette at edge of a small, dark loch. A tiny boy with light blond hair sits on a stone beside him, dirty-faced, hand lost in a packet of crisps.

I swallow heavily and turn the photos over. There is writing on the back of the first: *D.C. June, 1977.*

'What's the C for?'

'Campbell.'

'Duncan Campbell,' I say softly, and the only coherent thought I can grasp is that I never imagined myself as a Campbell. The kitchen floor seems to tilt away from me; I lean against the bunker and try to collect myself.

'Tell me what you know.'

'Ehm . . .' She wavers, mouth half open. 'They saw each other for a couple of years, on and off, while he was still in the army. He used to disappear without a word, not write to her for months, then turn up again as if he'd only been gone a week. They split for good, probably

211

just after that second photo was taken. You would have been . . . two and a half, maybe? Three at most.'

I sit at the table and my right leg jiggles up and down. Anger so heavy in my chest it's hard to breathe.

'He lives on Cauldhill Farm. He's been there all this time. You lied to me all these fucking years and I had to find out by accident. Do you want to tell me why, please?'

'Jesus,' she whispers and drags out a chair, sits heavily and covers her mouth with her hands. 'Well, for a start I didn't know until the other day that he was still living anywhere near here.'

I drum my thumb on the tabletop. 'You're trying to tell me that in thirty-odd years, you never saw him about? Mum never saw him?'

'I don't know. If mum did, she . . .' She squeezes her eyes shut and clenches her fists. 'I saw him in passing a few times, but that's it. He didn't want you. He wanted nothing to do with you. He didn't acknowledge you as his, he wouldn't allow her to put his name on your birth certificate. Alright? D'you understand?'

There isn't any sensible reply to this, so I stare at the table. The evening sun shines on it, illuminating dust and red wine stains.

'Sean, it's worse. He beat her up.'

'When?'

'More than once. She used to leave us at Granny's and the pair of them would go out and get hammered. She'd come home with a burst lip or a black eye, and she'd deny it was him. She'd say she'd fallen or run into a door . . . the usual excuses.'

She shakes her head and wipes tears from her eyes. 'She admitted it was him eventually. I think possibly he sexually abused her too. Made her do things that even

212

she thought were indecent. I'm not sure. Sometimes she said things like that for effect and I was never sure how true they were.'

We sit there for a minute or two, the clock ticking on the wall. My legs jiggle. Another crossroads, once again way beyond the boundaries of any map.

Eventually she closes her eyes and sighs. 'Maybe I should have told you before. Really Mum should have told you.'

My shoulders rise and fall and I chew on my bottom lip. 'Mum didn't give a crap about me, or anyone else for that matter.'

'That's not true.'

'It is, Janet. As far as I'm concerned, it always was.'

'She loved you. She was trying to protect you.'

'If she loved either of us, she would have got herself straight. She was a sick, selfish woman and you were just her helper. Fucking pathetic, the pair of you.'

'That's just cruel, Sean. I won't have you say that.'

'I'll say what I bloody like.' I stand up and swipe the photos from the table, slide them back into their envelope and stuff this into my rucksack. Then I thump out the kitchen door again.

Janet minces after me in her bare feet. 'Where you going now?'

I pretend not to hear her as I head down the garden path and grab the bike.

'Sean! What are you doing? Don't you dare go out there!'

I pause at the gate, turn to face her and lie through my teeth. 'I'm not going out there, alright. Just give me a fucking break, Janet. I'm going to clear my head.'

She steps back and watches me mount the bike. I push hard up the hill, past the field and out toward Rosewell,

213

pumping hard enough that there can be no spare room in my head for doubts.

It hardly takes any time to reach the rutted road to Cauldhill Farm, and within minutes I pass the drive. Molly's car is there, but I carry on past. The bike jitters over the potholes and gravel, then over the cattle grid and onto the muddy track up to Duncan's cottage. I haven't rehearsed what I'm going to say or the tone I'm going to take, because I don't know what state I'm going to find him in. But as I swing off the bike and lean it against the outside wall, I take a deep breath and prepare myself for a potential attack. I haven't got a weapon of any sort except my hands, though I know I could disarm him easily enough if he came at me with a knife. But still my heart begins to rev itself into combat mode.

A cloud obscures the sun, bringing a keen edge into the air and raising goose bumps on my arms. I bang on the door and shout, 'Duncan!'

There is no response at first except the rasping of crows on the roof and the distant bellow of sheep, and my face glows hot with frustration. Stupid old bastard must be out drinking himself legless. Then, maybe I'm the stupid one, to think he'd be safely at home while the pubs are still open.

But I bang again and wait there, hands poised at my sides in case something comes flying at me. After a moment, there's a clatter inside the cottage and a grumbling voice raised in complaint. I suck in a deep breath as the door creaks open.

We face each other. He wavers a little, exhaling toxic fumes into the already gamey air, brows knitting together. Drunk, but not paralytic. I suspect the only time he is even close to sober is first thing in the morning,

214

and that probably lasts only as long as it takes him to pour the hair of the dog down his gullet.

'Whit ye wantin?'

'I'd like to speak to you, Duncan.'

He glances over his shoulder and I look past him into a dank corridor with a muddy carpet and nicotine-yellow woodchip wallpaper. Added to the general stench of stale booze and fags is what smells suspiciously like sheep shit. This is my genetic inheritance: pervert, pisshead and in all probability, sheep-shagger to boot. Fucking great.

'I'm goan oot,' he replies in a voice that seems to mimic the crows that are nesting at the side of his chimney. He takes a step back and tries to swing the door closed, but I catch it.

'I know who you are. I think you'd better let me in.'

His chest swells. 'Are ye threatenin' me?'

I hold up my hands, palms toward him. 'Take it easy, aye? I only want to talk.'

'Dinnae fuck wi' me, son, I ken how tae fight.'

'So I hear. You slapped my ma around a few times and all.'

'Whae telt ye that?'

'Somebody who knows the truth.'

He swallows hard and stares at me, mouth half open, an argument hanging there in the entrance to it. But then he snaps his gob shut again and turns his back on me, shuffles down the corridor. I follow him inside, letting the rucksack slide off my shoulders, quietly unzipping it and removing the photographs.

Duncan shows me into a fusty lounge with an ash-dusted carpet, tatty but surprisingly good quality furniture, empty bottles lying around or stuck to shelves by their sticky remnants. The old black and white collie is lying in front of a fireplace with no fire in it. The dog

215

raises its head and blinks at me, then lets its chin fall back onto its paws.

Without an invitation, I sit myself on the least filthy armchair, drop the two photographs of Duncan onto the coffee table, then cross my legs and wait. His hand shakes as he bends slowly, fingers reaching toward the photos then pausing before touching them, as though they might burn him. His breathing is laboured and wheezy. He lingers there for a moment, staring without touching, then straightens up, turns away and mutters something.

'Turn around and face me, Duncan.'

He turns around again, but stares at the floor. 'D'ye want a drink or no?'

'No.'

A shrug. 'Suit yersel.' He shuffles across to the shelving unit against the far wall, twists the cap off a fresh bottle of supermarket whisky and fills a tumbler. He throws half of it straight down his throat then refills the glass and crosses the room again, sits across from me and stares at me with renewed clarity. 'I heard ye came a cropper in Afghanistan.'

I smile to cover my surprise. 'Word gets about, eh? Don't tell me you actually care.'

'I dinnae. Yer ainly living because yer ma remembered too late she wis a Pape and refused tae get rid o' ye. I telt her I didnae want the bairn. So if it wis some kind o' faither-son reunion ye wis wantin, I'm sorry tae disappoint ye.'

'Why the fuck would I want to lumber myself with a wasted old prick like you?'

'Dinnae speak tae me like that, boy, if ye ken whit's good fer ye.'

'I'll speak to you how I like.'

He takes another slug of whisky and his bristly jaws

216

work silently as he assesses me. 'Whit dae ye want? Money? As ye can see, I'm no exactly loaded.'

'To know the truth, Duncan, that's all.'

'Apparently ye ken it already.'

I shake my head. A battalion of questions has come marching into my mind, but I'll have to choose them carefully. My combative tone has knocked him into compliance for now, but it won't last. 'Not all of it. How'd you meet her?'

'Up the toon, I telt ye that before. The Scotsman bar in Cockburn Street. We were just back from a tour in Northern Ireland, and she was on the hunt. Bonny girl, yer ma, I mind that much.'

'How long were you together?'

He shrugs. 'I wouldnae say we were together. She kept comin' aifter us, I didnae . . .' He breaks off and stares out the window.

'You didn't what?'

'I wasnae in any fit state.'

'No change there, then. You're a pathetic lump of shite, Duncan, I'm surprised even the army wanted you.'

'Ye ken nothin' aboot me.'

'You got her pregnant. You beat her up, you humiliated her. You brought a child into this world and denied he had anything to do with you. You're a pathetic lump of shite, and you're a coward. That's about the sum of it, as far as I can tell.'

He explodes out of his seat with surprising agility for a man who looks like he could fall over his own shadow. One hand on the coffee table, he leans across and jabs a finger toward my face.

'Get oot ma hoose, or I'll fuckin' show ye what I did tae yer ma when she asked for it. She had a nasty tongue in her heid an' all.'

I draw down my poker face and refuse to flinch. 'I'll go when I'm ready. Sit down before you hurt yourself, Duncan.'

Scarlet circles appear on his cheeks and his mouth drops open, but he retreats back across the table and thumps into his chair.

'What about Molly Finlayson. Did you fuck her as well?'

'Did she tell ye that?'

'She said it wasn't her idea. She said she didn't want to do it.'

'Fucking bastard,' he whispers, so softly I can't really hear the words. But I can read the shapes of his lips just fine.

'If I'm a bastard, it's your fault. Did you rape her, then, Duncan?'

'No, I didnae. You've got it wrong.'

I lean across toward him. 'She as much as told me you did.'

In one fluid motion, he dives out of the chair, grasps an empty bottle and swings it in a sweeping arc toward the side of my head. I duck to the side of the table, catch his arm and twist it viciously back on itself, his hand automatically releasing the bottle as I force it behind his back. The dog erupts into a frenzy, growling and barking at my ankle. Duncan spews whisky fumes in my face and struggles, knocking over the coffee table as he tries to get purchase on me with his left hand and sweep my legs.

I could have him face down on the floor in a second, but instead I shove him away from me hard and let go. He stumbles, trips over the upturned table and falls on top of it.

He groans, as though the one burst of violence has

spent him completely, but by now rage is crashing through me. I swing for him with my right foot and nail him in the side of the abdomen: every hurt I've ever felt for the unfairness of the life he and my mother gave me, and every resentful thought that's darkened my mind on their account, all channelled through the toe of one muddy trainer and into the ribs of the man on the floor in front of me.

He gives a choked cry and flops onto his side, trapped between the legs of the upturned table. I kick him again, this time in the face, and watch blood explode from his nose. The dog launches itself toward me, and yelps with pain as I boot it away.

Duncan is still moving, a low whimper issuing from his throat as his hand creeps up toward his face. The sight of him is foul and painful, like a dying animal on the road. I want to finish the job. I stand over him, grasp his collar with my left hand and place my best right hook under his jaw. His head snaps backward.

I swing again, but someone screams my name behind me and breaks the spell. My fist is already moving, but it goes with less force and scuffs off Duncan's stubble.

'Sean, stop it! Oh my God, stop it!'

Hands lock onto me. Two sets of hands, dragging me backwards by the shoulders.

'Jesus Christ, you've fucking killed him!'

It's like someone's turned off a tap. I go limp and collapse backward, sitting on the floor with Duncan's blood splattered across my shirt. I am only vaguely aware of two women stooped over Duncan, speaking in words I can't make out. The energy and will to move have ebbed out of me, so I draw my knees up to my chest, rest my forehead against them and feel my throat closing.

The women move in and out of the room, bringing wet

cloths and tending to Duncan, ignoring me completely for a length of time that I can't measure. Eventually he begins to rouse himself. He staggers to the sofa and lies down again with a stream of curses, and a trickle of selfish relief creeps into me. A murder sentence for the worthless old wanker would have been suicide time.

I look up and my eyes begin to focus. Blood still damp on the floor, Duncan stretched on the sofa with a red-stained towel pressed over his nose. Molly is dabbing at a cut above his eye and Janet is holding a cold beer can over a vivid, creeping bruise on his ribs.

My breath shakes as I fill my lungs. 'Is he alright?'

Janet turns on me. 'He's a bloody mess. What in the name of God are you trying to do?'

I don't bother trying to answer. 'You followed me?'

'Of course I followed you. I'm not that stupid. I had to go to the farm and ask Molly to take me here. Jesus Christ, Sean, you've lost the fucking plot.'

Duncan ignores Janet and stares at Molly. 'I think maybe somebody else has lost the plot and all. Why does he think I raped you?' His voice is thick and muffled.

Molly's mouth falls open slightly, and she looks from him to me and back again. 'I never said that.'

'Tell him the truth or I will.'

She rises from her seat and refuses to look at any of us.

'Fucking tell him,' Duncan orders again.

'I am, alright!' she snaps, then blows loudly through pursed lips. 'It was Gillian's idea. Gillian Taylor, you remember her?'

I close my eyes and nod. Duncan makes jerky hissing sound, which is apparently a laugh. Tears drip from the corners of his eyes.

'Evil wee minx, she wis.'

Molly turns around, shoots him a look. 'We were

twelve. Bored, stupid and twelve. We ... took some photographs of ourselves that were ... well ... .basically pornographic, and left them in his house. I don't know what we thought. Maybe that he'd be interested. Maybe that he'd see us as women instead of little girls.'

'Dinnae believe that, by the way. She wanted me away, that's all, because the auld man didnae gie a toss aboot her.'

He turns back to Molly again, finger stabbing the air. 'I brought the photies tae the old man and telt him what ye'd done. You fucking accused me of taking them, and yer ma believed ye. She was all for havin' me put away. Tell him, hen. Tell him I never touched ye.'

Molly wilts onto a chair and covers her face with her hands. 'He never touched us. He never did anything wrong except drink too much, live off Dad's money and keep Dad's dirty little secrets. That was the last straw for Mum; that was the end of their marriage. This is my fault. If I'd told you the truth when you asked me, this wouldn't have happened.'

At this point Janet decides to leap in with both feet. 'It's not your fault, Molly. Sean did this, not you. He's ill, alright? He hears voices. His dead mate talks to him.' She turns on me. 'You need help. Do you see that now?'

The look she gives me, fear and disgust and heartbreak, I've seen before. She looked at me like that when Mum was dying and I refused to make my peace with her. Maybe then I deserved it, and maybe I do now, but the force of it is more than I can take. I launch myself to my feet and stumble out of the room.

'Sean, don't you leave,' Janet shouts after me. 'Sean!'

I'm already on the bike by the time she gets out the door.

'Sean, will you fucking stop!'

221

The bike chitters over the gravel, skidding as it hits larger stones. I clatter over the cattle grid and freewheel down the hill, legs pumping hard in high gear. The light is beginning to fade and there is still a bit of traffic on the main road, mostly coming the other way. One or two vehicles pass me on my side of the road, so close I feel the brush of displaced air against my cheek. I've got no helmet, no light, no reflectors. I don't particularly have a death wish, but then, I don't particularly have a life wish either.

Going home is not an option but I'm going to crash soon. Jack's only got the one bed, and he'll require explanations and cups of tea. I head back to the shop and let myself in the back door from the alley.

'Harry!' I call out, and receive only a wraithlike echo of my own voice. The shop is cavernous and gloomy, but turning on the lights will draw attention so I don't bother. I wheel the bike inside, lock the door behind me and switch off my mobile phone. Then I go to the kitchen and fill the kettle, make tea and sit at the sticky table, watch wisps of steam spiralling upward and wait for my breathing to slow.

Remember Macpherson. Never regret necessary actions. No matter how brutal, do not regret. Regret will kill you.

Macpherson was one of our instructors on the mountain leader course, a Scot of aristocratic northern breeding, arching public school vowels and an ice-scarred face. Rumour was he cut off his mate's foot to save him from gangrenous frostbite somewhere in the Himalayas. A hard bastard: a man who never spoke words he didn't live by.

I remember Captain Macpherson and his advice, and stare into my tea wondering how to define *necessary*.

222

After a while, when it has become truly dark and the worst pangs of hunger have been sated by half a packet of stale Hobnobs, I drag an old quilt to one of the mattresses at the back of the shop, kick off my trainers and curl up.

XXIII

Dreams of enemies and running with blocks of concrete on my feet, dreams I have to force myself out of like a drowning man writhing for the surface. I wake periodically to the sounds of our own little post-industrial skirmishes outside in the back alley: breaking glass, drunken laughter tipping over into rage, police sirens. Bawling voices, slurred, incomprehensible syllables.

Morning arrives with a headache behind both eyes, sinuses thick with mould and dust, and Harry, apparently unshaken by my dishevelled presence. Less shaken than I am, anyway, when he wakes me with a gentle pat on the shoulder.

'Jesus,' I blurt, sitting up, momentarily lost in a jumbled room with too much furniture.

'At ease, Sean, it's only me. Here.' He hands me a cup of tea, sits beside me and stretches his legs out. Faded jeans, dark green wool jumper, smells of coffee and wood smoke. 'You've been here all night?'

'Aye. Sorry, Harry, I . . .' I stop there, mouth open as it all comes back to me. Words seem pointless at this stage. Back to the wall right enough; there's nowhere to go from here. I pick up the tea, take a sip and wish the mug was big enough to hide my face.

'This can't be the nicest place to sleep,' he says after a moment. He leans forward slightly, turns his eyes to me in such a way that it's impossible to avoid his gaze. 'What's going on?'

'Just a bit of a . . .' my voice revs, splutters, fails. The mug trembles between my hands, my reflection shimmering in the vibrating liquid. 'Nothing.'

Harry is so still he's almost feline. A grizzled old cat waiting to pounce, watching me shiver like a mouse in his gaze. 'I think you'd better tell me whose blood that is.'

I glance down at my shirt, then at the shadowy bruises on the knuckles of my right hand. 'An old guy called Duncan Campbell. Turns out he's . . .' I can't say the words. My throat closes and my eyes start to burn. I close them, draw in a long breath, which catches and forces its way out in a strangled laugh. 'He's the guy who fucked my mother. He fucked her and beat her up and left her pregnant.'

'He's your father?' For the first time, his voice betrays note of surprise that he isn't able to hide in his beard. 'What happened last night?'

'He lives on Cauldhill Farm, as it turns out. I went out there to talk to him and he didn't like what I had to say. He came at me with a bottle, so I went for him. I wanted to kill him.'

I laugh again at Harry's earnest, worried face, but it's the kind of laugh that only brings you closer to tears. 'Relax, Harry, I didn't. He's doing a good job of it himself, bottle by bottle. You want to call the police? You can, I don't care.'

'I don't want to, but I would if I thought there was a reason. Why didn't you go home last night?'

'My sister thinks I've lost it completely. She'd have had me taken away in a padded van if she'd had her choice.'

'Does she know where you are?'

'No.'

He takes a deep breath. 'What about Duncan Campbell? How badly did you hurt him?'

'I broke his nose at the very least. Possibly a rib or two. Janet was there; she'd have got him help if he needed it. She likes looking after wasters; she's spent her life doing it.'

His fingers curl into his beard and he sits there for a moment, plotting his next move. Probably trying to work out whether Janet is right about my state of mind without having to ask too many questions.

'Is there anything I can help with?'

I shake my head, then drain my mug and set it on the floor. 'I just . . . don't know what to do, Harry.'

'Tell me what you mean.'

'I mean I . . .' I breathe deeply and try to find a passable explanation. 'All I want is to pick up and live a normal life, but I don't know what that is. I always thought there was something better than this, you know? I thought I could be better than just . . . a fatherless son of a bitch, but maybe Janet's right. Maybe I've lost the plot. Maybe it's more than my head can cope with.'

'Maybe it is, Sean. I don't know very many heads that could cope with everything you've been through. There's no shame in admitting it.'

'So . . . what? I'm just another casualty at the side of the fucking road, like Billy or Duncan, or my Ma for that matter?'

Harry smiles gently. 'Why should you end up like them?'

'I don't know how to come back from where I am at the moment.'

'Step by step, just like any other serious injury. Your

ear doesn't hold you back. If you'd lost a leg, I've no doubt that by now you'd be out running miles every day on a prosthetic. Why should this be so different?'

I run my fingers through sweaty, unwashed hair. 'It just is.'

He sighs. 'Would you mind if I told you what I see when I look at you?'

'You're the boss.'

'Are you going to listen?'

I remove my elbows from my knees and sit up, spread my fingers onto my filthy trousers and stare at them. There is dried blood under my nails. 'Fire away, then.'

He leans toward me so I have to make eye contact again. 'Sean, when I look at you, I absolutely do not see a fatherless son of a bitch. I see a very brave and intelligent and determined young man. I see someone who could have followed his parents down the road of addiction and had the strength of mind to choose not to. And I see someone who is punishing himself for choices made by other people. Your mother's drinking wasn't your fault. She didn't drink because of you; she didn't die because of you.'

'I didn't help her.'

'It wasn't in your control.' He punctuates this point with a little nod of his head. 'This country didn't commit to a string of unjust wars because of you. Your friend Mitch . . . didn't die because of anything you did wrong. Someone else placed that device there, not you. Mitch chose to save you. Do you hear me? That was his choice, and you are not to blame for his death. Carrying this stuff isn't like carrying a wardrobe on your back. This stuff will flatten you, my friend. It will, no matter how strong you are. You have to set it down. It's not your load to carry.'

227

'Whose is it, then?'

'God's, if you're that way inclined. Nobody's. You have to set it down, son.'

He looks at me with those armour-piercing eyes, giving me permission to cry. I look back and feel nothing. His eyes cut through an empty space.

'I understand what you're trying to do, Harry, but I can't.'

'Okay,' he says softly and places his hand on my back for a moment. 'I'll be back in five minutes. Don't go anywhere, alright?'

I nod and he gets up, scurries toward the back door, slips out and closes it gently. Alone again, I go to the loo, wash my face and run wet fingers through my hair. It makes me feel slightly less groggy but doesn't help my appearance much; I still look like an extra from a cheap zombie film.

Harry returns and hands me a warm, greasy paper parcel containing two bacon rolls. 'Breakfast.'

'Thank you.'

I follow him to the kitchen and demolish the first roll while he fills the kettle and makes a second round of tea.

'I'm sorry about this. I'll get you the money back.'

'I can afford a couple of bacon rolls. Here.' He places a mug in front of me and sits down opposite. For a minute or two, we lose ourselves in the comfort of salty meat and caffeine. I finish mine and tip back in my chair. The two front legs make a sticky sound as they lift off the floor.

'Mitch talks to me, Harry. I hear his voice in my deaf ear.'

Harry pauses chewing for a moment and looks at me, eyebrows arched, then swallows this information with a slug of tea.

'What does he say?'

I shrug. 'He commentates on whatever I happen to be up to. He sings, he . . . calls me an arsehole from time to time. He remarks about women. Sometimes he goes quiet for a while and then he just speaks up out of the blue.'

'When did you first hear him?'

'Just . . . the minute he died. We were thrown metres through the air and he was lying on top of me. His legs were blown clean off and he was bleeding out right there. His blood was so hot it felt like someone had poured a flask of tea all over me. I was clinging onto him, and . . . he told me to let him go. So I did, and that was it. Next thing I heard in that ear was him singing Hank Williams.'

'Hank Williams?'

'*Lost Highway*. He liked hillbilly music.'

Harry smiles for a moment, but it fades. 'Does he tell you to do things?'

'Sometimes.'

'Do you do them?'

I laugh. 'Only the sensible ones. Will I go out and murder someone because the voice in my head tells me to? No, of course I fucking won't. My sister thinks I will.'

Harry blows out a long breath but doesn't say anything.

So I try to force his hand. 'Do you?'

His reply is indirect, but clear enough. 'Have you ever spoken to a doctor or a counsellor about this?'

'Aye. They said it was trauma-induced psychosis or some bloody thing. They put me on medication, which totally strung me out but didn't get rid of Mitch.'

He considers this for a moment. 'Do you *want* to get rid of him?'

229

'I . . . want him to be at peace.'

'You think he's not? Do you think he's a ghost?'

'I think . . . it's him, somehow . . . part of him. Part of something that got left behind. I mean, you know I really am crazy now so I can't make it any worse by saying this. I think . . . he needs something from me before he can go.'

'What does he need?'

'I don't know that either.'

'Why don't you ask him?'

'I do. He says I have to figure it out by myself.'

Harry rubs his belly. 'Maybe he wants you to figure out what *you* need, Sean. Maybe you have to go away and figure it out.'

'Yeah, there's a place where people like me go away to figure things out, it's called the Royal Edinburgh. Billy and I could be roommates.'

'I wasn't suggesting that at all. I thought more on the lines of a holiday, somewhere away from here. A beach somewhere. Somewhere you can just relax and stop running for a few days. Have you had a holiday since you left the Marines?'

'No.' My eyes nip and I press my fingers into them. 'Ach, maybe you're right.'

'I also think you need to get some professional help.'

A wet blanket of disappointment settles over me. 'I knew we'd get round to this.' I stand up, walk toward the window, stare out at seagulls investigating rubbish in the grotty carpark behind the building. 'You're a counsellor, Harry, or at least you do a good impression of one. I can talk to you.'

'I'm your manager. It's not appropriate. Would you let me introduce you to someone?'

'Who?'

'Chick Thomson. He's a friend of mine, going back to our Navy days. He was a doctor for years, and when he retired he trained up as a counsellor. He works with a lot of ex-servicemen, and knows as much as anyone about Post Traumatic Stress. I think you'd like him.'

'You were in the Navy? Why didn't you tell me that?'

'I didn't want you to think I gave you the job out of sympathy, because I didn't. I never went to war. But we're not talking about me, Sean. Will you let me take you to meet Chick?'

Too worn down to protest, I shrug and lean my arse on the warm radiator. 'I'll think about it.'

He offers me a reassuring smile, though I think he'd prefer to drive me off to see his mate this very minute. 'That's good enough for now. Meantime, the crew'll be here soon. Maybe you should go home and get some rest.'

I nod. 'Thanks for . . . you know . . . being alright with me. I appreciate it.'

He dumps our dishes in the sink. 'You're welcome. And thank you for telling me about Mitch. Now get yourself home, get cleaned up and let your sister know where you are. I think maybe a few days off, eh? Take a week if you want.'

'What, just . . . now? Are you suspending me?'

'No, I'm asking you to take a few days off for the sake of your health. You're exhausted, I've been noticing that for a while now. You can take sick leave if you'd rather keep your annual. I'll help Jack in the van if I have to.'

'What about Chick Thomson?'

'You just let me know when you're ready.'

I take a deep breath and nod, anticipating pain and unpleasantness, as though I'm about to receive my first round of cancer treatment. Which, in a way, maybe I am.

231

XXIV

Back at the house I bolt two bowls of cornflakes and listen to last night's voicemails.

Janet: *Sean, I can't believe you. You're so fucking lucky I followed you, or you'd be in the bloody jail by now. You need to come home. We need to talk about this. Don't be a baby about this, please.*

Janet again: *Where the hell are you? Look, I'm sorry, alright? I guess this is partly my fault . . . I know it is. I should have told you before. But it still doesn't justify what you did. Duncan . . . he'll be alright, you just gave me a fright. Will you please call me?*

Molly: *It's me. I feel awful and I . . . don't really know what to say. Call me when you've calmed down a little. And please . . . don't do anything stupid, alright, Sean? I couldn't live with myself.*

Paula: *Hey. So ehm . . . Janet phoned me. I guess she thought you were with me. I wish you were with me too, but . . . well . . . you're not. Guess what? Eva slept six hours last night. I feel human again. Simple pleasures really are the best things in life at the end of the day. You know I really do love you, right? Maybe you don't, so I'm telling you. I always have. When I married Ewan . . . I wished it had been you standing there. Shocker, eh? Please call me, Sean. Let me know you're okay.*

Janet: *Oh, wee man, I'm sorry. Please just let me know you're alright.*

Three women and how many pleases? My face burns in a way that only happens when you know you've done something shamefully idiotic. More than that, I realise that my actions have been those of war: interrogating, intimidating, attacking. Brutally attacking with intent to kill. I have forgotten rules of engagement in normal peaceful civilian existence, or maybe excused myself from them for reasons that would never hold up anywhere except in my own head.

I stare at the phone for a moment with an invisible set of fingers around my throat, then switch it off again, wash my dishes and head upstairs. After a shower, I collapse face-first into my pillow.

Mrs McGrath, the Sergeant said, would you like a soldier of your son Ted?

My eyes open into the stale pillowcase and I turn over. 'Mitch . . .'

With a scarlet coat and a big cocked hat, Mrs McGrath, would you like that?

I sit up and look around, as if I might find him hovering somewhere just out of reach. 'I'm trying to sleep here.'

I'm trying to sing here. With a too-ri-ay-fol-diddle-aye-ay . . .

'After the kind of night I've had? Take your fucking *too-ri-diddly* shite and occupy somebody else's head.'

Well Captain dear, where have you been? Have you been sailing the Mediterranean? And have you news of my son Ted? Is he living or is he dead?

'Mitch, go and move something. Make the door creak or . . . do something ghostly. Prove you're not just a voice in my head.'

Then up comes Ted without any legs, and in their place two wooden pegs . . .

233

'Come on, buddy, you can do it.'

She kissed him a dozen times or two, and said My God, Ted, is that you?

He's fading out again. I think I can hear him laughing. 'Mitch . . . please?'

Oh was you drunk or was you blind, when you left your two fine legs behind? Or was it walking upon the sea that wore your two fine legs away?

'Mitch, it has to be you!' I'm shouting into the still, empty house, not a thump or a creak to be heard.

I'm beyond sleep now, wired and twitchy as I used to get before heading out on operations. Guys used to pace, chain smoke, wank furiously, fight, pack and unpack and pack their kit again: anything to kill the anticipation. I heard of people killing themselves with pills and of Americans who went mad and turned machine guns on their own men. I used to run in frustrated circuits around the perimeter of the camp, but Mitch would just sit and pick that guitar and sing. Eyes closed, smiling, content. I think he actually loved war.

Maybe we all did, once.

I get up again and dress myself in camo trousers and a black t-shirt, thick socks and boots. Then I drag my Bergen down from the top of the wardrobe and begin stuffing things into it: spare pants and socks, water-proofs, my favourite bandana, hat and gloves, knife, torch, camel pack for water, a couple of thin fleece tops, spare trousers, two packs of Ibuprofen tablets, first aid kit, midge spray, compass, OS maps, wallet, phone, toothbrush and towel, sleeping bag and bivvy bag, primus and billycan. Then I thump downstairs and raid the kitchen for any reasonably portable and non-perishable foods I can find: some cereal bars, a chorizo sausage,

234

raisins, a Soreen's fruit loaf, a pack of KitKats, a jar of peanut butter and a spoon.

Loaded up, Bergen slung over one shoulder, I leave the house again and walk toward the bus stop with the urgency of a man on the run from the law or his wife. The stop is busy, mainly with old grey women with walking sticks and young grey women with bairns in pushchairs. A couple of the younger ones stare at me and whisper comments, and I look purposefully at my phone so that they'll know I'm occupied by something important.

On the bus into Edinburgh I stare out the window and see little except the flotsam and jetsam of a throwaway world: blown plastic bags caught in hedges, fast food packaging strewn across sports pitches, Saddos in door-ways. The city looks ugly and has the feel of a place that is not so much suffering recession as terminal decline. There's too much shit in this nest. I want to leave. I want to go somewhere clean, wipe the memory files and start again.

I get off at Waverley Station and buy a single ticket to Fort William. Then I draw a couple of hundred quid out of the cashpoint, buy a kingsized bag of fruit pastilles, a little lined notebook and a large coffee to go, then hop onto the 10:15 train to Glasgow Queen Street.

I only get my phone out again once the train has cleared Edinburgh's dreary western reaches and is speed-ing into the West Lothian countryside. Pulling up Janet's number, I suck in a deep breath and steel myself for the inevitable lecture.

Her voice almost falls down the line at me. 'Sean? Oh thank God. Please tell me you're alright.'

'I'm alright. I'm sorry about last night.'

I can hear her sigh. 'Aye. Well . . . that makes two of us. Where did you sleep?'

'The shop. Is Duncan okay?'

'That depends how you define okay, I suppose. He says he's taken worse beatings.'

'He's inflicted worse too. He's done time for it.'

'That doesn't justify anything, Sean. But anyway, he's alive. I don't think he's fit to live up there on his own. The place is squalid and cold and miles from anywhere. He doesn't even have a phone. The poor man is totally isolated. I'd like to speak to Molly about trying to get him into some kind of sheltered housing.'

'It's up to you.'

'What do you think?'

'I have no opinion on the matter at all. You're the expert on these things; do what you think is best.'

'He's your father, Sean.'

'No, Janet, he isn't. He gave up any right to call himself that years ago. I want nothing to do with him.'

'You'd just see him suffer up there on that hill?'

'No more or less than anyone else. If you think he needs to live somewhere else, you see what you can do about it and try to convince him he's got to move.'

'I'd rather talk about this face to face.'

'I'm kind of tired of talking. Anyway, I'm on a train.'

Her calm tone cracks a little. 'You're on a train now? A train to where?'

'Fort William. I need to get out in the hills for a few days. Harry said I could have some time off.'

'How long?'

'I'll see how I feel. I'll call you, eh?'

There is a troubled pause. 'Sean . . . you will come back, won't you?'

'No, I'm just gonna to take off into the hills forever. For fucksake, Scotland's not that big.'

'That's not what I meant.'

'I know what you meant, and I cannae believe you're even asking.'

I can, Mitch interjects, and I put my fingers over my bad ear and stare out the window at a scrubby plantation of birch trees screening industrial waste ground.

'I just want you to be safe.'

I sigh. 'Okay, look, I'm taking a wee holiday and I'll be home in a few days. That's all, I promise.'

'You'd better.'

She's annoying me now. 'Aye, I will. See you later, alright?'

'Sean . . .'

'Goodbye, Janet.'

I end the call, sip my coffee and sit there absorbing the gentle rattle of the train. I think about calling Paula and decide against it, switch off the phone to save the battery. Then I stand and pull the Bergen down from the overhead rack, dig out the maps and heave the pack back up again.

The rest of the way to Glasgow, I plot a dozen or more possible routes through mountains that feel like old friends. The Ring of Steall, the Mamores, the Aonachs, the Devil's Staircase and the Glen Etive Slabs, the damp scramble through Glencoe's Lost Valley to the summit of Bidean nam Bian. The high windswept boglands of Rannoch Moor, where you hear nothing but air stirring the heather and the rasping calls of ravens. Places where we trained, hill tracks we ran light-footed in trainers or trudged in full webbing, rivers we forded, the best places to catch rabbits or poach salmon, ridges where we roped up and moved blind through winter blizzards, rock faces we climbed and abseiled down. Sometimes we felt like Boy Scouts, that we were out there for no reason other than the pure joy of being outside and of pushing our

237

bodies through cold and fatigue toward something like euphoria.

At Queen Street I switch to the West Highland Line and bag a table seat so I can continue perusing the maps, but at the last possible moment three red-faced Englishmen in their fifties pile on and breathlessly invade the table with wafts of beer and aftershave.

'It's your lucky day, mate,' says the man who squeezes in next to me. He produces a six-pack of Boddingtons cans from a plastic Tesco bag. He shares the beer out to his mates and offers a fourth to me. 'A little token of my gratitude for letting us share your table.'

'Nah, you're alright. Thanks anyway.'

'Go on, there's plenty more. We're on our jollies. Stag week. Mikey here's getting married next month.' His words are muddy over the grind of the diesel engine.

I glance up at Mikey, the man sitting across from me. He's got short-cropped hair in a suspect tone of reddish brown, puffy eyes and a Wasps rugby shirt.

'Congratulations.'

He laughs. 'Third time lucky, eh? Still, a good enough excuse for a party. Have a beer, Jock.'

Go on, Nic, you abstemious old monk, let your hair down.

Fuck off, Mitch.

I consider moving, but there aren't many free seats left and my choices seem now to be limited to sharing with fractious children or American tourists. Quickly I assess my options: revert to antisocial type, turn down the beer and pretend to sleep all the way to Fort William, or just take one and drink it for the sake of international relations.

I force a laugh. 'Alright, just the one. Thanks.'

'Good man,' says the boy next to me, sliding the can over.

238

I crack it open and raise it to my lips to catch the overflowing foam. It tastes surprisingly good and I swallow two or three mouthfuls before putting it down again. Mitch applauds in the background, makes some jeering remark about me popping my honorary cherry and starts to sing *Hearts of Oak*.

The grubby little diesel chuffer makes its way out of Glasgow's northern suburbs and up along the muddy shore of the Clyde. Mikey and his pals drink and plan a night on the town in Fort Bill: meal and pub crawl, followed by a boogie if such a thing can be found in the back of beyond. Tempted to wonder why they bothered to leave London for a second rate West Highland curry, I enjoy the warmth of the beer in my chest as I set about my maps again.

The man next to me says something. I glance up again to find him peering over my shoulder at the map.

'Pardon?'

'You going walking?'

'Aye.'

'Where you going?'

'Haven't decided yet. Wherever my feet take me.'

'We're doing The Ben tomorrow. Nevis.'

'Are you really?' A vision of them puking and farting their way up the tourist trail: heart attacks on legs. The kind of walkers the mountain rescue guys dread.

'You done it?'

I smile. 'Once or twice.'

Once or twice. You remember the last time?

Aye, I remember the last time. You nearly killed us down Five Finger Gully, you Taff bastard. You never did learn to navigate properly.

Only a fucking Yeti could have navigated through that storm.

239

'Sure he has,' says Mikey. Jock's a squaddie, ain't ya, Jock?'

'Say again?'

'I said you look like you're in the army.'

'I was a bootneck. In a past life.'

'Blimey,' says Mikey appreciatively. 'This guy knows a thing or two about the Scottish hills, then. They all train up here, don't ya? I saw a documentary thingy on telly about it. What's your name, by the way?'

'Sure as fuck isn't Jock, anyway.'

Mikey bellows with laughter. 'Fair comment. I'm Michael.' He offers his hand and we shake across the table.

'Sean.'

'Pleased to meet ya, Sean. These reprobates are Ed and Simon.'

I nod at the pair of them.

'What's a bootneck, then?' the one called Ed asks, looking up from The Sun to check me properly out for the first time.

'A fucking Royal Marine Commando.' Mikey punctuates each word and puffs out his chest as though I'm his long lost best mate. 'Sean here's one tough geezer. Bet you've seen some action, Sean, haven't ya.'

I swallow about a third of the can in a single draught and nod, feeling half cut already. 'You might say that.'

'Where you been, then?'

Ed swats him with his paper. 'Jesus wept, Michael, give the man a break why don't you? Maybe he don't want to talk about it.' He looks at me. 'Don't mind him, he's pissed as a fart.'

Mikey nods. 'He's right, I am. Don't mind me. I know a guy at work whose son was in the Paras. He went to Afghanistan and got blown up. Roadside bomb, bang, nothing left of him but a grease spot in the dust. Nineteen, he was. Only been there a couple of weeks, left his girl alone with a brand new baby. Tell me something, Jock, is it worth it? Are we winning?'

'Nuh.'

'Seriously?'

I shrug. 'I killed a kid on my last tour. Thirteen, maybe fourteen years old. He came running at me with an antique Kalashnikov that didn't even work, but I shot him between the eyes before I realised that. The word *winning* doesn't apply to anybody in Afghanistan except bent politicians and opium barons. Taliban are just biding their time, till we leave.'

Ed puts down his newspaper and they all look at me.

'You asked,' I say by way of an apology, then drink some more and look out at verdant, bracken-covered hillsides rising steeply away from the train. We are moving past our own store of weapons of mass destruction at Faslane, toward Arrochar and the bottleneck of Loch Lomond. The guys drink and chat more quietly now and I get the distinct impression I've spoiled their party.

I see the kid's face superimposed over my own reflection in the window. I see him lying across his mother's lap, eyes turned blankly toward the puffy white clouds, blood oozing brackishly from the wound the way it does when the heart has stopped pumping. It was the dirt smudged on his chin that made him look like he had stubble, but up close he was a boy playing the hero, trying to scare us with his father's clapped out rifle. A father long dead, a mother crying to Allah, asking him to take her too. Goats bleating in the background as though nothing had happened.

I dropped my own rifle then, as though it had suddenly become too hot to touch, turned away and spewed my last meal into a wadi. That was the moment I cracked; the thrill of battle finally ended there, frozen in the dead stare of a child. I had to wait out another three months for an IED to send me home.

We arrive at Crianlarich station and sit out the usual bumps and jostles as the Oban half of the train detaches. My hospitable English companions offer me another beer and I take it. We chat about weather in the hills, the joys that are to be found in Fort William of an evening and rugby, where at least the comforting choice between winning and losing still holds.

My head swims a little and my eyes close for a while, sleep pulling my chin toward my chest. By Bridge of Orchy I am feeling slightly sick and desperate to be off the train, and instead of going all the way to Fort William, I decide to get off at Rannoch Station. It's only thirteen miles or so across the moor to Kingshouse, likely to be blissfully deserted, and the fair weather appears to be holding. The moor will be a tapestry of spring wildflowers, all fragile pinks and yellows amongst the still dark heather and patches of verdant moss, sun shimmering off lochans like polished steel. Tomorrow, depending on weather and my mood I can tackle the Aonach Eagach or the Buachaille. A vision of myself – brief but visceral, as though it's happened in a dream-- spreading my arms, flying from The Chancellor over Glencoe, and blowing away to hell like a crow on the shoulder of the wind.

XXV

I am the only person to step onto the tiny platform at Rannoch Station. Head foggy from the beer, I delve into my provisions and break off about a quarter of the fruit loaf and eat it with some peanut butter. After a few slugs of water, I hoist the pack onto my back and, still working the sticky sweet and salty goo off the roof of my mouth, set out on the track heading west toward the mountains. The sun beams in rays through silver clouds, and the wind comes out of the southwest with the sweet smell of gorse blossom. Where the track is dry and easy to follow I run, and my head empties of everything except the physical process of lifting one foot after another.

Endorphins carry me to Kingshouse, but begin to drain as soon as I head down the gradual slope from the moor toward the old hotel. It's dusk by the time I arrive, and there are two tents tucked into the heather behind the pub already. I am lured by the smell of chips into the climber's bar at the back, and park myself at the last empty table. It doesn't take many bodies to fill the small room, with its carved high-backed seats, wood fire and walls hung with mountaineering photos.

I let the Bergen slide onto a bench, then head for the bar and wait my turn behind a couple of guys in boots and gaiters. They're boisterous as they gather their pints, laughing about some misadventure on the hill. I order lasagne and chips and, after only a moment of swithering, a pint of Guinness. Back at my seat, I sip it slowly and take stock of myself: the now familiar tightness at the backs of my knees, a grumble in the lower back and a bit of chafing around my right ankle. Thirteen miles wouldn't usually faze me, but running in boots, with a loaded pack, is something altogether different. I'm not sure I'd pass the ML course now, if I had it to do over.

I loosen the laces of my boots, soak in the warmth of the fire and try not to throw back the Guinness too fast. The door creaks open, letting in a blast of cold air and a young woman in a Nepali hat with ear flaps and a bright green North Face jacket. Slim legs, stiff brown walking boots. She stands for a moment looking around for a seat, then takes off her hat and runs her fingers through long, honey-blond hair. The other tables are all occupied by groups, so she fixes her eyes first on the spare seat at my table and then on me.

'Is anyone sitting here?' A wee hopeful smile and a nice accent: west of Scotland, educated, comfortable in itself.

I sit up a little straighter and return the smile. 'I think you are.'

'Oh God, thank you.' She peels off her jacket and drapes it over the back of the chair, then walks stiffly to the bar and places an order for food. After a couple of minutes she returns, carrying a pint. She puts it down, warms her hands in front of the fire, then sits. Closes her eyes for just a moment with the relief of being off her feet, and takes a long drink. Her cheeks glow in the dim, flickering light.

She groans softly. 'I'm totally jiggered.' Then she looks up at me and smiles again. 'I'm Laura.'

'I'm Sean.'

'Are you on the West Highland Way as well?'

I laugh. 'No, I'm walking Sean's Way.'

Her brows draw together. 'Where's that go, then?'

'I don't know, I'll tell you when I get there.'

This gets a clear, rich laugh out of her and she says something generally appreciative, which I don't catch over the testosterone-fuelled conversations going on around us. I lean toward her and rest on my elbows, and she does the same. This is about the point where Mitch could be expected to chime in, but I haven't heard from him since I left the train.

'What about you?'

'West Highland Way. I left Glasgow four nights ago.'

I'm concentrating intently on her words, which probably gives the impression that I'm coming onto her. But then, she doesn't seem to mind.

'You're on your own?' I ask.

'I'm celebrating my singleness after five years with the most uptight man on the face of the earth. I'm doing a Nancy Sinatra.' She holds up a boot. 'I've got blisters on both feet and the fucking pack is killing me, but I'm loving it. I've met some incredible people on the way. Today I met two women riding these black highland ponies across the moor. They're riding the drovers' roads all the way to London for charity. Amazing. It seems like everyone out here has a story.'

I take a drink and consider this. 'Out here you realise it's your story that makes you who you are. It's not your house or your job or what mobile phone you've got. When your life is stripped down to the things you can carry on your back, you realise that your stories are the only things that matter.'

And right on cue: *Listen to this rubbish. I forgot what a twat you are when you drink, Nic.*

I ignore him and focus on Laura's face.

'That is so fucking right,' she says, and looks at me as though this is the most profound thing she's ever heard. 'You know what? That's exactly why I left John. Because he defined his life by his mobile phone.'

'Most people do.' I glance up as a weedy young waiter arrives with an enormous plate of lasagne and salad, with a bowl of chips on the side. My stomach growls on cue. I dig my fork in and take a large bite, yaffel it down almost without chewing. After three or four bites, I remember my manners. 'Sorry, Laura. I've had nothing but fruit loaf and peanut butter since Waverley Station this morning.'

'Fruit loaf and peanut butter?'

I like the little wrinkles at the bridge of her nose. 'Protein and sugar. Keeps you going.'

She shakes her head. 'Sounds disgusting. How's the lasagne?'

I pause to taste it. 'Right now it's the best meal I've ever had. I could eat the table as well, mind you.'

The waiter reappears with her meal: a cheeseburger and more chips. She unwraps the cutlery from the paper napkin and starts eating, almost as greedily as I am. After a few minutes, she sits back and wipes tomato sauce off her mouth and says something into her napkin.

I wash down a mouthful and look up. 'Say again.'

She nods at her plate, then pats her tummy. 'You can have the rest of my chips.'

'You sure?'

'Aye, go for it.' She slides her plate toward me.

'Thanks.' I tip her chips onto my plate and use them to polish off the last of the tomato sauce. 'Total gannet, eh?'

'You looked like you needed them. Where did you walk from today?'

246

'Rannoch Station. I ran most of the way.'

'You *ran*?' She clocks my Bergen. 'With that thing on your back?'

'Yep.'

'Jesus. Isn't that just a little bit masochistic?'

'Yeah, probably.'

'Okay, let me guess.' She cocks her head to one side and studies me carefully. 'You're training for something. Everest. That marathon thingy across the Sahara.'

'Everest?' I laugh. 'No. Not training for anything. Just running.'

'Then you're running *from* something.'

I shrug and drain my pint. 'Possibly. What you drinking?'

She smiles. 'Best.'

I go to the bar and order pints for both of us, watch the rings of foam rising to the top of the Guinness and wonder what pathetic story I might be able to concoct for her. I've got six months to live. My wife has gone off with my best friend. I'm looking for God on the road. All of the above.

I head back to the table and sit down. We drink and chat about meaningless things for a while and then Laura goes to the bar again to buy another round.

'So is it a girl you're running from?' she asks when she sits down.

I take a long drink. 'No.'

'A boy then?'

I raise an eyebrow. 'No. Not quite. Would you have been disappointed if I'd said yes?'

She flushes. 'Maybe, but I'd have got over it. So, Sean of Sean's Way, are you going to tell me what lies at the end of your quest?'

'Ehm . . .' I laugh. 'The Holy Grail. The Ring. Yoda.

247

I don't know.' I sigh and rub my hand over my chin. 'A life that's . . . a little different from the one I've had up to now. I'm just in an in-betweeny kind of place, Laura.'

She leans toward me again, her chin resting on her palm. 'So am I. It's a wee bit scary and a wee bit exciting.'

'I don't think I've got to the exciting part yet.'

'I can read palms, you know. Let me see and I'll tell you.'

'I dinnae believe in all that.'

'Give us a paw.' She takes hold of my right hand and draws it toward her, turns it over and traces her fingertips very lightly over my skin. Her hair brushes my arm.

'Ah ha,' she says softly. 'There's a break in your lifeline, just here.' She taps the middle of my hand. 'It gets a little lost, but it starts again here. You'll find your way soon.'

'That's good to know.'

She looks up at me and laughs, still holding onto my hand. 'I am bullshitting, you know. I can't really read palms.'

'You're just teasing me.'

'No, I'm definitely not teasing you. Where are you sleeping tonight?'

'Honestly?'

She grins, shrugs. 'Just asking. I'm a bit drunk and you're a bit nice, so I'm asking.'

'Okay . . . I'm a bit drunk too, so I'll tell you. Outside. In my bivvy.'

'A bivvy? That's it? I've got a whole two-man tent to myself.'

'A veritable palace.'

'You can share my palace if you want to.'

I clear my throat in astonishment. 'So, what's the deal? Is it a man a night between Glasgow and Fort William?'

She sits back and lets her mouth hang open. 'Is that how I come over?'

'No. Sorry, I didn't mean that. I've had too much to drink.'

'So have I.' She drains her pint and stands up. 'I need a pee.'

She disappears into the Ladies' for a couple of minutes, comes out with a damp, red face and pulls on her jacket. 'Come on, then. Unless you'd rather be in your bivvy all night.'

I finish my own drink, grab my Bergen and follow her outside toward a compact pup tent on the other side of the burn. It's cold and mostly dark now, a brilliant spray of stars showing through deepest blue, the black brooding masses of the hills all around us. There is a rush of wind through the stand of Scots pines in front of the hotel and a little burble of water, muffled laughter coming from inside, the occasional whoosh of a car passing on the road.

'Well, here we are, home sweet home.' She stops in front of the tent and turns toward me, wavering a little as if a second thought has entered her mind. I stand there like a kid on the doorstep after a first date.

Get some, Marine. An American voice: Texan.

Fuck off, Mitch. Do I get no privacy at all?

Laura looks over my shoulder curiously. 'What was that?'

I turn. 'What?'

'I thought I just saw . . .' She pauses for a moment, scanning the heather behind us. 'Nothing. I thought I saw someone.'

'Who?' I ask, too quickly.

'I don't know.' She shivers. 'Somebody just walked over my grave, I think.'

I am tempted to agree with her. 'The moor's a creepy old place at night.'

'Aye. Anyway, come in.' She turns on her torch, kneels and crawls in, kicking her boots off in the bell end before pulling her feet inside. I pull my ground mat and grot bag out of the Bergen, squat down and arrange them inside beside hers, then pull off my own boots and get in. The tent is barely high enough to sit up in, and we huddle there still fully clothed, staring at each other nervously.

'What, no nightcap?' I ask to break the ice.

She laughs softly, switches off the torch, then leans toward me and kisses me. I twine my fingers in her hair and kiss her back, then find the zip of her jacket and slip the rustling material off her shoulders like Christmas wrapping. We undress each other hungrily, peeling away layers of sweaty fleece and wool. I hate to think what I smell like, but she smells of Avon Skin So Soft, woodsmoke and fresh air.

Sex in a backpacking tent is a bit of a logistical nightmare and really only lends itself to the missionary position, but it's warm and companionable. She giggles at me as I scuff my head off the roof and eventually subside onto the sleeping bag beside her, chest pumping and pulse racing in my ears.

We lie there for a few minutes, until the night air begins to sting our skin. I pull on a shirt and clean boxers, and she wriggles into some blue thermals, then sits cross-legged on her sleeping bag, switches on her torch and peels off her socks to examine her heavily-plastered feet. It's definitely not the normal way to charm someone you've just met in a pub, but when you're walking, normal rules cease to apply.

She smiles at me. 'Sorry, you might want to look away now.'

250

I sit up. 'Let's see those.'

'God, no, they're minging. You don't need to look at my feet.'

'I've seen worse things, believe me. Give 'em to me.'

She lies back and rests her feet on my lap. I shine the torch on them, gently peel away the plasters and inspect the blisters. A couple of them have already burst and rubbed themselves raw.

'Let's sort you out.' I reach for my pack and locate the first aid kit, pull out a needle and a lighter. 'I'm going to lance the ones that haven't burst already, alright?' I hold the needle in the flame for a moment to sterilize it.

'Is this what you do to all the girls?'

I laugh. 'Only the ones who yomp across Scotland in boots that don't fit properly. Just . . . lie still and I'll try not to stab you, right?'

'Great.' She closes her eyes and wiggles her pink-tipped toes. 'One prick and it's the bivvy for you.'

'You'll thank me for this tomorrow.' I lean down and set to work, delicately poking each firm blister until a little bead of liquid appears, then pressing cotton wool over it and squeezing out as much of the water as I can. When they're all done, I rub antiseptic cream on them and leave them unbandaged.

As I work, Laura finds the RMC flash stitched onto my Bergen, beside my name and stripes. 'McNicol,' she says softly, running her fingers over the dagger. 'Is this you? Sean McNicol. Sergeant.'

'Yep.'

'Royal Marine Corps. So that's how you know what to do about blisters.'

'Look after your feet. It's the first thing they teach you. I knew guys who dropped out of training because of blisters.'

'I don't blame them.' She smiles. 'Are you on leave?'

'No, I've been out a little while.'

'Is that why you're in an in-betweeny place?'

'Yeah. Well . . . sort of.'

'I understand,' she says, and to her credit doesn't ask any more. Instead, she yawns and wriggles her toes again. 'That's much better. Thank you, Sean.'

'You're welcome. Bandage them up in the morning. I think I've got one as well, here.' I peel my own sock down and examine the rubbed area on my ankle. 'Almost.'

She squirms around and looks at my ankle, then takes my foot onto her lap and massages it firmly with her thumbs. I lie back with my arms behind my head, and the aches seem to melt out of my body as she works away on one foot, then the other.

I close my eyes. 'That's incredible.'

'Mmm. They say there's a connection between every part of your body and a nerve somewhere in your foot. It's very effective pain relief.'

'Well, it's working a treat.'

'You've never had a foot rub before?'

'Not often. It's not something that's done in the Marines, as a matter of course. If there's any rubbing to be done, it's not usually of feet. I mean, maybe there's the odd guy with a fetish or something, but generally speaking . . .'

She giggles and begins to run her hand up my leg. 'I don't have to stop at feet.'

'Neither do I.' I turn onto my side and let my fingers work their way up the inside of her own leg, until they find their way into her thermals. She breathes deeply, then slips her hand round the back of my head and pulls me toward her.

After a second go-round, I lie beside her and we don't talk for a few minutes. The wind pushes at the walls of the tent and makes the pine branches creak. Maybe it's just the beer or the afterglow of sex, but a fragile peace has fallen over me like a feather come to rest on a fencepost. I hardly dare to breathe for fear of sending it sailing upward again, but for now it lingers. Duncan Campbell, Molly and her photographs and Cauldhill Farm might be a thousand miles away.

My eyes begin to close as fatigue catches up with me. It's all I can do to force myself up again, locate my toothbrush, pull on some clothes, slide my feet into my boots and stumble outside for a swamp and a notional wash. I run the brush over my teeth, splash my face with cold water from the burn and take a long swig from my camel pack, then walk for a minute or two along the drive toward the road to clear my head. There is laughter coming from inside the pub, but outside it's still and, although there is still a blue-ish glow in the west, extremely dark. The Milky Way is a vivid bandolier across the sky, dizzying to look at. I tilt my head back and stare up until I feel tiny and lost and in danger of being swept away into space.

I won't tell Paula if you won't. It'll be our little secret.

'Oh fucking hell, Mitch, what are you trying to do?'

She loves you, Nic. Honest to God, real life, grown up LURVE, while you're rolling in the heather with a stranger. You want to sort out your priorities, buddy boy.

I leave the drive and head for the trees, thankfully remembering that beer makes me prone to shouting. I reply in a barely controlled whisper, 'We haven't committed to anything. You remember. You heard me. She'll understand.'

She'll say she does.

'So . . . what? What you trying to say?'

I'm saying, don't blow it. I'm saying mind where you go this time, my friend.

'I always minded where I went.'

You were depressed and punishing yourself for the kid, and it made you careless. You still are. Harry was right. About blaming yourself for other people's decisions. What's the bloody point of that?

I open my mouth to deny this, but even in my semi-intoxicated state I can see the ridiculousness of lying to a voice in my head. 'We should never have been there in the first place. We had no business being there.'

Well, the next time you happen to bump into Tony Blair you can tell him.

'What do you think, Mitch?'

I think men fight because it's in our nature to fight. Like baboons. We justify it with politics because we like to think we're cleverer than they are, but we're not. So there's no point worrying about what should or shouldn't happen, because it's always going to happen.

'So that makes it alright?'

Was it alright to kick the shite out of Duncan? Was doing that any more justified because you have business with him?

'No.'

Ah, Hallelujah! He's capable of answering a question. Let me ask another one. Are you capable of letting anyone love you? And are you capable of loving them back? Or is resentment the best you can manage?

'That's three questions, and I don't know.'

Come on, let's have an answer.

'That is my fucking answer! I don't know!'

Now I am properly shouting. My voice seems to reverberate off the surrounding hills, and I cringe at the sound of it.

Well figure it out. There. That's your hint.

'My hint?' I whisper.

Figure it out.

I stand there, wishing all of a sudden that I didn't have to go back to Laura's tent. If she was sound asleep and I could retrieve my gear without waking her, I would happily melt away into the blackness of the moor.

Laura is dozing in her sleeping bag when I crawl in beside her. She wriggles closer and nuzzles her cheek into the crook of my shoulder. I lie there with my arm around her and my eyes wide open as she drifts off. Wind pushes at the tent and footsteps pass by, bursts of drunken laughter, the trickle of water in the burn. The pub grows quiet, the wind strengthens and weakens and sleep stays just out reach.

So I lie awake and a route begins to unfold itself in my mind, the path through the mountains clear as the contours of a lover's body, until I arrive at what seems an appropriate end point. What happens when I get there is less clear, but in a way it doesn't matter. As Mitch always said, the fixed points on the map matter less than the road you take between them.

I open my eyes to sunlight, the incessant twitter of a skylark and a dull, dehydrated throb in my head. Laura is still out cold beside me: a lumpy red sleeping bag with a fringe of yellow hair poking out the top. As quietly as I can, I extract myself and crawl out into the cold damp morning, my mouth thick with the tastes of sex and beer. A wave of dizziness passes over me and I step delicately across the heather in my bare feet, kneel beside the burn, plunge my hands into the water and bring up two big cupped handfuls to my face. It's so cold that my breath catches in my chest and my teeth ache.

There is nobody about and the road is quiet; it must still be very early. I sit by the burn for a minute or two in my tee-shirt and boxers, then go back to the tent, pull on my trousers and socks and begin stuffing my sleeping bag into its sack.

Laura stirs. She unzips her sleeping bag a little, raises her head and looks at me, then at her watch. There are creases from her sleeping bag across her face.

'It's not even five.' Her voice crackles with sleep.

'I'm gonna get moving,' I say softly, pulling the drawstring around the top of the stuffsack.

'Which way are you going?'

'To Kinlochleven, then up over the Mamores.'

She sits up, rubs her eyes. 'I'll see you over the Devil's Staircase if you want to wait a bit.'

I pause to consider this, then smile. 'Sean's Way needs to be walked alone, I'm afraid.'

Laura doesn't protest, but watches me as I press a couple of ibuprofen tablets out of the packet and wash them down with water from my camel pack. Then I break off a wedge of fruit loaf and chew on it as I stow the rest of my gear and lace up my boots.

'Bite?' I offer her a bit of the fruit loaf.

A pained expression crosses her face. 'No thanks. I can't eat this early.'

'Okay.' I pop the last of it into my mouth, then stick my arms into the sleeves of the old standard issue green woolly pully which has been with me since Lympstone. 'I had a very nice night. Thank you.'

'So did I. I hope Sean's Way takes you where you need to go.'

I nod. 'Me too.' Then I lean in and kiss her once, on the cheek. 'Cheers, Laura. Look after those feet.'

We part without exchanging numbers and I swing my Bergen onto my back and follow the little wooden waymarks for the West Highland Way, heading toward the mouth of Glencoe.

XXVI

At Altnafeadh I get out my primus and make tea, have a cereal bar and an apple, and watch a raven rising from the craggy face of the Buachaille.

Raven or eagle? Macpherson asked us once, mid-way through our ML training. We were huddled around a meagre campfire, shivering against a Hebridean November howler, half starving after days of foraging. *If you had the choice to be one or the other, which would you be?*

Eagle, we answered, to a man.

Raven, said Macpherson. *The eagle's hunt won't always be successful, no matter how good he is. The raven eats what he finds, and he can always find something. That's why he's laughing, chaps.*

I drink my tea and watch the raven. He laughs his familiar coarse laugh, like a chesty old miner, circling above the mountains. The sun climbs higher and steam begins to rise from the peat, along with clouds of midges which promise misery later on if the wind doesn't pick up. A couple of walkers are now making their way toward me from the direction of Kingshouse, another couple behind them.

I pull off my jumper again, pack up quickly to avoid the onset of the West Highland Way morning rush hour, and make my way up the Devil's Staircase at a jog.

I trot into Kinlochleven a couple of hours later,

head for the Co-op, stock up on food and water (*Sorry Macpherson*, I think as I stand in the queue to pay for my provisions, *my scavenging days are well and truly behind me*). Then I make my way through the village, across the bridge over the river Leven and up the steep track that leads through the Mamore Forest. It has become almost hot and I sweat out the remnants of last night's Guinness as I reach the top of the incline and head into the Lairig Mor, which leads between the Mamores toward Fort William.

I camp wild beside a little tumbledown wall, the remnant of one of the many shielings that used to populate this glen. It's a mild, dry evening and I make a fire, boil my kettle over it to save gas, drink tea and eat a couple of Cornish pasties warmed over the fire, dried fruit, chocolate. Little rustles and snaps make me start from time to time, and I have to take a deep breath and remind myself where I am. I am too far into the wilderness for any Kinlochleven chavs to claim I've stolen their boozing spot, and Scotland's wilderness is a defeated landscape, emptied by force, with nothing left to pose any threat except weather. And even that is subdued tonight.

So I sit very still and listen to the cries of oystercatchers, the far-off bleating of sheep and the wind in the grass. Words come to my mind, form themselves into sentences and fall apart again: things I should have said, and things I still have to say. Things I might once have been ashamed of, but which no longer seem shameful. Sometimes I am almost aware of him sitting beside me, but he's quiet, as though he understands that I need time to gather my thoughts before I can answer his questions.

I sleep hard and in the morning leave the West Highland Way and head north into the Mamores, following a semi-circular line of peaks from Stob Bàn to An

259

Gearanach. Sometimes I pass other walkers and we stop to chat for a few minutes, sharing information about the condition of the path or the weather back where we came from. There's rain coming in tomorrow, I'm told. It's hard to believe, looking out at an almost cloudless blue sky, but things change brutally up here. Rain on low ground could fall as snow up here, even in May.

The end of the third day brings me down into the verdant glen below the waterfall of An Steall Bàn. I camp in a little hollow filled with wood sorrel and bluebells and wake up to the sound of the persistent, pattering rain that has moved in overnight. The sphagnum moss is like a wet sponge under me.

In the meagre shelter of my bivvy I eat two cereal bars, more peanut butter and a bunch of raisins, and manage to boil up some water for tea. I wriggle into my waterproofs and force myself out into the rain, packing up quickly, trying and failing to keep things dry. Above me, the hills disappear into mist and I pull my map and compass out of my pack and keep them handy in my jacket pocket.

It's a long, bleak slog over the Grey Corries in the cloying mist, which gathers like ghosts in the hollows and threatens to lead me in the wrong direction more than once. As I climb the rain congeals into sleet, then back to rain again as I drop down, and in some places ground blizzards obscure the path so navigating becomes a technical affair. After four days, I'm tired and my knees have begun to ache in earnest. My pace has slowed and I can hear Macpherson bellowing through the mist: *Let's get moving, ladies! My granny could have climbed this hill by now, with two hip replacements and a fucking colostomy bag!* I can't lift my legs any faster. Twice I slide and land heavily on loose, wet scree. Pain judders through my body, but I get up again and force myself to keep moving. I don't even let myself sit down to eat.

As I walk, I dig down into layers of memory, past Afghanistan, Mitch, the Marines, to those shadowy remnants of childhood which serve as my rather shoogly foundations. Janet was right; the brain blocks things out for good reason. I sift through redacted history. I turn over fragments: my mother arguing with a man in a swing park; a man, possibly the same one, in our front room doing his best to ignore my efforts to maul him with a stuffed monkey. So many guys progressed meaninglessly in and out of her life that I never paused before to wonder who this particular gaunt, angry person was.

No doubt she would have thought she loved him. Mum thought she loved all of them, even if they only hung about for a few days. And no doubt she would have pressed a pack of frozen peas to her battered face and accepted his fumbling, gutless apologies time and time again. Janet would have been around, at least sometimes, and would have had very clear memories of him. She must have witnessed their fights, and I wonder what it's cost her to keep them secret all these years.

She was right about another thing: I have not found a father. I have found a decaying wraith who will soon leave this world for some black place, with or without help from me. Anything he might once have been, before the army and the drink and the years of hollow lonely life on that hill, is dead already.

That will not be my life. This is the one thought that keeps me going as a mixture of sleet and sweat drips down the back of my neck. The RMC took me apart and rebuilt me once, and Afghanistan has taken me apart again. The pieces are so small and jumbled now, I can put them back in any order I want. Or not, as the case may be.

I stand at the cairn at the top of Stob Coire na Ceannain and shout it into mist so thick my words echo back at me: 'THAT WILL NOT BE MY FUCKING LIFE!' I shout it three times, until my voice breaks.

By the time I stumble down into the relative civilisation of Spean Bridge, ten hours after crawling out of my bivvy this morning, conscious thought has dissolved into a haze of pain, cold and hunger. The only place open is the aptly named Commando Bar at the Spean Bridge Hotel, so I go inside and pointedly ignore the tourists and RMC memorabilia on the walls on my way to the Gents. Leaving little muddy pools on the floor, I pull off my boots, strip off my sodden waterproofs, shirt and socks and dig into the rucksack for dry kit. Dressed and slightly drier, I stand at the sink and hold my peat-stained hands under the warm water until my fingers thaw enough to move freely again. I down a couple more ibuprofen tablets, empty my camel pack and refill it with fresh water, then gather my gear and mop up after myself as best I can with a paper towel. At the bar I order a steak pie and boiled spuds, a pint of Best and a double Glenlivet.

I find a seat in the back corner of the pub, subside onto the bench, splash a little water into the whisky and take a large sip. Even watered down it burns in my belly and makes me shudder, but almost immediately its heat squeezes into my bones. I close my eyes and lean my head back against the bench, slip my feet out of my unlaced boots and sit there in my socks. The voices around me melt into each other and become indistinguishable, and I doze, dream that I'm walking on a crust of deep snow into an arctic blue sky. A sky with no stars and no end, a sky that could sweep you off the earth and swallow you. Mitch is walking in front of me, leaving no footprints at all.

Then I'm falling. I'm shouting for him but he can't hear me. I hit some kind of bottom and my eyes pop open. My shoulders snap back against the upholstered seat. I am dizzy from the whisky and blood rushes in my ears.

After a while my food arrives and I eat mechanically, hand to plate to mouth and back again until the white china is polished clean and the hollow ache in my belly has disappeared. I order sticky toffee pudding and coffee, finish them quickly, then slide my feet into my boots and pull on my clammy, smelly anorak. At the bar I ask for another double measure of whisky, knock it back and pay up.

I head outside, sit on a bench and pull my phone out of my rucksack, lace up my boots while I'm listening to the voicemails. There are only three: two tremulous and frustrated messages from Janet, which I disregard, and one from Molly:

I'm afraid I've turned your life on its head at a time when you needed things to be stable; it seems I have a talent for doing that to people. I hope you're going to be okay, and I hope you come home soon. I want to talk to you about the farm. I honestly would like you to help me with my idea. Call me, alright?

I look up. The clouds have started to break in the face of a stiff breeze from the northwest. Gradually the hills emerge from their cloaks of mist, their snowy tops glowing pink and gold. It is light long into the evening now, so I stand, hoist my Bergen onto my back and start walking again on wobbly legs.

263

XXVII

The Commando Memorial occupies a hillside a mile or so above Spean Bridge. The three bronze soldiers stand on their plinth looking out over the commanding mass of Scotland's highest mountains: the Grey Corries, the Aonachs and Ben Nevis, its hunched, bulky top in clear view. The only other people here are a group of young men, snapping photos of the memorial and of the sun just slipping down behind the hills. I sit on a bench for a little while, eyes on them, waiting for them to leave. They're big, fit buggers with short hair, possibly soldiers but more likely students. They glance at me a few times and I sit there like some kind of half-cracked assassin, still enough to feel my body sway with my own pulse, pretending I'm made of stone. One guy whispers to his mate, and at last they head down the hill to the car park.

When they've driven away I head for the little garden of remembrance, which has been built more recently to the side of the original memorial. It is a low, circular granite wall framing a ring of memories: flowers, impromptu crosses, wreaths of poppies, candles, photographs, faces fixed in time.

I look at each one, walking slowly around the circle with sweating palms. I find four men I knew: snipers Ryan Brigham and Joshua Meeks, who were blown to oblivion by an American airstrike outside of Basra, Colin Richards who was shot in the head within a week of arriving in Helmand on his first operation, and Mitch. A smile like the moon in his passing out photo, a boy's face as yet untarnished by the job he has signed himself up for. A wreath of poppies has been left under the photo, with a message on laminated plastic card: "To our Gareth. We never needed proof that you were a hero. *Gorwedd mewn hedd*. With love, always. Mam and Dad."

I drop to my knees and sit on my heels. 'I walked here for you, you bastard. I hope you're listening.'

I've been listening to you whinging for two years now. It took you long enough.

'Why did you do it, Mitch? I didn't want you to die for me.'

Like I said, maybe you should have watched your feet a bit more carefully that day then.

'I'm sorry mate. I'm so fucking sorry. I just didn't see it. I was tired of watching my feet. Tired of watching other guys' backs. Just . . . tired of all of it. You know I was.'

Would you rather I had let you cop it?

'Yes.'

Fucking get to it then, if that's what you really want.

I drop my pack onto the ground and pull my FS knife out of the side pocket, unsheathe it, tilt it to catch the last of the light. It's a brutal thing, purchased years ago in a fit of pride, never used in anger except on small animals destined for a billy can.

The wind pushes at my back like a hand and my heart thunders. I sit with my back to the stone wall, push up my sleeve and press the point into the tender skin on the inside of my elbow. Very slowly, I draw it down the length of my forearm, raising a hairline of blood. I smear the blood across my skin like finger paint. Then I draw another line parallel to the first, and then a third. Finally I pause at the blue ridge of the radial artery at the wrist. The pressure in my chest makes it hard to breathe.

Is this your final answer, or would you like to phone a friend?

'I'm not listening to this. You're dead, alright? Shut the fuck up for once. Just stop talking!'

If you end yourself in a Scottish sheep field I fucking swear that I will never stop talking. I will personally torment your cowardly soul for eternity.

I press the tip down until it punctures the skin, but at the very last moment I pull the blade away from my wrist and instead drag seven inches of honed Sheffield steel across the inside of my left hand.

The pressure releases, breath explodes from my lungs in a gasp and I shout into the gathering darkness: 'YOU BASTARD, MITCH!'

I open my palm to see blood seeping out of the gash, stare at it until my vision blurs and tears burn down my cheeks. 'I fucking loved you, alright? There's your answer.'

I loved you too. I'd have given up women for you. What else could I have done that day?

'I'd have done the same for you. You know I would.'

I know, Nic.

The knife falls onto the ground and I press my hands over my face, blood mixing with tears and snot. I'm rocking back and forth in the gravel, gut contracting so hard that I can barely force in a breath. It feels like I might cry forever.

Minutes – hours – lifetimes later, I become aware of a ferocious ache in my hand and cramp in my knees. The tears begin to choke themselves off, but I am shivering with pain and cold and pure fatigue.

'Mitch? You still here?'

Are you?

'Apparently.'

What now, boss?

I pause for a moment, listening to the wind in the trees and the cry of gulls. 'I guess my name wasn't on that one.'

I could have told you that, but you wouldn't listen.

'What about you?'

I'm tired, Sean. You've knackered me out.

'Stay with me just a wee bit longer.'

Alright. You'd better sort that hand out.

My breath shakes and I'm starting to feel light-headed, possibly shocky. One-handed I dig into my pack and find the first-aid kit and head torch. I flush my hand with a little water and examine the wound; it's long and deep and will need stitching. For now, I dab some antiseptic on it and bandage it tightly. Then I pull on my hat and jumper, coorie into my sleeping bag, sit back and nibble some chocolate. The wind cuts my cheeks and stars are appearing through the empty blue all around me. I draw my knees up to my chest and hug them.

A crow startles to my right and I look up. Mitch is sitting beside me in his combats, long legs stretched in front of him, back against the stones and arms crossed over his chest. He appears to be sleeping, his face clean-shaven and unlined, mouth curled into a wee smile. His skin looks warm and solid enough to touch, but I don't try. He'll vanish if I try.

I pull my sleeping bag up around my shoulders and lean against the stone ring beside him, wishing I could lean against him instead. My head swims and I feel like I'm fading in and out of consciousness. 'I'm tired too, Mitch. Can I sleep now?'

He opens his eyes and looks at me, speaks to me clearly as a living man sitting right there. 'Do one last thing for me, bud. Send word home. Tell them you're okay.'

I don't question him. I get my phone out a final time, switch it on and tap in a text to the first person that comes to mind. I hit send and shove the phone back into the bag without waiting for a response.

'Alright now?'

'Alright, Sean. Now get some kip.'

I close my eyes and huddle down beside him, wondering as I have so many times before, whether we will survive the night.

****

I realise through closed eyelids that the first rays of sun are spilling over the hills and, with some relief, that I am not dead. A step closer toward consciousness and I'm confronted by a parade of discomforts: pain, cold, dehydration, a numb arse and a desperately full bladder. The wind moves in the grass and down the hill the tree branches creak. My eyes are crusty with dried tears and take a minute to focus. Mitch has gone and left no indentation in the gravel to indicate he was ever here.

'Mitch?'

Nothing but the tireless wind in the grass and the ache of loss in my chest.

It's very tempting to swamp the sleeping bag rather than face the effort of moving. I weigh it up for a few seconds and eventually conclude that, since I have so spectacularly failed to despatch myself, I will have to walk off this hill and get myself to hospital. Probably better not to have to do it with sodden breeks.

I take a deep breath and my head pounds. A fearsome

burn radiates from my left hand up my arm. The bandage is stained with fresh blood, so I clutch my hand to my chest and slowly uncross my cramped legs, pull them toward me and struggle out of the bag. My legs feel about as substantial as wet spaghetti as I stagger a few steps away, pee into the heather, then lurch back and subside onto my sleeping bag again. I gulp a couple of ibuprofens and most of my remaining water. The earth spins beneath me and I lean back, close my eyes and sit very still, fighting down a wave of nausea.

I doze again and wake to the bleep of my phone in my pack. I groan, then pull out the phone and squint at the words on the screen:

Was sleeping-- just got your text. Where the F are you? And don't say it if you don't mean it. P.

Then I read the text that I only vaguely remember sending her last night:

I am alive. I love you too. Will call you tomorrow. S.

'Jesus,' I mutter. That's me committed then. I rub my cheek, consider my next move and after a moment, text her again:

Heading into Ft William. Hopefully catch train to E-burgh today. Don't want to go to Janet's. Can I come to yours? PS- I did mean it.

The reply is almost immediate: *Yes.*

I pocket the phone. My head feels a little clearer, but my hand is throbbing and sticky. Cautiously I turn my palm up and open my fingers to have a look. They move freely, which means I probably haven't sliced any tendons, but the bandage is gory and saturated. I pack it with cotton wool, wrap the last of my gauze around it and pull it tight. I splash a little water onto a fleece towel, scrub my face, then do my best to stow my gear one handed.

The sleeping bag proves impossible, so I fold it and lay it beside Mitch's picture. Then I tear a page out of my little notebook and write on it:

Sleep well, mate. And thanks (Kajaki, Afghanistan, 27/04/2009). SMcN.

I slip the note inside the sleeping bag, swing my pack over my shoulder and walk out toward the road.

XXVIII

A soft breeze drives me along the road, and water from the recent rain splatters up onto my legs, peppering my skin with muddy brown spots. I've been on the bike every day the last two weeks, exploring farm tracks and paths I never knew existed, pushing up and over the Moorfoots or the Lammermuirs or following the East Lothian coast, speeding past patchworks of red poppies, oilseed rape, coarse tan barley, brave stands of oak and ash and Scotch pine, stubbly rows of tatties, wind turbines, sheep, rusted-out cars, old pit workings and lime kilns, refurbished cottages and derelict ones, defunct railways and disembodied brick chimneys on heathery hillsides: a rural landscape where there used to be industry.

The country around my home is beautiful in a way I've never noticed before, and I begin to believe that if green things can survive the black wounds of coal mining then a man can live with war in his blood.

It's been three weeks since I came home from Fort William with a line of tidy black stitches in my left hand. The scar curves down from the base of my index finger to the middle of my palm, dangerously close to the artery I'd first aimed for. One more whisky, a second's less hesitation, it would have been mission accomplished. I could tell the doc who stitched me up at Belford Hospital had second thoughts about letting me go. It still aches a little, and the healing skin itches: reminders of a place I never want to be again. I find myself curling my fingers protectively or hiding my hand in my pocket so that I don't have to answer questions.

The GP who removed my stitches back at Eskbridge Health Centre agreed to sign me off for a few more weeks and suggested a prescription for Prozac, which I refused. However silent she may be, Mum's ghost still hangs about me, shrivelled and toxic. I do this clean or not at all.

As soon as the stitches were out, I wheeled my bike out of Janet's shed and headed out of town. It helps to get moving again. Every day I go a little further. Every day the vice loosens its grip just a little and the road unfolds like pages of the map that were previously hidden. I start to look ahead, anticipating crossroads, wondering which way I might go.

This morning I'm not going very far: only to the end of the road past Cauldhill Farm. With a jangle of nerves I clatter over the cattle grid and push up the hill, swing off the bike and leave it against the wall of Duncan's cottage. I bang on the door and after a minute, it creaks open. He stands there, wavering slightly, regarding me silently with bloodshot eyes. The long straight bridge of his nose is flattened and puffy, and the bruises on his cheeks and under his eyes have not yet faded completely. The skin of his face is pallid and yellowish and the contours of his skull are clearly visible underneath. He looks like a re-animated corpse and smells about the same but seems lucid, if only temporarily.

Then he laughs in my face, so hard I actually flinch.

'Dinnae tell me ye've come tae apologise.'

And bang goes any contrition that might have motivated me to come out here. Actually I don't know why I've come here, beyond some probably childish desire to

272

close a wound. You'd think maybe I'd have learnt better by now.

'No, you know what? Fuck you. That's what I came to say. For what you did to my mum and me. Fuck you, Duncan.'

He softens. 'That's mair like it. I dare say, I deserve it.'

'Aye, you do.' I begin to back away. 'I won't bother you again. We pass each other in the road, we don't know each other.'

'Nae argument there. But seein' as yer here, would ye gie a message tae yer sister. Tell her thanks but nae thanks.'

'What for?'

'The hoose. She's tryin' tae get me shifted. I've nae plan tae end ma days in a poxy bedsit in the toon somewhere, in a stair fu' o junkies? Nae danger.'

'You'd rather stay here?'

'Aye. I've got mates, much as ye may find that hard tae believe. They look aifter me. In a few months, maybe a year, yis can cairry ma corpse off the hill and dae whit yis like wi' the place.' He hawks and spits onto the ground beside my feet. 'Is that all ye wis wantin?'

'Aye.' I shrug. 'Suit yourself. I'll see you later then.'

'I doubt that,' he replies. For a moment, his eyes meet mine and we understand each other clearly. Questions hang between us like over-inflated soap bubbles, and burst into nothing.

I step back without a further word, and he pushes the door shut with an anticlimactic click. I swallow hard, then turn away, grab the bike and cycle away from the house. Then I stop, swill water around my mouth and spit it into the dirt. I can't decide whether I'm relieved, disappointed or maybe just incapable of figuring it out by myself. Some things, it seems, the brain just isn't programmed for.

273

Instead of heading down the hill again, I go up the way, standing on the pedals and grinding over the rutted track as fast as my lungs and thighs will allow. A half mile or so beyond Duncan's cottage, the track reaches a saddle and begins to descend into an area of forest plantation. I leave it behind and turn onto the little path that leads more steeply uphill to my right. Barely more than a sheep trail, it follows a line of wire fencing toward the brow of the hills. The path becomes narrower and more difficult as I ascend: rocky and criss-crossed by heather and little rivulets of water. Eventually it becomes too boggy and I have to dismount, sling the bike over my right shoulder and continue on foot to the top of the hill.

When I get there, I sit in the waving grass, gather my knees to my chest and look down across fields and hills, straight lines of tarmac, farm houses, villages and towns, shimmery water. I can see Cauldhill Farm, and the silver glimmer of Molly's car in the drive. I can see the old coal bings and our little humble housing estate at the edge of Eskbridge. Across the Forth, the Lomond Hills, the Ochils and the Trossachs are in clear view. Beyond them, shadowy lines between land and sky, hazy patches of brightness which could be cloud or could be snow.

I try my luck, and whisper, 'Mitch?'

He doesn't answer.

I close my eyes and try to picture him. I imagine him waking up in my sleeping bag in the stone circle where I left it, reading my note and slipping it into his pocket. He stands up on two whole, undamaged legs, steps out of the sleeping bag and begins to walk. I see him walk uphill, toward the snow still lying on the high tops. His stride has purpose and he knows his destination, even if I don't.

'I miss you, bud.'

A skylark twitters an answer, and I smile. Then I get up, strap my helmet back onto my head, put on my sunglasses and climb onto the bike. I look back down the path and a thrill of fear courses through me; the hill looks even steeper from the top. Another man would drink himself blind; this is my version. If go flying arse over tit and break something, the only person who might conceivably come to my rescue anytime soon is Duncan. Dear old Dad. Wiping out is not an option.

'Mind where you go this time, Nic,' I say, and swallow heavily. Then I release the brake and begin to roll downhill.

Adrenaline hammers through me like a hit of Dexedrine. I skid to a halt outside our back fence, open the gate and roll along the path. I peel my fingers off the handlebars and shake life back into them, leave the bike out to wash down later, and flop onto the soft, dry lawn, pull off my helmet, shoes and socks. My pulse is rushing in my ears, my shirt is soaked in sweat and I am splattered with mud from my ankles to my face.

I feel almost dizzy, so I lie back in the grass and stare up at the cloudless sky. Immediately I am caught in a riptide of memory and panic. My mouth fills with the taste of blood and I have such an intense sensation of falling that my fingers scrabble for handfuls of earth to hang onto. They scrape Afghan dust.

The flashback goes as quickly as it came, but leaves my heart skittering around my chest like a trapped hare. My instinct is to turn onto my belly and crawl for cover, but since that would only confirm to Brenda Fairbairn and any other curtain-twitching neighbours that I am completely cracked, I don't do it. Janet would be mortified.

It takes all of my will to lie still and look up at that view. I breathe in for a count of ten and out again, unwind my fingers from the grass and wait for my pulse to slow.

'I'm here,' I say aloud just to reassure myself, and take another deep breath.

I close my eyes for a few moments, then open them again. The sky is still blue overhead, but the appearance of a little wispy cloud is immeasurably comforting. I am in Scotland, where a blue sky never lasts all that long.

Ten or fifteen minutes pass by and I'm still lying here. Nothing has fallen on me or blown up under me. The sun is hot on my skin. The gate opens and I lift my head from the grass to see Paula, pushing Eva in her pram.

'Hi.'

'Hi,' she says, and laughs at the sight of me. 'I was helping Mum in the garden and I saw you go by on the bike. I wondered if maybe you'd like to come down to the beach with us?'

'I might. It's a beach kind of day.' I drop my head back down again. 'It's good to see you.'

'Sean . . .'

'What?'

'Why are you lying on the ground?'

'I'm looking at the sky.'

'Right . . .' She parks Eva and drops down onto the lawn beside me, stretches out and looks up. 'Why?'

'No reason.' I should tell her. One day I will.

'It's very blue today,' she says after a few seconds.

'Yes it is.'

She turns her head and looks at me, brushes my fingertips with her own.

'Are you okay?'

'Mmm. I think so.'

'What are you thinking about?'

'Mitch. Just . . . something he said to me one time. It kind of stuck with me.'

She brushes a lock of hair away from her lips and looks curious. 'Are you going to tell me?'

'These American Marines had got their vehicle stuck in the mud trying to cross the Helmand River, and we got called in to help them dig it out. Inevitably we came under fire like fish in a barrel, and it was just about the most ridiculous situation I think I've ever been in. I remember lying on my stomach, trying to shelter behind a rut in the mud or some bloody thing, and I asked Mitch how the hell we got there. And he said to me, *there's only two fixed points on this map, Nic. You can't go back to the first and you sure as hell can't avoid the second. Everything else is up for grabs.*'

'So . . . what does that mean?'

'I guess it means that there's no master plan. You can only take the direction you think is right at the time. Sometimes it leads you into the shit, and sometimes it leads you out.'

She props herself up on an elbow and runs her finger along the inside of my left hand, tracing the lines that have been interrupted by the knife scar. I think briefly of my evening with Laura at Kingshouse, and wonder if maybe she really did know how to read palms after all.

Paula sighs, then laughs softly. 'And how do you know which is which?'

The grass tickles the back of my neck as I shake my head. 'I have absolutely no idea.'